The Dancing Floor

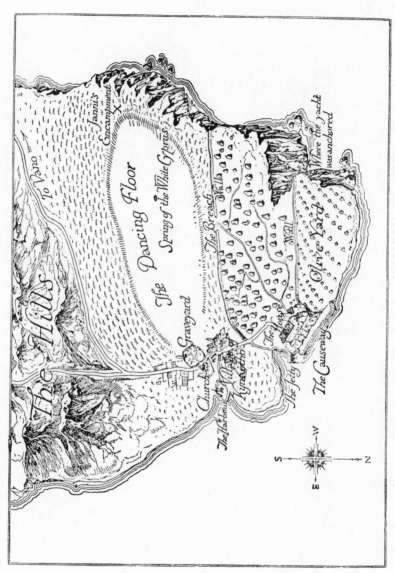

THE ISLAND OF PLAKOS AS SEEN FROM THE NORTH

THE
DANCING
FLOOR

JOHN BUCHAN

"Quisque suos patimur Manes"
VIRGIL, *Aeneid*, vi.743

THREE RIVERS BOOKS

First published 1926 by Hodder & Stoughton Ltd.
This edition published 1982 by
Three Rivers Books Ltd.
Mill Green, Bampton, Oxfordshire

Copyright the Rt. Hon. Lord Tweedsmuir, CBE

ISBN 0-907951-02-3

Printed in Great Britain by
The Thetford Press Ltd., Thetford, Norfolk

Dedication

TO

HENRY NEWBOLT

Note

An episode in this tale is taken from a short story of mine entitled " Basilissa," published in *Blackwood's Magazine* in 1914.

J. B.

PART I

*This story was told me by Leithen, as we were return-
ing rather late in the season from a shooting holiday
in North Ontario. There were few passengers, the
weather was a succession of snow blizzards and gales,
and as we had the smoking-room for the most part
to ourselves, we stoked up the fire and fell into a mood
of yarns and reminiscences. Leithen, being a
lawyer, has a liking for careful detail, and his tale
took long in the telling ; indeed, snatches of it filled
the whole of that rough October passage. The version
I have written out is amplified from his narrative,
but I think it is accurate, for he took the trouble to
revise it.*

Romance (he said) is a word I am shy of using.
It has been so staled and pawed by fools that the
bloom is gone from it, and to most people it stands
for a sugary world as flat as an eighteenth-century
Arcadia. But, dry stick as I am, I hanker after
my own notion of romance. I suppose it is the
lawyer in me, but I define it as something in life
which happens with an exquisite aptness and a
splendid finality, as if Fate had suddenly turned
artist—something which catches the breath because it is so wholly right. Also for me it must
happen to youth. I do not complain of growing
old, but I like to keep my faith that at one stage
in our mortal existence nothing is imposs███ ▓▓It

is part of my belief that the universe is on the whole friendly to man and that the ordering of the world is in the main benevolent. . . . So I go about expecting things, waiting like an old pagan for the descent of the goddess. And once—only once—I caught the authentic shimmer of her wings.

I

My story begins in January 1913, when I took my nephew Charles to dine with the Amysforts for a ball they were giving. Balls are not much in my line, for when I came first to London it was the foolish fashion of young men not to dance, but to lounge superciliously in doorways, while their elders took the floor. I had a good deal of work on hand, and I meant to leave immediately after dinner, but the necessity of launching Charles made me linger through the first few dances. My nephew was a cheerful young gentleman in his second year at Oxford, and it presently appeared that he did not want for friends of his own age. There was a perpetual bandying of nicknames and occult chaff with other fresh-coloured boys.

One in particular caught my attention. He was a tall young man of about Charles's age, who was not dancing but stood beside one of the windows with his head silhouetted against a dark curtain. He was uncommonly handsome after the ordinary English pattern, but our youth is mostly good to behold and that would not have fixed my attention. What struck me was his pose. He was looking at the pretty spectacle with a curious aloofness—with eyes that received much but gave out nothing. I have never seen anyone so completely detached, so clothed with his own atmosphere, and since that is rare at the age of twenty, I asked Charles if he knew him.

" Rather. It's old Milburne. He's up at Magdalen with me. First string for the 'Varsity mile. Believed "—his voice became reverential—" to be going to knock five seconds off his last year's time. Most awful good chap. Like me to introduce you ? "

The young man in response to my nephew's beckoning approached us. " Hullo, Vernon, how's life ? " said my nephew. " Want to introduce you to my uncle — Sir Edward Leithen — big legal swell, you know — good fellow to have behind you if you run up against the laws of England."

Charles left us to claim a partner, and I exchanged a few commonplaces with his friend, for I too—*consule Planco*—had run the mile. Our short talk was the merest platitudes, but my feeling about his odd distinction was intensified. There was something old-fashioned in his manner—wholly self-possessed yet with no touch of priggishness— a little formal, as if he had schooled himself to be urbanely and delicately on his guard. My guess at the time was that he had foreign blood in him, not from any difference of colouring or feature, but from his silken reserve. We of the North are apt to be angular in our silences ; we have not learned the art of gracious reticence.

That boy's face remained clearly fixed in my memory. It is a thing that often happens to me, for without any reason on earth I will carry about with me pictures of some casual witnesses or clients whom I am bound to recognise if I ever see them again. It is as freakish a gift as that which makes some men remember scraps of doggerel. I saw the face so vividly in my mind that, if I had been an artist, I could have drawn it accurately down to the finest lines of the mouth and the wary courtesy of the eyes. I do not suppose I gave the meeting another conscious thought, for I was desperately busy at the time, but I knew that I had added another portrait to the lumber-room of my absurd memory.

I had meant to go to Scotland that Easter vacation to fish, but a sudden pressure of Crown cases upset all my plans, and I had to limit my holiday to four days. I wanted exercise, so I took it in the most violent form, and went for a walk in the Westmorland hills. The snow lay late that year, and I got the exercise I sought scrambling up icy gullies and breasting north-easters on the long bleak ridges. All went well till the last day, which I spent among the Cartmel fells, intending to catch a train at an obscure station which would enable me to join the night mail for London at Lancaster. You know how those little hills break down in stony shelves to the sea. Well, as luck would have it, I stepped into a hole between two boulders masked with snow, and crawled out with the unpleasing certainty that I had either broken or badly wrenched my ankle. By the time I had hobbled down to the beginning of the stone-walled pastures I knew that it was a twist and not a break, but before I reached a road I knew also that I would never reach the station in time for my train.

It had begun to snow again, the spring dusk was falling, and the place was very lonely. My watch told me that even if I found a farm or inn and hired a trap I should miss my train. The only chance was to get a motor-car to take me to Lancaster. But there was no sign of farm or inn— only interminable dusky snowy fields, and the road was too small and obscure to make a friendly motor-car probable. I limped along in a very bad temper. It was not a matter of desperate urgency that I should be in London next morning, though delay would mean the postponement of a piece of business I wanted to get finished. But the prospect was black for my immediate comfort. The best I could look forward to was a bed in a farm- or a wayside public-house, and a slow and painful journey next day. I was angry with myself for my clumsiness. I had thought my ankles beyond reproach, and it was ridiculous that after three days on rough and dangerous mountains I should come to grief on a paltry hillock.

The dusk thickened, and not a soul did I meet. Presently woods began to creep around the road, and I walked between two patches of blackness in a thin glimmer of twilight which would soon be gone. I was cold and hungry and rather tired, and my ankle gave me a good deal of pain. I tried to think where I was, and could only remember that the station, which had been my immediate objective, was still at least six miles distant. I had out my map and wasted half a dozen matches on it, but it was a map of the hill country and stopped short of my present whereabouts. Very soon I had come to a determination to stop at the first human habitation, were it a labourer's cottage, and throw myself upon the compassion of its inmates. But not a flicker of light could I see to mark the presence of man.

Then something white glimmered faintly on my left, and I saw that it was a wicket gate. This must mean a house near at hand, so I hopefully pushed it open and entered. I found myself in a narrow path running among fir-trees. It was nearly pitch-dark in that place, and I was in fear of losing the road, which was obscured by the fallen snow, and getting lost in a wood. Soon, however, I was clear of the firs and in more open country among what looked like beeches. The wind, too, had swept the path bare, and there was just enough light to make it out as it twined up and down a little glade. I suspected that I was in a demesne of some considerable house, and the suspicion became a certainty when my track emerged on a broad gravel drive. After that my way was clear. The drive took me into a park—I knew it was a park because of the frequent swing-gates for cattle—and suddenly it bore to the right and I saw half a dozen irregularly placed lights high up in the air before me. This was the house, and it must be a large one, for some of the lights were far apart.

Five minutes later I found myself ringing the bell in a massive pillared porch, and explaining my case to a very old butler, to whom I gave my card.

" I've had an accident on the hills," I said, " and twisted my ankle rather badly. I wonder if I might ask for some assistance—to get to an inn or a station. I'm afraid I don't in the least know where I am."

" This is Severns Hall, sir," said the man. " My

master is Mr Vernon Milburne. If you will come
in, sir, I will acquaint him with the position."
"Mr Vernon Milburne?" I cried. "I believe
I have met him. I think he is at Oxford with my
nephew."
"Mr Milburne is a member of the University of
Oxford," said the ancient man. He led me into
a vast hall of the worst kind of Victorian Gothic,
in which a big bright wood fire crackled. When
he saw me clearly the butler proved a very angel
of mercy. "I think, sir, you should first have a
little refreshment," he said, and brought me a
whisky-and-soda. Then, while I thawed my
frozen bones before the logs, he departed to seek
his master.

I was too preoccupied with my own grievances
to feel much interest in the fact that I had stumbled
upon the dwelling of the boy who had so intrigued
me at Lady Amysfort's ball. But as I warmed my
hands at the blaze it did occur to me that this was
the last kind of house I would have linked him
with—this sham-mediæval upholstered magnificence. It was Gothic with every merit of Gothic
left out, and an air of dull ecclesiasticism hung
about it. There was even an organ at one end,
ugly and staring, as if it had come out of some
nouveau riche provincial church. Every bit of
woodwork was fretted and tortured into fancy
shapes.

I heard a voice at my elbow.

"I think we have met before, Sir Edward," it
said. "I am so sorry for your misfortune. Let's
get the boot off and look at the ankle."

"It's only a sprain," I said. "I really don't
want to bother you. If you would be so very kind

as to lend me a car to take me to Lancaster, I can
manage to travel all right. I ought to be in London to-morrow morning."

" Nonsense ! " He smiled in a pleasant boyish
way. " You are going to stay here to-night, and
if you're well enough I'll send you into Lancaster
to-morrow. You look simply fagged out. Let's
get the boot off and see if we need a doctor."

He summoned the butler, and the two of them
soon had my foot bare, while the boy, who seemed
to know something about sprains, ran a light hand
over the ankle bone.

" Nothing very bad here," he said ; " but it must
have been jolly painful to walk with. We'll
bandage it and you need only limp for a day or
two. Beaton, find out if Sir Edward's room is
ready. You'd better have a hot bath and then
we'll do the bandaging. After that you'll want
some food. I'll lend you a dressing-gown and dry
clothes."

The next hour was spent in restoring me to some
ease of body. Severns might be an ugly house,
but whoever built it had a pretty notion of comfort
in bedrooms. I had two rooms, each with a
cheerful fire, and when I had had my bath the two
Samaritans bandaged my ankle as neatly as a
hospital nurse, and helped me into a suit of flannels.
Then Vernon disappeared, and when he returned
he was dressed for dinner. A table had been laid
for me in the sitting-room, and Beaton was waiting
to ask me what I would drink.

" Champagne," said Vernon. " I prescribe it."

" But you're making far too much fuss about
me," I protested. " I can easily dine downstairs
with you."

" I think you ought to dine here. You've put yourself in my hands and I'm your medical adviser."

He saw me start my meal before he left me.

" Do you mind if I say good night now ? " he said. " You ought to get to bed pretty soon, and I have some work I want to do after dinner. Sound sleep and pleasant dreams."

I dined excellently, and after a single pipe was resolutely put to bed by Beaton the butler. They were benevolent despots in this house who were not to be gainsaid. I was sufficiently weary to be glad to go to sleep, but before I dropped off I wondered just a little at the nature of my reception. There were no other guests, Beaton had told me, and it seemed odd that a boy of nineteen alone in this Gothic mausoleum should show so little desire for human companionship. I should have expected, even if I were not allowed downstairs, to have had him come and talk to me for an hour or so before turning in. What work had he to which he was so faithful ? I remembered that Charles had mentioned that he was a bit of a swell at his books, but, as Charles himself had been ploughed for Pass Mods, that might mean very little. Anyhow, there was something morbid about a conscience which at nineteen forced its possessor to work in vacation time after dinner. He had been immensely hospitable, but obviously he had not wanted my company. That aloofness which I had remarked at Lady Amysfort's ball had become a heavy preoccupation. His attitude had been courteously defensive ; there had been a screen which robbed his kindness of all geniality. I felt quite distinctly that there was something in or about the house, something connected with himself, from which I was being resolutely excluded.

I slept well, and was awakened by Beaton bringing my early tea. He had undrawn the curtains and opened one of the windows, and a great flood of sunlight and spring airs was pouring through. The storm had passed and April was in her most generous mood. My ankle felt lumpish and stiff, but when Beaton examined it he pronounced that it was mending nicely. "But you can't press on it to-day, sir," he added. "Mr Vernon won't let you move to-day. . . . Breakfast will be laid in the sitting-room, and Mr Vernon's compliments and he proposes to join you at nine o'clock. I will return and bandage the ankle and assist you to rise as soon as Prayers are over."

Presently, as I lay watching a ridge of distant hill seen through the window and trying to decide what it could be, the sound of singing rose from some room below me. It must be Prayers. The old-fashioned hymn tune reminded me of my childhood and I wondered how many young men of to-day kept up the fashion of family worship when alone in a country house. And then I suddenly remembered all about the Milburnes, for they had been my mother's friends.

Humphrey Milburne had been a rich Lancashire cotton-spinner, whose father or grandfather—I forget which—had been one of the pioneers of the industry. I don't think he had ever concerned himself greatly with business, for his *métier* had always been that of the devout layman who is more occupied with church affairs than any bishop. He had been a leader of the Evangelical party, a vigorous opponent of ritualist practices, and a noted organiser of religious revivals. Vague memories of him came back to me from my child-hood, for my own family had been of the same persuasion. I had a recollection of a tall bearded man who on a visit to us had insisted on seeing the children, and had set me on his knee, and had asked me, a shivering self-conscious mite, embarrassing questions about my soul. I remembered his wife, Lady Augusta, more clearly. She was a thin little woman who never seemed to be separated from a large squashy Bible stuffed with leaflets and secured by many elastic bands. She had had a knack of dropping everything as she moved, and I had acted as page to retrieve her belongings. She had been very kind to me, for to her grief she had then no children. . . . I remembered that a son had at last been born—" a child of many prayers," my mother had called him. And then came a vague recollection of a tragedy. Lady Augusta had died when the boy was an infant and her husband had followed within the year. After that the Milburnes passed out of my life, except that their nurse had come to us when I was at Eton, and had had much to say of young Master Vernon.

My vague remembrance seemed to explain my host. The child of ageing parents and an orphan from his early years—that would account for his lack of youthful spontaneity. I liked the notion of him I was acquiring ; there was something quaint and loyal in his keeping up the family ritual —an evangelical athlete with the looks of Apollo. I had fancied something foreign in his air, but that of course was nonsense. He came of the most prosaic British stock, cotton-spinning Milburnes, and for his mother a Douglas-Ernott, whose family was the quintessence of Whig solidity.

I found Vernon waiting for me in the sunny sitting-room, dressed in rough grey homespun and with an air of being ready for a long day in the open. There was a change in him since the night before. His eyes were a little heavy, as if he had slept badly, but the shutters were lifted from them. His manner was no longer constrained, and the slight awkwardness I had felt in his presence was gone. He was now a cheerful communicative undergraduate.

" Beaton says you had a good night, sir, but you mustn't use that foot of yours. You can't think of London to-day, you know. I've nothing to do except look after you, so you'd better think of me as Charles with a nephew's privileges. It's going to be a clinking fine day, so what do you say to running up in the car to the moors above Shap and listening to the curlews ? In the spring they're the jolliest things alive."

He was a schoolboy now, looking forward to an outing, and we might have been breakfasting in Oxford rooms before going out with the Bicester. I fell into his holiday mood, and forgot to tell him that I had long ago met his parents. He lent me an ulster and helped me downstairs, where he packed me into the front of a big Daimler and got in beside me. In the clear spring sunshine, with the park a chessboard of green grass and melting snow, and the rooks cawing in the beech tops, Severns looked almost venerable, for its lines were good and the stone was weathering well. He nodded towards the long façades. " Ugly old

thing, when you think of Levens or Sizergh, but
it was my grandfather's taste and I mean to
respect it. If we get a fine sunset you'll see it
light up like an enchanted castle. It's something
to be able to see the hills from every window, and
to get a glimpse of the sea from the top floor.
Goodish sport, too, for we've several miles of
salmon and sea trout, and we get uncommon high
birds in the upper coverts."

We sped up by winding hill-roads to the moors,
and there were the curlews crying over the snow-
patched bent with that note which is at once
eerie and wistful and joyful. There were grouse,
too, busy about their nesting, and an occasional
stone-chat, and dippers flashing their white waist-
coats in every beck. It was like being on the roof
of the world, with the high Lake hills a little fore-
shortened, like ships coming over the horizon at
sea. Lunch we had with us and ate on a dry bank
of heather, and we had tea in a whitewashed
moorland farm. I have never taken to anyone
so fast as I took to that boy. He was in the highest
spirits, as if he had finished some difficult task,
and in the rebound he became extraordinarily
companionable. I think he took to me also, for
he showed a shy but intense interest in my doings,
the eagerness with which an undergraduate prospects the channels of the world's life which he is
soon to navigate. I had been prepared to find a
touch of innocent priggishness, but there was
nothing of the kind. He seemed to have no dogmas
of his own, only inquiries.

" I suppose a lawyer's training fits a man to
examine all kinds of problems—not only legal
ones," he asked casually at luncheon. " I mean

he understands the value of any sort of evidence, for the principles of logical proof are always the same ? "

" I suppose so," I replied, " though it's only legal conundrums that come my way. I was once asked my opinion on a scientific proof—in the higher mathematics—but I didn't make much of it—couldn't quite catch on to the data or understand the language."

" Yes, that might be a difficulty," he admitted. " But a thing like a ghost story for instance—you'd be all right at that, I suppose ? "

The boy had clearly something in his head, and I wondered if the raw magnificence of Severns harboured any spooks. Could that be the reason of his diffidence on the previous evening ?

When we got home we sat smoking by the library fire, and while I skimmed *The Times* Vernon dozed. He must have been short of his sleep and was now making up for it in the way. of a healthy young man. As I watched his even breathing I decided that here there could be no abnormality of body or mind. It was like watching a tired spaniel on the rug, too tired even to hunt in his dreams.

As I lifted my eyes from the paper I saw that he was awake and was looking at me intently, as if he were hesitating about asking me some question.

" I've been asleep," he apologised. " I can drop off anywhere after a day on the hills."

" You were rather sleepless as a child, weren't you ? " I asked.

His eyes opened. " I wonder how you know that ? "

" From your old nurse. I ought to have told you that in my boyhood I knew your parents a little. They stayed with us more than once. And Mrs Ganthony came to my mother from you. I was at Eton at the time, and I remember how she used to entertain us with stories about Severns. You must have been an infant when she left."

" I was four. What sort of things did she tell you ? "

" About your bad nights and your pluck. I fancy it was by way of censure of our declamatory habits. Why, after all these years I remember some of her phrases. How did the thing go ? ' What fidgeted me was the way his lordship 'eld his tongue. For usual he'd shout as lusty as a whelp, but on these mornings I'd find him with his eyes like moons and his skin white and shiny, and never a cheep the whole blessed night, with me lying next door, and a light sleeper at all times, Mrs Wace, ma'am.' Was Mrs Wace a sort of Mrs Harris ? "

He laughed merrily. " To think that you should have heard that ! No, she was our housekeeper, and Ganthony, who babbled like Sairey Gamp, made a litany of her name. That's the most extraordinary thing I ever heard."

" You've outgrown that childish ailment anyhow," I said.

" Yes. I have outgrown it." My practice with witnesses made me detect just a shade of hesitation.

At dinner he returned to the subject which seemed to interest him, the exact nature of the legal training. I told him that I was an advocate,

not a judge, and so had no need to cultivate a
judicial mind.

"But you can't do without it," he protested.
"You have to advise your client and pronounce
on his case before you argue it. The bulk of your
work must be the weighing of evidence. I should
have thought that that talent could be applied
to any subject in the world if the facts were sufficiently explained. In the long run the most
abstruse business will boil down to a fairly simple
deduction from certain data. Your profession
enables you to select the relevant data."

"That may be true in theory but I wouldn't
myself rate legal talent so high. A lawyer is apt
to lack imagination, you know." Then I stopped,
for I had suddenly the impression that Vernon
wanted advice, help of some kind—that behind
all his ease he was profoundly anxious, and that a
plea, almost a cry, was trembling on his lips. I
detest confidences and labour to avoid them, but
I could no more refuse this boy than stop my ears
against a sick child. So I added, "Of course
lawyers make good confidants. They're mostly
decent fellows, and they're accustomed to keeping
their mouths shut."

He nodded, as if I had settled some private
scruple, and we fell to talking about spring salmon
in the Tay.

"Take the port into the library," he told Beaton.
"Sir Edward doesn't want coffee. Oh, and see
that the fire is good. We shan't need you again
to-night. I'll put Sir Edward to bed."

There was an odd air of purpose about him, as
he gave me his arm to the library and settled me
with a cigar in a long chair. Then he disappeared

for a minute or two and returned with a shabby little clasped leather book. He locked the door and put the key on the mantelpiece, and when he caught me smiling he smiled too, a little nervously.

" Please don't think me an ass," he said. " I'm going to ask a tremendous favour. I want you to listen to me while I tell you a story, something I have never told to anyone in my life before. . . . I don't think you'll laugh at me, and I've a notion you may be able to help me. It's a confounded liberty, I know, but may I go on ? "

" Most certainly," I said. " I can't imagine myself laughing at anything you had to tell me ; and if there's anything in me that can help you it's yours for the asking."

He drew a long breath. " You spoke of my bad nights as a child and I said I had outgrown them. Well, it isn't true."

II

When Vernon was a very little boy he was the sleepiest and healthiest of mortals, but every spring he had a spell of bad dreams. He slept at that time in the big new night-nursery at the top of the west wing, which his parents had built not long before their death. It had three windows looking out to the moorish flats which run up to the fells, and from one window, by craning your neck, you could catch a glimpse of the sea. It was all hung, too, with a Chinese paper whereon pink and green parrots squatted in wonderful blue trees, and there seemed generally to be a wood fire burning. He described the place in detail, not as it is to-day, but as he remembered it.

Vernon's recollection of his childish nightmares
was hazy. They varied, I gathered, but narrowed
down in the end to one type. He used to find himself in a room different from the nursery and bigger,
but with the same smell of wood smoke. People
came and went, such as his nurse, the butler,
Simon the head keeper, Uncle Appleby his guardian,
Cousin Jennifer, the old woman who sold oranges
in Axby, and a host of others. Nobody hindered
them from going away, and they seemed to be
pleading with him to come too. There was danger
in the place; something was going to happen in
the big room, and if by that time he was not gone
there would be mischief. . . . But it was quite clear
to him that he could not go. He must stop there,
with the wood smoke in his nostrils, and await the
advent of the something. But he was never quite
sure of the nature of the compulsion. He had a
notion that if he made a rush for the door at
Uncle Appleby's heels he would be allowed to
escape, but that somehow he would be behaving
badly. Anyhow, the place put him into a sweat of
fright, and Mrs Ganthony looked darkly at him in
the morning.

Those troubled springs continued—odd inter-
ludes in a life of nearly unbroken health. Mrs
Ganthony left because she could not control her
tongue and increased the boy's terrors, and Vernon
was nine—he thought—before the dream began to
take a really definite shape. The stage was
emptying. There was nobody in the room now but
himself, and he saw its details a little more clearly.
It was not any apartment in Severns. Rather
it seemed like one of the big old panelled chambers
which he remembered from visits to the Midland

country houses of his mother's family, when he had arrived after dark and had been put to sleep in a great bed in a place lit with dancing firelight. In the morning it had looked only an ordinary big room, but at that hour of the evening it had seemed an enchanted cave. The dream-room was not unlike these, for there was the scent of a wood fire and there were dancing shadows, but he could not see clearly the walls or the ceiling, and there was no bed. In one corner was a door which led to the outer world, and through this he knew that he might on no account pass. Another door faced him, and he knew that he had only to turn the handle for it to open.

But he did not want to, for he understood quite clearly what was beyond. There was a second room just like the first one ; he knew nothing about it except that opposite the entrance another door led out of it. Beyond was a third chamber, and so on interminably. There seemed to the boy to be no end to this fantastic suite. He thought of it as a great snake of masonry, winding up hill and down dale away to the fells or the sea. . . . Yes, but there *was* an end. Somewhere far away in one of the rooms was a terror waiting on him, or, as he feared, coming towards him. Even now it might be flitting from room to room, every minute bringing its soft tread nearer to the chamber of the wood fire.

About this time of his life the dream was an unmitigated horror. Once it came while he was ill with a childish fever, and it sent his temperature up to a point which brought Dr Moreton galloping from Axby. In his waking hours he did not, as a rule, remember it clearly ; but during the fever,

asleep and awake, that sinuous building, one room
thick, with each room opening from the other, was
never away from his thoughts.   It amazed him to
think that outside were the cheerful moors where
he hunted for plovers' eggs, and that only a thin
wall of stone kept him from pleasant homely things.
The thought used to comfort him when he was
awake, but in the dream it never came near him.
Asleep, the whole world seemed one suite of rooms,
and he, a forlorn little prisoner, doomed grimly
to wait on the slow coming through the many
doors of a fear which transcended word and
thought.

He became a silent, self-absorbed boy, and,
though the fact of his nightmares was patent to
the little household, the details remained locked
up in his head.   Not even to Uncle Appleby would
he tell them, when that gentleman, hurriedly
kind, came to visit his convalescent ward.   His
illness made Vernon grow, and he shot up into a
lanky, leggy boy.   But the hills soon tautened
his sinews, and all the time at his preparatory
school he was a healthy and active child.   He told
me that he tried to exorcise the dream through his
religion—to " lay his burden on the Lord," as the
old evangelical phrase has it ; but he signally
failed, though he got some comfort from the
attempt.   It was borne in on him, he said, that
this was a burden which the Lord had laid quite
definitely on him and meant him to bear like a
man.

He was fifteen and at Eton when he made
the great discovery.   The dream had become almost a custom now.   It came in April at Severns
about Easter-tide—a night's discomfort (it was

now scarcely more) in the rush and glory of the holidays. There was a moment of the old wild heart-fluttering ; but a boy's fancy is more quickly dulled than a child's, and the endless corridors were now more of a prison than a witch's ante-chamber. By this time, with the help of his diary, he had fixed the date of the dream ; it came regularly on the night of the first Monday of April. Now the year I speak of he had made a long expedition into the hills, and had stridden home-ward at a steady four miles an hour among the gleams and shadows of an April twilight. He was alone at Severns, so he had had his supper in the big library, where afterwards he sat watching the leaping flames on the open stone hearth. He was very weary, and sleep fell upon him in his chair. He found himself in the wood-smoke chamber, and before him the door leading to the unknown. . . . But it was no indefinite fear that now lay beyond. He knew clearly—though how he knew he could not tell—that each year the something came a room nearer, and was even now but twelve rooms off. In twelve years his own door would open, and then——

He woke in the small hours, chilled and mazed, but with a curious new assurance in his heart. Hitherto the nightmare had left him in gross terror, unable to endure the prospect of its recurrence, till the kindly forgetfulness of youth relieved him. But now, though his nerves were fluttering, he perceived that there was a limit to the mystery. Some day it must declare itself and fight on equal terms.

The discovery opened a new stage in his life. As he thought over the matter in the next few days he had the sense of being forewarned and prepared for some great test of courage. The notion exhilarated as much as it frightened him. Late at night, or on soft dripping days, or at any moment of lessened vitality, he would bitterly wish that he had been born an ordinary mortal. But on a keen morning of frost, when he rubbed himself warm after a cold tub, or at high noon of summer, the adventure of the dream almost pleased him. Unconsciously he must have braced himself to a harder discipline. His fitness, moral and physical, became his chief interest for reasons that would have been unintelligible to his friends or his masters.

He passed through school—as I knew from Charles—an aloof and rather splendid figure, a magnificent athlete with a brain as well as a body, a good fellow in everyone's opinion, but a grave one. He could have had no real intimates, for he never shared the secret of the spring dream. At this period, for some reason which he could not tell, he would have burned his hand off sooner than breathe a hint of it. Pure terror absolves from all conventions and demands a confidant, so terror, I think, must have largely departed from the nightmare as he grew older. Fear, indeed, remained, and awe and disquiet, but these are human emotions, whereas terror is of hell.

Had he told anyone, he would no doubt have become self-conscious and felt acutely his difference from other people, so it was a sound instinct which kept him silent. As it was, he seems to have been an ordinary schoolboy, much liked, and, except at odd moments, unaware of any brooding destiny. As he grew older, and his ambition awoke, the moments when he remembered the dream were apt to be disagreeable, for a boy's ambitions are strictly conventional and his soul revolts at the abnormal. By the time he was ready for the university he wanted above all things to run the mile a second faster than anyone else, and he had hopes of academic distinction, for he was an excellent classic. For most of the year he lived with these hopes and was happy; then came April, and for a short season he was groping in dark places. Just before and after each dream he was in the mood of exasperation; but when it actually came he was plunged in a different atmosphere, and felt the quiver of fear and the quick thrill of expectation.

During his first year at Oxford he had made an attempt to avoid it. He and three others were on a walking tour in Brittany in gusty spring weather, and came late one evening to an inn by an estuary where sea-gulls clattered about the windows. Youth-like they made a great and foolish feast, and sat all night round a bowl of punch, while school songs and " John Peel " contended with the dirling of the gale. At daylight they took the road again, without having closed an eye, and Vernon told himself that he was rid of his incubus. He wondered at the time why he was not more cheerful, for to his surprise he had a sense of loss, of regret, almost of disappointment.

" That was last year," he said, and he opened the little locked diary and showed me the entry. " Last night I went to bed not knowing what to think, but far more nervous than I had been since I was a baby. I hope I didn't show it, but I wasn't much in the mood for guests when you turned up."

" What happened ? " I asked eagerly. " Did the dream come back ? "

He nodded and passed me the diary so that I could read that morning's entry. The dream had not failed him. Once more he had been in the chamber with the wood fire ; once again he had peered at the door and wondered with tremulous heart what lay beyond. For the something had come nearer by two rooms, and was now only seven doors away. I read the bare account in his neat, precise handwriting, and it gave me a strong impression of being permitted to peep through a curtain at a stage mysteriously set. I noticed that he had added some lines from Keats's " Indian Maid's Song " :

> " I would deceive her,
> And so leave her,
> But ah ! she is so constant and so kind."

There was a mark of exclamation against the " she," as if he found some irony in it.

III

He seemed to be waiting for me to speak, waiting shyly and tensely like a child expecting the judgment of an elder. But I found it hard to know what to say.

" That is a very wonderful story ! " I ventured at last. " I am honoured that you should have chosen me to tell it to. Perhaps it will be a relief to you to know that someone else understands what you are going through. . . . I don't suppose you want sympathy, but I would like to congratulate you on your fortitude."

" I don't need sympathy—or congratulation. But I want help—the help of your brain and your experience. . . . You see, in seven years some tremendous experience is coming to me, and I want —I'd like—to know what it is."

" I wonder if a good doctor wouldn't be the best person to consult."

" No, no," he cried almost angrily. " I tell you there's nothing pathological about it—not now that I'm a man. I don't want it exorcised as if it were an evil spell. I think—now—that I'd break my heart if it all vanished into moonshine. . . . I believe in it as I believe in God, and I'm ready to face whatever is coming. But I want to be forewarned and forearmed, if possible, for it's going to be a big thing. If I only knew something about what was coming—even the smallest something ! "

Those were the days before psycho-analysis had become fashionable, but even then we had psychologists, and in my bewilderment I tried that tack.

" Might not it all spring from some fright— some strange experience at any rate—which you had as a baby ? Such things often make an abiding impression."

He smiled. " You're still thinking it is pathological. Fright would account for recurring nightmares, but surely not for a thing so rational as this—a fixed day every year, the same room, the time limit. It would not explain the thing moving on a room last year when I had no dream."

" I suppose not," I admitted. " Have you looked up your family history ? I have heard stories of inherited obsessions and premonitions— what they call a ' weird ' in Scotland."

" I thought of that, but there's nothing—nothing. There are no Milburne records much beyond my grandfather, and by all accounts they were the most prosaic kind of business men. My mother's family—well, there's plenty of records there and I've waded through most of the muniment room at Appleby. But there's no hint of anything mysterious in the Douglas-Ernotts. They were a time-serving lot, who knew how the cat was going to jump, but they kept out of crime and shunned anything imaginative like the plague. I shouldn't think one of them had ever an ambition which couldn't be put in terms of office or money, or a regret except that he had missed a chance of getting at the public purse. True-blue Whigs, all of them."

" Then I'm hanged if I know what to say. But, now you've told me, I want you to remember that you can always count on me. I may not be able to help, but I'm there whenever you want me. Perhaps—you never know—the thing will reveal itself more clearly in the next seven years and come within the scope of my help. I've taken a tremendous liking to you, my dear chap, and we're going to be friends."

He held out his hand.

" That's kind of you. . . . Shall I tell you what I think myself ? I was taught to believe that everything in our lives is foreordained by God. No caprice of our own can alter the eternal plan. Now, why shouldn't some inkling of this plan be given us now and then—not knowledge, but just an inkling that we may be ready ? My dream may be a heavenly warning, a divine foreshadowing—a privilege, not a cross. It is a reminder that I must be waiting with girt loins and a lit lamp when the call comes. That's the way I look on it, and it makes me happy."

I said nothing, for I did not share his Calvinism, but I felt that suddenly that library had become rather a solemn place. I had listened to the vow of the young Hannibal at the altar.

I

I HAVE a preposterous weakness for youth, and I
fancy there is something in me which makes it
accept me as a coæval. It may be my profession.
If you are a busy lawyer without any outside
ambitions you spend your days using one bit of
your mind, and the rest remains comparatively
young and unstaled. I had no wife and few near
relations, and while I was daily growing narrower
in my outlook on the present and the future I
cherished a wealth of sentiment about the past.
I welcomed anything which helped me to recapture
the freshness of boyhood, and Vernon was like a
spring wind in my arid life. Presently we forgot
that I was nearly twice his age, and slipped into
the manner of contemporaries. He was far more
at his ease with me than with the men of his own
year. I came to think that I was the only person
in the world who *knew* him, for though he had an
infinity of acquaintances and a good many people
who ranked as friends I suppose I was his only
comrade. For I alone knew the story of his
dreams.

My flat in Down Street became his head-quarters
in London, and I never knew when he would stick
his head into my Temple chambers and insist on
our dining or lunching together. In the following

winter I went to Oxford occasionally, nominally to visit Charles ; but my nephew led a much occupied life, and it generally ended by my spending my time with Vernon. I kept a horse with the Bicester that season and we hunted occasionally together, and we had sometimes a walk which filled the short winter day, and dined thereafter and talked far into the night. I was anxious to learn how his contemporaries regarded him, and I soon found that he had a prodigious reputation, which was by no means explained by his athletic record. He at once impressed and puzzled his little world. I think it was the sense of brooding power about him which attracted people and also kept them at a respectful distance. His ridiculous good looks and his gentle courtesy seemed to mark him out for universal popularity, but there was too much austerity for a really popular man. He had odd ascetic traits. He never touched wine now, he detested loose talk, and he was a little intolerant of youthful follies. Not that there was anything of the prig in him—only that his character seemed curiously formed and mature. For all his urbanity he had a plain, almost rugged, sagacity in ordinary affairs, a tough core like steel harness under a silk coat. That, I suppose, was the Calvinism in his blood. Had he been a less brilliant figure, he would probably have been set down as " pi."

Charles never professed to understand him, and contented himself with prophesying that " old Vernon would be the devil of a swell some day." On inquiry I found that none of his friends forecast any special career for him ; it would have seemed to them almost disrespectful to condescend upon

such details. It was not what Vernon would do
that fired their sluggish imaginations, but what
they dimly conceived that he already was.

There was the same fastidiousness about all his
ways. I have never known a better brain more
narrowly limited in its range. He was a first-class
" pure " scholar and had got a Craven and been
proxime for the Hertford. But he .was quite in-
capable of spreading himself, and his prospects
looked bad for " Greats " since he seemed unable
to acquire the smattering of loose philosophy
demanded by that school. He was strictly cir-
cumscribed in his general reading ; I set it down
at first to insensitiveness, but came soon to think
it fastidiousness. If he could not have exactitude
and perfection in his knowledge, he preferred to
remain ignorant. I saw in him the makings of a
lawyer. Law was just the subject for a finical,
exact and scrupulous mind like his. Charles had
once in his haste said that he was not a man of the
world, and Charles had been right. He was a man
of his own world, not the ordinary one. So with
his intellectual interests. He would make his own
culture, quite regardless of other people. I fancy
that he felt that his overmastering private problem
made it necessary to husband the energies of his
mind.

During that year I think he was quite happy
and at peace about the dream. He had now
stopped hoping or fearing ; the thing had simply
become part of him, like his vigorous young body,
his slow kindliness, his patient courage. He
rarely wanted to talk of it, but it was so much in
my thoughts that I conducted certain researches
of my own. I began by trying the psychological

line, and plagued those of my acquaintances who
had any knowledge of that dismal science. I cannot say I got much assistance. You see I had to
state a hypothetical case, and was always met by
a demand to produce the patient for cross-examination—a reasonable enough request, which of course
I could not comply with. One man, who was full
of the new Vienna doctrine, talked about " com-
plexes " and " repressions " and suggested that
the dream came from a child having been shut up
by accident in a dark room. " If you can dig the
memory of it out of his subconsciousness, you
will lay that ghost," he said. I tried one evening
to awake Vernon's earliest recollections, but nothing emerged. The dream itself was the furthest-
back point in his recollection. In any case I
didn't see how such an explanation would account
for the steady development of the thing and its
periodicity. I thought I might do better with
family history, and I gave up a good deal of my
leisure to the Douglas-Ernotts. There was
nothing to be made of the Ernotts—gross utilita-
rian Whigs every one of them. The Douglas
strain had more mystery in it, but the records of
his branch of the great Scottish house were scanty,
and sadly impersonal. Douglases many had
endured imprisonment and gone to the scaffold,
but history showed them as mere sounding names,
linked to forays and battles and strange soubri-
quets, but as vague as the heroes of Homer. As
for the Milburnes, I got an ancient aunt who had
known Vernon's father to give me her recollections,
and a friend on the Northern Circuit collected for
me the Lancashire records. The first of them had
been a small farmer somewhere on the Ribble ;

the second had become a mill-owner; and the
third in the early nineteenth century had made
a great fortune, had been a friend of William
Wilberforce and later of Richard Cobden, and had
sat in the first Reform parliament. As I looked
at the portrait of that whiskered reformer, bland and
venerable in his stiff linen and broadcloth, or at
the early Millais of his son, the bearded Evangelical,
I wondered what in them had gone to the making
of Vernon. It was like seeking for the ancestry of
a falcon among barnyard fowls.

II

In the spring of 1914 I badly needed a holiday,
and Lamancha asked me to go cruising in his
yacht. He gave me permission to bring Vernon,
whom he knew slightly, for I wanted to be near
him on the first Monday of April. We were to
join the yacht at Constantinople, and cruise through
the Northern Ægean to Athens, and then by way
of the Corinth canal to Corfu, where we would
catch the steamer for Brindisi and so home.
Vernon was at first a little disinclined, for he had
a notion that he ought to be at Severns, but when
he allowed himself to be persuaded he grew very
keen about the trip, for he had been little out of
England.

He and I travelled by the Orient Express to
Constantinople, and after three days there and one
day at Brousa shaped our course westward. We
landed one morning on the Gallipoli peninsula,
and found birds' eggs on Achi Baba where in a
year's time there was to be nothing but barbed
wire and trenches. We spent a day at Lemnos,
which at that time few people had visited except

the British Navy, and then turned south. On the first Monday of April we had half a gale, an uncomfortable thing in those shallow seas. It blew itself out in the afternoon, and after tea we anchored for the night under the lee of a big island. There was a little bay carved out of the side of a hill; the slopes were covered with heath and some kind of scrub, and the young green of crops showed in the clearings. Among the thyme of the nearest headland a flock of goats was browsing, shepherded by a little girl in a saffron skirt, who sang shrilly in snatches. After the yeasty Ægean the scene was an idyll of pastoral peace. Vernon had all day shown signs of restlessness, and he now proposed a walk; so, leaving the others playing bridge, we two were put ashore in the dinghy.

We walked southward towards the other horn of the bay, past little closes of fruit blossom, and thickets of wildwood, and stony patches of downland bright with anemones and asphodel. It was a strange, haunted world, bathed in a twilight of gold and amethyst, filled with a thousand aromatic scents, and very silent except for the wash of the waves and a far-off bleating of goats. Neither of us wanted to talk, being content to drink in the magic of the evening. Vernon walked like a man in a dream, stopping now and then to lift his head and stare up the long scrubby ravines to the sharp line of the crest.

Suddenly a cuckoo's note broke into the stillness and echoed along the hillside. When it died away it seemed to be answered by a human voice, sweet and high and infinitely remote, a voice as fugitive as a scent or a colour.

Vernon stopped short.

" Listen to that," he cried. " It is the Spring Song. This has probably been going on here since the beginning of time. They say that nothing changes in these islands—only they call Demeter the Virgin Mary and Dionysos St Dionysius."

He sat down on a boulder and lit his pipe. " Let's burn tobacco to the gods," he said. " It's too enchanted to hurry through. . . . I suppose it's the way I've been educated, but I could swear I've known it all before. This is the season of the Spring Festival, and you may be sure it's the same here to-day as it was a thousand years before Homer. The winter is over and the Underworld has to be appeased, and then the Goddess will come up from the shades."

I had never heard Vernon talk like this before, and I listened with some curiosity. I am no classical scholar, but at that moment I too felt the spell of a very ancient and simple world.

" This was the beginning of the year for the Greeks, remember," he went on—" for the Greeks as we know them, and for the old Mediterranean peoples before them whose ritual they absorbed. The bones of that ritual never altered. . . . You have to begin with purification—to feed the ghosts of the dead in the pot-holes with fireless and wine-less sacrifices and so placate them, and to purify your own souls and bodies and the earth by which you live. You have your purgation herbs like buckthorn and agnus castus, and you have your *pharmakos*, your scapegoat, who carries away all impurities. And then, when that is done, you are ready for the coming of the Maiden. It is like Easter after Good Friday—the festival after the fast and penitence. It is always the woman that simple folk worship—the Mother who is also the Maid. Long ago they called her Pandora or Persephone, and now they call her the Blessed Virgin, but the notion is the same—the sinless birth of the divine. You may be sure it is she whom the peasants in this island worship, as their fathers did three thousand years ago—not God the Father.

" The Greeks had only the one goddess," he went on, " though she had many names. Later they invented the Olympians—that noisy, middle-class family party—and the priests made a great work with their male gods, Apollo and the like. But the woman came first, and the woman remained. You may call her Demeter, or Aphrodite, or Hera, but she is the same, the Virgin and the Mother, the ' mistress of wild things,' the priestess of the new birth in spring. Semele is more than Dionysos, and even to sophisticated Athens the Mailed Virgin of the Acropolis was more than all the pantheon. . . . Don't imagine it was only a pretty fancy. The thing had all the beauty of nature, and all the terror too." He flung back his head and quoted some sonorous Greek.

" What's that ? " I asked.

" Euripides," he replied. " It has been well translated," and he quoted :

" ' For her breath is on all that hath life, and she floats in the air
Bee-like, death-like, a wonder.'

" I can see it all," he cried. " The sacred basket, the honey and oil and wine, the torches crimsoning the meadows, the hushed quiet people waiting on the revelation. They are never more than a day or two from starvation all the winter, and the coming of the Maiden is a matter for them of life and death. They wait for her as devout souls to-day wait for the Easter Resurrection. I can hear the ritual chant and the thin clear music of the flutes. . . . Yes, but they were seeing things which are now hid from us—Dionysos with his thyrsus, and goat-feet in the thickets, and the shadows of dancing nymphs ! If you starve for three months and put your soul into waiting for the voice from heaven you are in the mood for marvels. Terror and horror, perhaps, but unspeakable beauty, too, and a wild hope. That was the Greek religion, not the Olympians and their burnt offerings. And it is the kind of religion that never dies."

I thought this pretty good for the scion of an evangelical family, and I said so.

He laughed. "It isn't my own creed, you know. I dislike all kinds of priestcraft. But, though I'm a stout Protestant, I'm inclined to think sometimes that it is a pity that we have departed from the practice of all other religions and left out the Mother of God. . . . Let's go on —I want to see what is on the other side of the cape."

Beyond the little headland we came suddenly on a very different scene. Here was the harbour of the island. Beside a rude quay some fisher-boats lay at anchor with their brown sails furled. Along the water-front ran a paved terrace, a little dilapidated and with bushes growing in the cracks of the stones. Above rose a great building, show-

ing to seaward as a blank white wall pierced with
a few narrow windows. At first sight I took it
for a monastery, but a second glance convinced
me that its purpose had never been religious. It
looked as if it had once been fortified, and the
causeway between it and the sea may have mounted
guns. Most of it was clearly very old, but the
architecture was a jumble, showing here the
enriched Gothic of Venice and there the straight
lines and round arches of the East. It had once,
I conjectured, been the hold of some Venetian
sea-king, then the palace of a Turkish conqueror,
and was now, perhaps, the manor-house of this
pleasant domain. The owners, whoever they
might be, were absent, for not a chimney smoked.

We passed the quay and wandered along the
great terrace, which was as solidly masoned as a
Roman road. For a little the house hung sheer
above us, its walls level with the rock, with in
three places flights of steps from the causeway
ending in small postern doors. Obviously the
main entrance was on the other side. There were
no huts to be seen, and no sign of life except a
little group of fishermen below on the shore, who
were sitting round a fire over which a pot was
boiling. As we continued along the terrace beyond
the house we came to orchards and olive yards,
no doubt part of the demesne, and had a glimpse
of a rugged coast running out into the sunset.

The place impressed even my sluggish fancy.
This great silent castle in the wilds, hung between
sky and earth, and all rosy in the last fires of the
sun, seemed insubstantial as a dream. I should
not have been surprised if it had vanished like a
mirage and left us staring at a bare hillside. Only

the solid blocks of the causeway bound us to
reality. Here, beyond doubt, men had lived and
fought far back in the ages. The impression left
on my mind was of a place inhabited for æons,
sunk for the moment in sleep, but liable to awake
suddenly to a fierce life. As for Vernon he seemed
positively rapt.

" There's your castle in Spain," he cried. " Odd
thing ! but I seem to have seen all this before. I
knew before we turned the corner that there were
olive trees there, and that the rocks tumbled just
in that way into the cove. Listen ! "

The sound of voices drifted up from the beach,
and there was a snatch of a song.

" That's Antiphilos of Byzantium—you remember in the *Anthology*—the fisher-boys singing round
the broth-pot. Lord ! what a haunted spot !
I'd like to spend the night here."

I can give no reason for it, but I suddenly
felt a strange uneasiness, which made me turn
back and stride at a good pace along the terrace.
We seemed to have blundered outside the ordinary
natural world. I had a feverish desire to get
away from the shadow of that pile of masonry, to
get beyond the headland and in sight of the yacht.
The place was wonderful, secret, beautiful, yet
somehow menacing. Vernon clearly felt nothing
of all this, for he grumbled at my haste. " Hang
it, we're not walking for a wager," he complained.
" There's loads of time before dinner. . . . I want
to stay on here a bit. I never saw such a
place."

At the beginning of the paved terrace close to
the quay we came suddenly upon two men, probably from the fishermen's party we had seen on

the shore. They were well-set-up fellows, with handsome clear-cut faces, for the true Greek strain is still found in the islands. We came on them by surprise as we turned the corner of a rock, and they may have thought from our direction that we were coming from the house. Anyhow they seemed to get the fright of their lives. Both leaped aside and looked at us with startled angry eyes. Then they flung up their right hands ; and for a moment I thought they were going to attack us.

But they contented themselves with spitting on their breasts and each holding out a clenched fist with the little finger and the thumb extended. I had seen this before—the ancient protection against the evil eye. But what impressed me was the expression in their faces. It was at Vernon that they stared, and when their stare moved from him it took in the pile of the house above. They seemed to connect us in some way with the house, and in their eyes there was an almost animal fear and hate. . . . I looked after them when they had passed, and observed that they were hurrying with bent heads up the path which may have led to their village.

Vernon laughed. " Queer chaps ! They looked as scared as if they had seen Pan."

" I don't like this place," I told him when we were approaching the dinghy. " Some of your infernal gods and goddesses have got loose in it. I feel as if I want to run."

" Hullo ! " he cried. " You're getting as impressionable as a minor poet. . . . Hark ! There it is again ! Do you hear ? The Spring Song ? "

But the thin notes which drifted down from the

upland no longer seemed to me innocent. There
was something horrible about that music.

Next morning, when we were steaming south
in calm weather with the island already dim behind
us, I found Vernon smoking peacefully on deck
and looking at sea-birds through a glass. He
nodded gaily as I sat down beside him.

" I had the dream all right—one room nearer.
But the room in which I wait has changed. It
must be due to being out here, for hitherto I've
always spent April in England. I suppose I
furnished it unconsciously with things I had seen
at home—there was a big lacquer cabinet for one
thing, and something like pictures or tapestry on
the walls—and there were great silver fire-dogs.
But now it's quite bare. The same room of course
—I couldn't mistake it—but scarcely any furniture in it except a dark lump in a corner. . . . Only
the fire-dogs are the same. . . . Looks as if the
decks were being cleared for action."

I had expected to find him a little heavy about
the eyes, but he appeared as fresh as if he had just
come from a morning swim, and his voice had a
boyish carelessness.

" Do you know," he said, " I've lost every scrap
of funk or nervousness about the dream ? It's a
privilege, not an incubus. Six years to wait !
I wish I knew how I was going to put them in.
It will be a dull business waiting."

III

Fate contrived that to Vernon, as to several
million others, the next four years should scarcely

deserve the name of dull. By the middle of August I was being cursed by a Guards sergeant in Chelsea barrack yard, and Vernon was training with his Yeomanry somewhere in Yorkshire.

My path was plain compared to that of many honest men. I was a bachelor without ties, and though I was beyond the statutory limit for service I was always pretty hard trained, and it was easy enough to get over the age difficulty. I had sufficient standing in my profession to enable me to take risks. But I am bound to say I never thought of that side. I wanted, like everybody else, to do something for England, and I wanted to do something violent. For me to stay at home and serve in some legal job would have been a thousand times harder than to go into the trenches. Like everybody else, too, I thought the war would be short, and my chief anxiety was lest I should miss the chance of fighting. I was to learn patience and perspective during four beastly years.

I went to France in October '14, and Vernon dined with me before I started. He had got a curious notion into his head. He thought that the war would last for full six years, and his reason was that he was convinced that his dream had to do with it. The opening of the last door would be on the battlefield—of that he was convinced. The consequence was that he was in no hurry. My nephew Charles, who was in the same Yeomanry, spent his days pleading to be sent abroad and trying to exchange into any unit he thought would get away first. On the few occasions I met him he raved like a lunatic about the imbecility of a Government that kept him kicking his heels in England. But Vernon, the night he dined with me, was as placid as Buddha. " I'm learning my job," he said, " and I've a mighty lot to learn. I ought to be a fair soldier in six years' time—just when the crisis is due." But he was very anxious about me, and wanted to get into the Guards to be beside me. Only his fatalism kept him from agitating for a change, for he felt that as he had begun in the Yeomanry, Providence most likely meant him to ·continue there. He fussed a good deal about how we were to correspond, for I seemed to have taken the place of his family. But on the whole I was happy about him, his purpose was so clear and his mind so perfectly balanced. I had stopped thinking seriously about the dream, for it seemed only a whimsy in the middle of so many urgent realities.

I needn't tell you the kind of time I had in France. It was a long dismal grind, but I had the inestimable advantage of good health, and I was never a day off duty because of sickness. I suppose I enjoyed it in a sense ; anyhow I got tremendously keen about my new profession, and rose in it far quicker than I deserved. I was lucky, too. As you know, I stopped something in every big scrap—at Festubert, Loos, Ginchy, Third Ypres, Cambrai and Bapaume—so that I might have covered my sleeve with wound-stripes if I had been so minded. But none of the damage was serious and I can hardly find the marks of it to-day. I think my worst trial was that for more than three years I never had a sight of Vernon.

He went out in the summer of '15 to the Dardanelles and was in the Yeomanry fight at Suvla, where a bit of shrapnel made rather a mess of his left shoulder. After that he was employed on various staff jobs, and during '16 was engaged in some kind of secret service in the Ægean and the Levant. I heard from him regularly, but of course he never spoke of his work. He told me he had learned modern Greek and could speak it like a native, and I fancy he had a hand in Venizelos's revolution. Then he went back to his regiment, and was in the " Broken Spurs " division when the Yeomanry were dismounted. He was wounded again in Palestine in '17, just before the taking of Jerusalem, and after that was second in command of a battalion.

When I was on leave in February '18 Charles dined with me at the Club—a much older and wiser Charles, with an empty sleeve pinned to his tunic, who was now employed in home training.

" It's a bloody and disgusting war," said my nephew, " and if any fellow says he likes it, you can tell him from me that he's a liar. There's only one man I ever met who honestly didn't mind it, and that was old Vernon, and everybody knows that he's cracked."

He expatiated on the exact nature of Vernon's lunacy.

" Cracked—as—cracked, and a very useful kind of insanity, too. I often wished I had half his complaint. He simply didn't give a hang for the old war. Wasn't interested in it, if you see what I mean. Oh, brave as you-be-damned, of course, but plenty of other chaps were brave. His was the most cold-blooded, unearthly kind of courage. I've seen the same thing in men who were sick of life and wanted to be killed and knew they were going to be killed, but Vernon wasn't that sort. He had no notion of being killed—always planning out the future and talking of what he was going to do after the war. As you know, he got badly mauled at Suvla, and he nearly croaked with malaria in Crete, and he had his head chipped at Neby Samwil, so he didn't bear what you might call a charmed life. But some little bird had whispered in his ear that he wasn't going to be killed, and he believed that bird. You never saw a fellow in your life so much at his ease in a nasty place.

" It wasn't that he was a fire-eater," Charles went on. " He never went out to look for trouble. It was simply that it made no difference to him where he was or what he was doing—he was the same composed old fish, smiling away, and keeping quiet and attending to business, as if he thought the whole thing rather foolishness."

" You describe a pretty high class of soldier," I said. " I can't understand why he hasn't gone quicker up the ladder."

" I can," said Charles emphatically. " He was a first-class battalion officer but he wasn't a first-class soldier. The trouble with him, as I say, is that he wasn't interested in the war. He had no initiative, you understand—always seemed to be thinking about something else. It's like Rugby football. A man may be a fine player according to the rules, but unless his heart is in the business and he can think out new tactics for himself he won't be a great player. Vernon wasn't out to do anything more than the immediate situation required. You might say he wasn't dead-set enough on winning the war."

I detected in Charles a new shrewdness. " How did the others get on with him ? " I asked.

" The men believed in him and would have followed him into hell, and of course we all respected him. But I can't say he was exactly popular. Too dashed inhuman for that. He ought to fall in love with a chorus-girl and go a regular mucker. Oh, of course, I like him tremendously and know what a rare good fellow he is ! But the ordinary simple-minded, deserving lad jibs at Sir Galahad crossed with the low-church parson and the 'Varsity don."

The Broken Spurs came to France in the early summer of '18, but I had no chance of meeting them. My life was rather feverish during the last weeks of the campaign, for I was chief staff-officer to my division, and we were never much out of the line. Then, as you know, I nearly came by my end in September, when the Boche made quite a good effort in the way of a gas attack. It was a new gas, which we didn't understand, and I faded away like the grin of the Cheshire cat, and was pretty ill for a time in a base hospital. Luckily it didn't do me any permanent harm, but my complexion will be greenery-yallery till the day of my death.

I awoke to consciousness in a tidy little bed to learn that the war was all but over and the Boche hustling to make peace. It took me some days to get my head clear and take notice, and then, one morning, I observed the man in the bed next to me. His head was a mass of bandages, but there was something about the features that showed which struck me as familiar. As luck would have it, it turned out to be Vernon. He had been badly hit, when commanding his battalion at the crossing of the Scheldt, and for a day or two had been in grave danger. He was recovering all right, but for a time neither of us was permitted to talk, and we used to lie and smile at each other and think of all the stories we would presently tell.

It was just after we got the news of the Armistice that we were allowed to say how d'ye do. We were as weak as kittens, but I, at any rate, felt extraordinarily happy. We had both come through the war without serious damage and a new world lay before us. To have Vernon beside me put the coping-stone on my contentment, and I could see that he felt the same. I remember the thrill I had when we could stretch out our arms and shake hands.

Slowly we began to build up each other's records for the four years. I soon knew, what I had guessed before, the reason of that inhuman composure which Charles had described. Vernon had had a complete assurance that his day of fate was not due yet awhile, and therefore the war had taken a second place in his thoughts. Most men who fought bore the marks of it in harder lines about the mouth and chin and older eyes. But Vernon had kept his youth intact. His face had always had a certain maturity beyond his years, and his eyes had been curiously watchful. These traits were perhaps slightly intensified, but otherwise I noticed no difference.

" You remember what I told you when we last met in October '14 ? " he said. " I was wrong and I'm rather sorry. I thought the war would last for six years and that the last stage of my

dream would be in the field. That would have
been such a simple and right solution. As it is,
I must wait."

I asked if the dream had come regularly in the
past four years.

" Quite regularly," was the answer. " The room
hasn't changed either, except that the dark shadow
in the corner has moved, so I think it must be a
human figure. The place is quite bare and empty
now, except for the silver fire-dogs. . . . I think
there is a little window in the wall, rather high up."

" You have only two years more to wait," I
said, " less—a year and a half." It was then
November '18.

" I know. . . . But I am impatient again. I
thought the climax would come in the war, so I
stopped speculating about it. . . . I thought I would
be called on as a soldier to do something very
difficult, and I was quite ready. . . . But that has
all gone, and I am back in the fog. I must think
it all out again from the beginning."

THE immediate consequence of peace was to keep Vernon and myself apart. You see, we neither of us got better very quickly. When his wounds were healed a kind of neuritis remained; he was tortured with headaches, didn't sleep well, and couldn't recover his lost weight. He was very patient and cheerful about it, and did obediently what he was told, for his one object seemed to be to get fit again. We returned to England together, but presently the doctors packed him off abroad with instructions to bask in the sun and idle at a Riviera villa which had been dedicated to such cases. So I spent a lonely Christmas in London.

Heaven knows I had nothing to complain of compared with most fellows, but 1 count the six months after the Armistice the most beastly in my life. I had never been seriously ill before, all the four years of war I had been brimming over with energy, and it was a new experience for me to feel slack and under-engined. The gas had left a sort of poison in my blood which made every movement an effort. I was always sleepy, and yet couldn't sleep, and to my horror I found myself getting jumpy and neurotic. The creak of a cart in the street worried me so that I wanted to cry; London noise was a nightmare, and when I tried the country I had a like horror of its silence. The thing was purely physical, for I found I could think quite clearly and sanely. I seemed to be two persons, one self-possessed enough watching the antics of the other with disgust and yet powerless to stop them.

Acton Croke was reassuring. " You're a sick man, and you've got to behave as such," he told me. " No attempt to get back into harness. Behave as if you were recovering from a severe operation—regular life, no overstrain physical or mental, simply lie fallow and let nature do its work. You have a superb constitution which, given a chance, will pick up its balance. But don't forget that you're passing through a crisis. If you play the fool you may have indifferent health for the rest of your days."

I was determined that at all events that mustn't happen, so I was as docile as a good child. As I say, I had mighty little to complain of, when you consider the number of good men who, far seedier than I, came back to struggle for their daily bread. I had made a bit of money, so I had a solid hump to live off. There was a dearth at the time of leaders at the Bar, and I could have stepped at once into a bigger practice than I had ever dreamed of. Also, I had a chance, if I wished, of becoming one of the law officers of the Crown. I was still a member of Parliament, and at the December election, though I had never gone near the place, my old constituency had returned me with a majority of more than ten thousand. A pretty gilded position for a demobbed soldier ! But for the present I had to put all that aside and think only of getting well.

There has been a good deal of nonsense talked

about the horror of war memories and the passionate desire to bury them. The vocal people
were apt to be damaged sensitives, who were
scarcely typical of the average man. There were
horrors enough, God knows, but in most people's
recollections these were overlaid by the fierce
interest and excitement, even by the comedy of it.
At any rate that was the case with most of my
friends, and it was certainly the case with me. I
found a positive pleasure in recalling the incidents
of the past four years. The war had made me
younger. You see—apart from regular officers—
I had met few of my own year and standing. I
had consorted chiefly with youth, and had recovered the standpoint of twenty years ago. That
was what made my feeble body so offensive. I
could not regard myself as a man in middle age,
but as a sick undergraduate whose malady was
likely to keep him out of the Boat or the Eleven.

You would have laughed if you could have seen
the way I spent my time. I was so angry with
my ill health that I liked to keep on reminding
myself of the days when I had been at the top of
my form. I remember I made out a complete
record of my mountaineering exploits, working
them out with diagrams from maps and old
diaries, and telling myself furiously that what I
had once done I could do again. . . . I got out my
old Oxford texts and used to construe bits of the
classics, trying to recapture the mood when those
things meant a lot to me. . . . I read again all the
books which used to be favourites but which I
hadn't opened for a score of years. I turned up
the cram books for the Bar exams, and the notes
I had taken in my early days in chambers and the

reports of my first cases. It wasn't sentiment, but a deliberate attempt to put back the clock, and, by recalling the feelings of twenty-five, to convince myself that I had once been a strong man. . . . I even made risky experiments. I went up to Oxford in vacation and managed to get put up in my old diggings in the High. That would have been intolerable if they had recalled war tragedies, but they didn't. The men who had shared them with me were all alive—one a Colonial bishop, one a stockbroker, another high up in the Indian Civil Service. It did me good to see the big shabby sitting-room where, in my day, a barrel of beer had adorned one corner. In March, too, I spent three nights at a moorland inn on the Borders which had once been the head-quarters of a famous reading-party. That was not quite so successful, for the weather and the food were vile, and I was driven to reflect on the difference of outlook between twenty and forty-three.

Still my childishness did me good, and I began slowly to gain ground. The spring helped me, which was early that year, you remember, so that the blossom had begun on the fruit trees in the first days of April. I found that it was the time just before the war that it comforted me most to recall, for then I had been healthy enough and a creature more near my present state than the undergraduate of twenty. I think, too, it was because those years were associated with Vernon. He was never much out of my mind, and the reports from him were cheering. The headaches had gone, he had recovered his power of sleep, and was slowly putting on weight. He had taken to sailing a small boat again, had bought a racing cutter, and had come in third in one of the events at the Cannes Regatta.

I had this last news in a letter which reached me while I was staying at Minster Carteron, and it turned my mind back to the yachting trip I had made with Vernon in 1914 in the Ægean. It revived the picture I had almost forgotten—the green island flushed with spring, the twilight haunted with wild music, the great white house hanging like a cliff over the sea. I had felt the place sinister—I remembered the two men with scared faces and their charm against the evil eye —and even after five years a faint aura of distaste lingered about the memory. That was sufficient to awake my interest, and one afternoon I rummaged in the library. Plakos had been the island's name, and I searched for it in gazetteers.

It was the day of the famous April snowstorm which wrought such havoc among English orchards. The windows of the great room were blurred with falling snow, and the fires on the two hearths were hissing and spluttering while I pursued my researches. Folliot, I remember, was dozing beside one of them in an arm-chair. You know old Folliot, with his mild cattish ways and his neat little Louis Napoleon beard. He wants to be the Horace Walpole of our time, and publishes every few years a book of reminiscences, from which it would appear that he has been the confidant of every great man in Europe for the last half-century. He has not much of a mind, but he has a good memory, and after all there is a faint interest about anybody who has dined out in good company for fifty years.

I woke the old fellow when I dropped by misad-

venture a big atlas on the floor, and he asked
testily what I was after.

"I'm trying to find a beastly Greek islet," I
said. "You haven't by any chance in your
travels visited a place called Plakos ? "

The name roused him. "No," he said, "but
of course I have often heard of it. It belonged to
Shelley Arabin."

"Now, who on earth was Shelley Arabin ? "

"You young men!" old Folliot sighed. "Your
memories are so short and your ignorance so vast.
Shelley Arabin died last year, and had half a
column in *The Times,* but he will have a chapter
in my memoirs. He was one of the most
remarkable men of his day. Shelley Arabin—
to think you never heard of him! Why, I knew
his father."

I drew up an arm-chair to the hearth opposite
him. "It's a foul afternoon," I said, "and
there's nothing to do. I want to hear about
Shelley Arabin. I take it from his name that he
was a Levantine."

Folliot was flattered by my interest. He had
begun to bore people, for the war had created a
mood unfavourable to his antique gossip. He
still stayed a good deal in country houses, but
spent most of his time in the libraries and got
rather snubbed when he started on his reminiscences.

"Bless you, no! A most ancient English
house—the Arabins of Irtling in Essex. Gone out
for good now, I fear. As a boy I remember old
Tom Arabin—a shaggy old bandit, who came to
London once in five years and insulted everybody
and then went back again. He used to dine with

my family, and I remember watching him arrive, for I had a boyish romance about the man who had been a friend of Byron. Yes, he was with Byron when he died at Missolonghi, and he was an intimate of all the poets of that time—Byron, Shelley —he called his son after Shelley—Keats too, I think—there's a mention of him in the *Letters* I'm almost sure—and he lived with Landor in Italy till they quarrelled. A most picturesque figure, but too *farouche* for comfort. With him a word was a blow, you understand. He married —now, who did he marry?—one of the Manorwaters, I fancy. Anyhow, he led her the devil of a life. He bought or stole or acquired somehow the island of Plakos, and used it as a base from which to descend periodically upon the civilised world. Not a pleasant old gentleman, but amazingly decorative. You may have seen his translation of Pindar. I have heard Jebb say that it was a marvellous piece of scholarship, but that his English style was the exact opposite of everything that Pindar stood for. Dear me! How short the world's memory is!"

"I want to hear about his son," I said.

"You shall—you shall! Poor Shelley, I fear he had not the kind of upbringing which is commonly recommended for youth. Tom disliked his son, and left him to the care of the family priest—they were Catholics of course. All his boyhood he spent in that island among the peasants and the kind of raffish company that his father invited to the house. What kind of company? Well, I should say all the varieties of humbug that Europe produces—soldiers of fortune and bad poets and the gentry who have made their

native countries too hot for them. Plakos was the
refuge of every brand of outlaw, social and political.
Ultimately the boy was packed off to Cambridge,
where he arrived speaking English a generation
out of date and with the tastes of a Turkish pasha,
but with the most beautiful manners. Tom, when
he wasn't in a passion, had the graciousness of
a king, and Shelley was a young prince in air and
feature. He was terribly good-looking in a way
no man has a right to be, and that prejudiced him
in the eyes of his young contemporaries. Also
there were other things against him."

" How long did Cambridge put up with him ? "
I asked.

" One year. There was a scandal—rather a
bad one, I fancy—and he left under the blackest
kind of cloud. Tom would not have him at home,
but he gave him a good allowance, and the boy
set up in London. Not in the best society, you
understand, but he had a huge success in the half-
world. Women raved about him, and even when
his reputation was at its worst, he would be seen
at a few good houses. . . . I suppose a lawyer does
not concern himself with poetry, but I can assure
you that Shelley Arabin made quite a name for
himself in the late eighties. I believe bibliophiles
still collect his first editions. There was his epic
on the Fall of Jerusalem—a very remarkable
performance as a travesty of history. And there
were his love sonnets, beautiful languid things
quite phosphorescent with decay. He carried
Swinburne and Baudelaire a stage further. Well,
that mood has gone from the world and Shelley
Arabin's reputation with it, but at one time sober
critics felt obliged to praise him even when they

detested him. He was a red-hot revolutionary, too, and used to write pamphlets blackguarding British policy. . . . I saw quite a lot of him in those days, and I confess that I found him fascinating. Partly it was his beauty and his air, partly that he was like nobody I had ever met. He could talk wonderfully in his bitter, high-coloured way. But I never liked him. Oh no, I never liked him. There was always a subtle cruelty about him. Old Tom had been a blackguard, but he had had a heart—Shelley behind all his brilliance was ice and stone. I think most people came to feel this, and he had certainly outstayed his welcome before he left London."

" What made him leave ? "

" His father's death. Tom went out suddenly from old age just before the war between Greece and Turkey. Shelley left England with a great gasconade of Greek patriotism—he was going to be a second Byron and smite the infidel. By all accounts he did very little. I doubt if he had old Tom's swashbuckling courage : indeed I have heard ugly stories of the white feather. . . . Anyhow England knew him no more. He married a girl he met in Rome—Scotch—a Miss Hamilton, I think, but I never knew of what Hamiltons. He treated her shamefully after the Arabin tradition. She did not live long, and there were no children, I believe, and now Shelley is dead and the Arabins are extinct. Not a pleasant family, you will say, and small loss to the world. But there was a certain quality, too, which under happier circumstances might have made them great. And assuredly they had looks. There was something almost unholy about Shelley's beauty in his early

days. It made men instinctively dislike him.
If I had had a son I should have liked him to be
snub-nosed and bullet-headed, for ugliness in
the male is a security for virtue and a passport to
popularity."

This was probably a sentence from one of Folliot's
silly books of reminiscences. My curiosity about
Plakos was not exhausted and I asked what kind
of life had been lived there. " The house is a
tremendous affair," I said, " with room for a
regiment."

" I know," said Folliot, " and it was often full.
I had always a great curiosity to go there, though
I dare say I should have found the atmosphere too
tropical for my taste. Shelley never invited me,
but if I had arrived he could scarcely have turned
me away. I entertained the notion at one time,
but I kept putting it off till my taste for that kind
of adventure declined. . . . No, I have never been
nearer Plakos than Athens, where I once spent a
fortnight when Fanshawe was our Minister there.
I asked about Shelley, of course, and Fanshawe
gave me an ugly report. Plakos, you must know,
is a remote and not over-civilised island where
the writ of the Greek Government scarcely runs,
so it was very much a patriarchal despotism. I
gathered that Shelley was not a popular landlord.
There had been many complaints, and one or
two really horrid stories of his treatment of the
peasantry. It seemed that he saw a good deal
of company, and had made his house a resort for
the rascality of Europe. The rascality—not merely
the folly, as in his father's time. The place fairly
stank in Fanshawe's nostrils. ' The swine still
calls himself an Englishman,' he told me, ' still

keeps his English domicile, so we get the blame of his beastliness. And all the while, too, he is sluicing out venom about England. He is clever enough to keep just inside the tinpot Greek law. I'd give a thousand pounds to see him clapped in gaol.' "

I had heard all I wanted to know, and picked up a book, while Folliot busied himself with the newspaper. A little later he interrupted me.

" I have just remembered something else. You knew Wintergreen, the archæologist ? He was at the British School in Athens, and then excavated Hittite remains in Asia Minor. Poor fellow, he died of dysentery as an intelligence officer in Mesopotamia. Well, Wintergreen once spoke to me of Plakos. I suppose he had been there, for he had been everywhere. We were talking, I remember, one night in the club about Gilles de Rais—the French Bluebeard, you know, the friend of Joan of Arc—and I asked if anything approaching that kind of miscreant still existed on the globe. Somebody said that the type was fairly common in the East, and mentioned some Indian potentate. Wintergreen broke in. ' You don't need to go to the East,' he said. ' You can find it in Europe,' and he started to speak of Shelley Arabin. I don't recollect what exactly he said, but it was pretty bad, and of course strictly libellous. By his account Shelley had become a connoisseur and high-priest of the uttermost evil, and the cup of his iniquities was nearly full. It seemed that Wintergreen had been in the island excavating some ancient remains and living among the peasants, and had heard tales that sickened him. He thought that some day soon the great

house would go flaming to heaven, set alight by
an outraged people.

" Well, it hasn't happened." Folliot returned
to his *Times*. " Shelley has died in his bed, which
is perhaps more than he deserved. Not agreeable
people, I fear. It is a good thing that he left
no posterity."

That evening I thought a good deal about
Plakos. I was glad to have discovered the reason
for the aversion which I had felt on our visit, and
was inclined to believe that I must be a more
sensitive person than my friends would admit.
After that the subject passed from my mind.

By the end of April I was so much recovered
that I went back to my practice at the Bar, and
was almost snowed under by the briefs which
descended on my shoulders as soon as there was
a rumour of my return. It would have been a
difficult job to select, and I dare say I should have
slipped into overwork, had I not been made a
Law Officer. That, so to speak, canalised my
duties, and since my task was largely novel and,
at the moment, of extraordinary interest, the
change completed my convalescence. In May I
was my normal self, and when Vernon returned to
England in June he found me eating, sleeping
and working as in the old days—a fitter man,
indeed, than in 1914, for the war seemed to have
drawn off the grosser humours of middle life.

Vernon, too, was fit again. If a young man
starts with a fine constitution and a strong character and applies all the powers of his mind to
the task of getting well, he is almost certain to
succeed. He came back to London a lean, sun-

burnt creature, with an extraordinarily *rarified*
look about him. He had lost nothing of his
youth, indeed he scarcely looked his twenty-five
years ; but he had been fined down and tautened
and tested, so that his face had a new spirituality
in it as if there was a light shining behind. I
have noticed the same thing in other cases of head
wounds. You remember how Jim Barraclough,
who used to be a heavy red-haired fellow, came out
of hospital looking like a saint in an Italian primitive.

Vernon was changed in other ways. You see,
he belonged to a generation which was nearly
cleaned out by the war, and he had scarcely a
friend of his own year left except my nephew
Charles. That should not have meant so much
to him as to other people, for he had never depended
greatly on friends, but I think the thought of all
the boys who had been at school and college with
him lying under the sod gave him a feeling of
desperate loneliness, and flung him back more
than ever on himself. I could see that even I
meant less to him than before, though I still
meant a good deal.

I was partly to blame for that, perhaps. The
war had altered everybody's sense of values, and
unconsciously I had come to take his dream less
seriously. I had got into a mood of accepting
things as they came and living with short horizons,
and the long perspective which dominated his
thoughts seemed to me a little out of the picture.
I was conscious of this change in myself, and
strove not to show it, but he must have felt it,
and the blinds came down ever so little between
us. For it was clear that the dream meant more

than ever to him. He was in the last lap now,
had rounded the turn and was coming up the
straight, and every nerve and sinew were on the
stretch. I couldn't quite live up to this ardour,
though I tried hard, and with that lightning
instinct of his he was aware of it, and was sparing
of his confidences. The thing made me miserable,
for it increased his loneliness, and I longed for the
next year to be over and the apocalyptic to be
driven out of his life. The mere fact that I took
for granted that nothing would happen showed
that I had lost my serious interest in his dream.
Vernon had to outgrow a childish fancy, as one
outgrows a liability to chicken-pox—that was all.

He had become harder too, as a consequence of
loneliness. You remember that curious summer
of 1919 when everybody was feverishly trying
to forget the war. They were crazy days, when
nobody was quite himself. Politicians talked and
writers wrote clotted nonsense, statesmen chased
their tails, the working-man wanted to double
his wages and halve his working hours at a time
when the world was bankrupt, youth tried to make
up for the four years of natural pleasure of which
it had been cheated, and there was a general
loosening of screws and a rise in temperature.
It was what I had looked for, and I sympathised
with a good deal of it, but, Lord bless me! Vernon
was like an Israelitish prophet at a feast of Baal.
I recalled what Charles had said about him in the
war, and I wondered if Charles had not been right.
Vernon seemed destitute of common humour.

I took him to dine at the Thursday Club, which
had just been started. There he behaved well
enough, for he found people who could talk his

own language. But I noticed how complete was
his apathy when politics were the subject of conversation. He was as uninterested in the setting
to rights of the world as a hermit in a cell. He
was oddly uncompanionable, too. Burminster's
rollicking chaff got nothing out of him but a
Monna Lisa smile. " What has happened to the
boy ? " that worthy asked me afterwards. " Shell-
shock or what ?   Has he left a bit of his mind
out in France ?   He's the most buttoned-up thing
I ever struck."

He was worse with the ordinary young man.
I gave a dinner or two for him, and, as we had one
club in common, we occasionally found ourselves
together in smoking-room gatherings. I had an
immense pity for youth struggling to adjust its
poise, and often I could have found it in my heart
to be annoyed with Vernon's uncanny balance,
which was not far from egotism. These poor
lads were splashing about in life, trying to find
their feet, and for their innocent efforts he had
only a calm contempt. He sat like a skeleton at
the feast, when they chattered about their sporting
and amorous ventures and discussed with abysmal
ignorance how money was to be made in a highly
expensive world. I have a vivid recollection of
his courteous insulting aloofness.

" What rot to say that the war has done any
good," he remarked to me once as we walked back
to the flat. " It has killed off the men, and left
only the half-wits."

Charles, now endeavouring without much success to earn a living in the City, was vehement on
the subject, and he had a characteristic explanation. " Vernon has become a wonderful old

fossil," he said. " Not gone to seed, like some of
the rest, but a fossil—dried up—mummified. It
isn't healthy, and I'm pretty certain about the
cause. He's got something on his mind, and I
shouldn't be surprised if he was preparing to come
an everlasting cropper. I think it's a girl."

It certainly was not a girl. I often wished it
had been, for to a fellow as lonely as Vernon the
best cure, as I saw it, would have been to fall in
love. People had taken furiously to dancing, and
that summer, though there were no big balls, every
dinner party seemed to end in a dance, and every
restaurant was full of rag-time music and ugly
transatlantic shuffling. For youth it was a good
way of working off restlessness, and foolish middle
age followed the guiding of youth. I had no fault
to find with the fashion. The poor girls, starved
for four years of their rights, came from dull war-
work and shadowed schoolrooms determined to
win back something. One could forgive a good
deal of shrillness and bad form in such a case. My
one regret was that they made such guys of themselves. Well-born young women seemed to have
taken for their models the cretinous little oddities
of the film world.

One night Vernon and I had been dining at the
house of a cousin of mine and had stayed long
enough to see the beginning of the dance that
followed. As I looked on, I had a sharp impression of the change which five years had brought.
This was not, like a pre-war ball, part of the
ceremonial of an assured and orderly world. These
people were dancing as savages danced—to get
rid of or to engender excitement. Apollo had
been ousted by Dionysos. The nigger in the band

who came forward now and then and sang some
gibberish was the true master of ceremonies. I
said as much to Vernon, and he nodded. He was
watching with a curious intensity the faces that
passed us.

" Everybody is leaner," I said, " and lighter
on their feet. That's why they want to dance.
But the women have lost their looks."

" The women ! " he murmured. " Look at
that, I beseech you ! "

It was a tall girl, who was dancing with a handsome young Jew, and dancing, as I thought, with
a notable grace. She was very slim and clearly
very young, and I dare say would have been
pretty, if she had let herself alone. I caught a
glimpse of fine eyes, and her head was set on her
neck like a flower on its stalk. But some imp had
inspired her to desecrate the gifts of the Almighty.
Her hair was bobbed, she had too much paint and
powder on her face, she had some kind of barbaric
jewels in her ears which put her head out of drawing, and she wore a preposterous white dress.
Don't ask me to describe it, for I am not an expert
in millinery ; but it seemed to me wrong by every
canon of decency and art. It had been made, no
doubt, with the intention of being provocative,
and its audacious lines certainly revealed a great
deal of its wearer's body. But the impression
was rather of an outrage perpetrated on something
beautiful, a foolish ill-bred joke. There was an
absurd innocence about the raddled and half-clad
girl — like a child who for an escapade has
slipped down to the drawing-room in her night-
gown.

Vernon did not feel as I felt. His eyes followed

her for a little, and then he turned to me with a face like stone.

" So much for our righteous war," he said grimly. " It's to produce *that* that so many good fellows died."

EARLY in November I went down to Wirlesdon for the first big covert shoot. I am not a great performer with the gun, and you will not find me often in the first flight in the hunting-field, but, busy as I was, I made time now for an occasional day's shooting or hunting, for I had fallen in love with the English country, and it is sport that takes you close to the heart of it. Is there anything in the world like the corner of a great pasture hemmed in with smoky-brown woods in an autumn twilight: or the jogging home after a good run when the moist air is quickening to frost and the wet ruts are lemon-coloured in the sunset ; or a morning in November when, on some upland, the wind tosses the driven partridges like leaves over tall hedges, through the gaps of which the steel-blue horizons shine ? It is the English winter that intoxicates me more even than the English May, for the noble bones of the land are bare, and you get the essential savour of earth and wood and water.

It was a mild evening as we walked back from the last stand to the house, and, though so late in the year, there was still a show in the garden borders. I like the rather languid scent of autumn flowers when it is chastened by a touch of wood smoke from the gardeners' bonfires ; it wakes so many memories and sets me thinking. This time my thoughts were chiefly of Vernon, whom I had not

seen for several months. We were certainly
drawing apart, and I didn't see how it could be
avoided. I was back in the ordinary world again,
with a mighty zest for it, and he was vowed and
consecrated to his extraordinary obsession. I
could not take it seriously myself, but about one
thing I was grave enough—its effect on Vernon.
Nothing would happen when next April came—
of that I was convinced, but if nothing happened
what would Vernon do ? The linch-pin would be
out of his life. At twenty-six with a war behind
him a man should have found his groove in life,
but at twenty-six Vernon would be derelict, like
one who has trained himself laboriously for an
occupation which is gone. I put aside the notion
that anything could happen, for in my new mood
I was incredulous of miracles. But my scepticism
did not dispel my anxiety.

The hall at Wirlesdon is a big comfortable stone-
flagged Georgian place, and before one of the fire-
places, with two great Coromandel screens for a
shelter, there was the usual encampment for tea.
It was a jolly sight—the autumn dusk in the tall
windows, the blazing logs and the group of fresh-
coloured young faces. I had gone straight to the
covert-side that morning, so I had still to greet my
hostess, and I was not clear who were staying in
the house. Mollie Nantley, busied in making tea,
muttered some indistinct introductions, and I bowed
to several unfamiliar young women in riding-habits
who were consuming poached eggs. I remembered
that this was the Saturday country for the Mivern,
and presently one of the red backs turned towards
me, and I saw that it was Vernon.

The Mivern cut-away became him uncommonly

well, and his splashed breeches and muddy boots
corrected the over-precision which was apt to
be the fault of his appearance.   Once he would
have made a bee-line towards me, but now he
contented himself with a smile and a wave of his
hand.   We were certainly drifting apart. . . . He
was talking to one of the Nantley girls, a pretty
shy creature, just out of the schoolroom, and
Tom Nantley, her father, made a third in the
conversation.   As I drank my tea I looked round
the little gathering.   There were Bill Harcus and
Heneage Wotton and young Cheviot who had been
of the shooting party.   Lady Altrincham was
there with her wonderful pearls—she is one of
those people whose skin nourishes pearls and she
is believed to take them to bed with her.   Young
Mrs Lamington, who had been walking with the
guns, was kicking the burning logs with her man-
nish shoes and discussing politics with the son of
the house, Hugo Brune, who was in Parliament.
There were several girls, all with clear skins and
shorn curls and slim straight figures.   I found
myself for the first time approving the new fashion
in clothes.   These children looked alert and vital
like pleasant boys, and I have always preferred
Artemis to Aphrodite.

But there was one girl who caught and held my
eyes.   She had been hunting, and her flat-brimmed
hat was set deep on her small head and rather
tilted back, for her bobbed hair gave it no support.
Her figure in a well-cut coat and habit was grace-
ful and workmanlike, and there was a rakish
elegance about her pose, as she stood with one
foot on the stone curb of the hearth, holding a
tea-cup as a Wise Virgin may have carried a lamp.

But there was little of the Wise Virgin about her
face. Any colour the weather might have whipped
into it had disappeared under a recent powdering,
and my impression was of very red lips against a
dead white background. She had been talking
over her left shoulder to her hostess, and now her
eyes were roaming about the place, with a kind
of arrogant nonchalance. They met mine, and I
saw that they were curiously sullen and masterful. Then they passed from me, for a middle-
aged lawyer did not interest them, dwelt for a
moment on Cheviot and Wotton, who were having
an argument about woodcock, and finally rested
on Vernon. She had the air of being bored with
her company.

Vernon, talking idly to Tom Nantley, suddenly
found himself addressed.

" Your mare wants practice in jumping stone
walls," she said. " You'll cut her knees to ribbons.
Better try her in caps next time."

You can cut into a conversation gracefully, and
you can cut in rudely. This girl did it rudely.
I could see Vernon's face harden as he replied that
this bit of the Mivern country was strange to him.

" It's the only decent going in the shire. I'm
sick of the rotten pastures in the vale country.
What on earth does one hunt for except for
pace ? "

" Some of us hunt to follow hounds," was
Vernon's curt rejoinder.

She laughed—a rather ugly hard little laugh.
" Follow your grandmother ! If hounds are all
you care about you may as well go beagling !
Give me a cigarette, will you ? "

" Sorry. I haven't any," he replied.

Several men proffered cases. "You'll find heaps, Corrie dear," Mollie Nantley said, "in the box behind you." The girl reached behind her for the box and offered it to Vernon. When he declined she demanded a match, and Vernon, with an ill grace, lit her cigarette. It was plain that he detested her manners.

So most certainly did I. The little incident I had witnessed was oddly ill-bred and brazen. And yet "brazen" was not quite the word, for it implies self-consciousness. This masterful girl had no shadow of doubt as to her behaviour. She seemed to claim the right to domineer, like a barbaric princess accustomed to an obsequious court. Yes, "barbaric" was the right epithet. Mollie had called her "Corrie" and the name fitted her. No doubt she had been baptized Cora or Corisande, names which for me recalled the spangles and saw-dust of a circus.

She had decided that Vernon was the most interesting of the lot of us, and she promptly annexed him, moving to his side and swinging on an arm of a tapestry chair. But Vernon was a hard fellow to drive against his will. His air was a frigid courtesy, and presently he went up to his hostess. "We must be off, Lady Nantley," he said, "for it's getting dark and we are eight miles from home." He collected two of the men and three of the hunting girls, like a chaperone at a ball, shook hands with Mollie and Tom, nodded to me, and marched to the door.

The girl, who was apparently my fellow-guest, followed him with her eyes, and her scarlet lips seemed to twitch in a flicker of amusement. If she had been rude, so had been Vernon, and, had

she known it, it was something of a triumph
to have cracked his adamantine good manners.
When the party had gone, she strolled to the front
of the hearth, stretched her arms above her head,
and yawned.

" Lord, how stiff I am ! " she proclaimed.
" Heigho for a bath ! I hope you've the right
kind of bath salts, Mollie, or I'll be on crutches
to-morrow. Come and talk to me, Dolly ! " She
picked up her crop, made a noose with the lash
around the waist of one of the daughters of the
house and drew her with her. The child, to my
surprise, went smilingly.

I, too, had a bath, and read papers till it was
time to dress. I felt happier about Vernon, for
the sight of his unmistakable ill-temper seemed
to bring him into the common human category.
I had never seen him show dislike so markedly to
any human being as to that atrocious girl, and I
considered that it would be a good thing if his
Olympian calm could be ruffled more often in the
same way. I wondered casually who she could
be, and why the Nantleys should have her to
stay. Probably she was some daughter of pro-
fiteers who had bought her way into an unfamiliar
world, though that would not explain her presence
at Wirlesdon. But an ill-bred young woman did
not interest me enough for my thoughts to dwell
long on her, and my only prayer was that I might
not be placed next her at dinner.

It was a very young party which I found as-
sembled in Mollie's sitting-room, and a hasty
glance convinced me that I would be sent in with
Mrs Lamington. Old Folliot was there, and
presently he sidled up to me to tell me a new

piece of gossip.   Having been out all day in strong
air I was ravenous, and impatient for the announce-
ment of dinner.

" Now, who are we waiting for ? " Tom Nantley
fussed around.   " Oh, Corrie, of course.   Corrie
is always late.   Confound that girl, she has
probably gone to sleep in her bath.   Pam, you
go and dig her out. . . . Hullo, here she comes at
last ! "

In her hunting-kit she had looked handsome
in an outlandish way, but as she swept down—
without any apology—on our hungry mob there
was no question of her beauty.   For one thing she
walked superbly.   Few women can walk, and
the trouble about the new fashion in clothes is
that it emphasises ugly movement.   She wore a
gown of a shade of green which would have ruined
most people's looks, but she managed to carry it
off, and something more.   For a young girl she
was far too heavily made up, but that too she
forced one to accept.   I suddenly had a new view
of her, and realised that there was quality here,
a masterfulness which might charm, an arrogance
which perhaps was not *blasé* but virginal.

I realised, too, that I had seen her before.   This
was the girl whom Vernon and I had watched at
my cousin's dance in July.   I wondered if he
had understood this in their encounter at the
tea-table.

I had barely recovered from this surprise, when
I had another.   Folliot's hand was on my arm
and he was purring in my ear :

" We talked once of Shelley Arabin, and I told
you he left no children.   My memory betrayed
me, for that young lady is his daughter.   She

has the true Arabin eyes and all their unfathomable
conceit. She is what in my day we would have
called ' shocking bad form.' Rather common, I
think."

From which I knew that she must have dealt
hardly with old Folliot.

At dinner I sat between Mollie and Mrs Lamington, and since my hostess had the garrulous Cheviot
on her right hand, I devoted myself to my other
neighbour. That charming lady, who gives to
political intrigue what time she can spare from
horseflesh, had so much to tell me that I had no
need to exert myself. She was eloquent on the
immense importance of certain pending Imperial
appointments, especially on the need of selecting
men with the right kind of wives, the inference
being that George Lamington's obvious defi-
ciencies might be atoned for by the merits of his
lady. I must have assented to everything that
she said, for she told Mollie afterwards that the
war had improved me enormously and had
broadened my mind. But as a matter of fact
I was thinking of Miss Arabin.

She sat nearly opposite to me, and I could
watch her without staring. Her manner seemed
to alternate between an almost hoydenish vivacity
and complete abstraction. At one moment she
would have her young neighbours laughing and
protesting volubly, and then she would be apparently deaf to what they said, so that they either
talked across her or turned to their other partners.
. . . In these latter moods her eyes seemed almost
sightless, so wholly were they lacking in focus or
expression. Sometimes they rested on the table
flowers, sometimes on the wall before her, some-

times on Mrs Lamington and myself—but they
were always unseeing. Instead of their former
sullenness, they seemed to have a brooding innocence. . . . I noticed, too, the quality of her voice
when she spoke. It was singularly arresting—
clear, high and vital. She talked the usual
staccato slang, but though she rarely finished a
sentence grammatically, the cadence and intonation
were always rounded off to a satisfying close.
Only her laugh was ugly, as if it were a forced
thing. Every other sound that came from her
had a musical completeness.

She had the foreign trick of smoking before the
close of dinner, and, as if to preserve her beautiful
fingers from contamination, before lighting a
cigarette she would draw on to her right hand a
silk glove of the same colour as her gown. The
Nantleys seemed to be accustomed to this habit,
but it at last withdrew Mrs Lamington from her
Imperial propaganda.

" What an extraordinary young woman ! " she
whispered to me. " Who is she ? Is she a little
mad, or only foreign ? "

I paraphrased old Folliot in my reply : " Pure
English, but lives abroad."

The green glove somehow recalled that April
evening at Plakos. This outlandish creature was
interesting, for God knew what strange things
were in her upbringing and her ancestry. Folliot
was an old fool ; she might be odious, but she was
assuredly not " common." As it chanced the
end of dinner found her in one of her fits of
absent-mindedness, and she trailed out of the
room with the other women like a sleep-walker.
The two youngsters who had been her com-

panions at table stared after her till the door closed.

Later in the drawing-room I returned to my first impression. The girl was detestable. I would have liked a sleepy evening of bridge, but the young harpy turned the sober halls of Wirlesdon into a cabaret. She behaved like a man-eating shark, and swept every male, except Tom Nantley, Folliot and myself, into her retinue. They danced in the library, because of its polished empty floor, and when I looked in I saw that the kind of dances were not what I should have chosen for youth, and was glad that Pam and Dolly had been sent to bed. I heard a clear voice declaring that it was " devilish slow " and I knew to whom the voice belonged. At the door I passed old Folliot on his way to his room, and he shook his head and murmured " Common." This time I almost agreed with him.

In the drawing-room I found my hostess skimming the weekly press and drew up a chair beside her. Mollie Nantley and I count cousinship, though the relation is slightly more remote, and she has long been my very good friend. She laid down her paper and prepared to talk.

" I was so glad to see Colonel Milburne again. He looks so well too. But, Ned dear, you ought to get him to go about more, for he's really a little old-maidish. He was scared to death by Corrie Arabin."

" Well, isn't she rather—shall we say disconcerting ? More by token, who is she ? "

" Poor little Corrie ! She's the only child of a rather horrible man who died last year—Shelley Arabin. Did you never hear of him ? He married

a sort of cousin of mine and treated her shamefully. Corrie had the most miserable upbringing
—somewhere in Greece, you know, and in Rome
and Paris, and at the worst kind of girls' school
where they teach the children to be snobs and
powder their noses and go to confession. The
school wouldn't have mattered, for the Arabins
are Romans, and Corrie couldn't be a snob if she
tried, but her home life would have ruined St
Theresa. She was in London last summer with
the Ertzbergers, and I was rather unhappy about
her living among cosmopolitan Jew *rastaquouères*,
so I am trying to do what I can for her this winter.
Fortunately she has taken madly to hunting and
she goes most beautifully. She has never had a
chance, poor child. You must be kind to her,
Ned."

I said that I was not in the habit of being brutal
to young women, but that she was not likely to
want my kindness. " She seems to be a success
in her way. These boys follow her like sheep."

" Oh, she has had one kind of success, but not
the best kind. She casts an extraordinary spell
over young men, and does not care a straw for
one of them. I might be nervous about Hugo,
but I'm not in the least, for she is utterly sexless
—more like a wild boy. It is no good trying to
improve her manners, for she is quite unconscious
of them. I don't think there is an atom of harm
in her, and she has delightful things about her
—she is charming to Pam and Dolly, and they
adore her, and she is simply the most honest
creature ever born. She must get it from her
mother, for Shelley was an infamous liar."

Mollie's comely face, with her glorious golden-red

hair slightly greying at the temples, had a look of compassionate motherliness. With all her vagueness, she is one of the shrewdest women of my acquaintance, and I have a deep respect for her judgment. If she let her adored Pam and Dolly make friends of Miss Arabin, Miss Arabin must be something more than the cabaret girl of my first impression.

" But I'm not happy about her," Mollie went on. " I can't see her future. She ought to marry, and the odds are terribly against her marrying the right man. Boys flock after her, but the really nice men—like Colonel Milburne—fly from her like the plague. They don't understand that her bad form is not our bad form, but simply foreignness. . . . And she's so terribly strong-minded. I know that she hates everything connected with her early life, and yet she insists on going back to that Greek place. Her father left her quite well off, I believe—Tom says so and he has looked into her affairs—and she ought to settle down here and acclimatise herself. All her superficial oddities would soon drop off, for she is so clever she could make herself whatever she wanted. It is what she wants, too, for she loves England and English ways. But there is a touch of ' daftness ' about her, a kind of freakishness which I can never understand. I suppose it is the Arabin blood."

Mollie sighed.

" I try to be tolerant about youth," she added, " but I sometimes long to box its ears. Besides, there is the difficulty about the others. I am quite sure of Corrie up to a point, but I can't be responsible for the young men. George Cheviot shows every inclination to make a fool of himself about her, and what am I to say to his mother ? Really, having Corrie in the house is like domesticating a destroying angel."

" You're the kindest of women," I said, " but I think you've taken on a job too hard for you. You can't mix oil and wine. You'll never fit Miss Arabin into your world. She belongs to a different one."

" I wonder what it is ? "

" A few hours ago I should have said it was the world of cabarets and Riviera hotels and Ertzbergers. After what you have told me I'm not so sure. But anyhow it's not our world."

As I went to bed I heard the jigging of dance music from the library, and even in so large a house as Wirlesdon its echoes seemed to pursue me as I dropped into sleep. The result was that I had remarkable dreams, in which Miss Arabin, dressed in the spangles of a circus performer and riding a piebald horse, insisted on my piloting her with the Mivern, while the Master and Vernon looked on in stony disapproval.

The next morning was frosty and clear, and I came down to breakfast to find my hostess alone in the dining-room.

" Corrie behaved disgracefully last night," I was informed. " She started some silly rag with George Cheviot and made hay of Mr. Harcus's bedroom. Tom had to get up and read the Riot Act in the small hours. I have been to her room and found her asleep, but as soon as she wakes I am going to talk to her very seriously. It is more than bad manners, it is an offence against hospitality."

I went to church with Tom and his daughters,

and when we returned we found Miss Arabin
breakfasting before the hall fire on grapes and
coffee, with the usual young men in attendance.
If she had been given a lecture by her hostess,
there was no sign of it in her face. She looked
amazingly brilliant—all in brown, with a jumper
of brown arabesque and long amber ear-rings. A
russet silk glove clothed the hand in which she
held her cigarette.

Vernon came over to luncheon and sat next to
Mollie, while at the other end of the table I was
placed between Miss Arabin and Lady Altrincham.
The girl scarcely threw a word to me, being
occupied in discussing quite intelligently with
Hugo Brune the international position of Turkey.
I could not avoid overhearing some of their talk,
and I realised that when she chose she could behave
like a civilised being. It might be that Mollie's
morning discourse had borne fruit. Her voice
was delightful to listen to, with its full clear tones
and delicate modulations. And then, after her
habit, her attention wandered, and Hugo's platitudes fell on unheeding ears. She was staring
at a picture of a Jacobean Nantley on the wall,
and presently her eyes moved up the table and
rested on Vernon.

She spoke to me at last.

" Who is the man next to Mollie—the man who
came to tea last night ? You know him, don't you?"

I told her his name.

" A soldier ? " she asked.

" Has been. Does nothing at present. He has
a place in Westmorland."

" You are friends ? "

" The closest." There was something about the

girl's brusqueness which made me want to answer in monosyllables. Then she suddenly took my breath away.

"He is unhappy," she said. "He looks as if he had lost his way."

She turned to Hugo, and, with an urbanity which I had thought impossible, apologised for her inattention and took up the conversation at the point at which she had dropped it.

Her words made me keep my eyes on Vernon. Unhappy! There was little sign of it in his lean smiling face, with the tanned cheeks and steady eyes. Mollie was clearly delighted with him; perhaps her maternal heart had marked him down for Dolly. Lost his way? On the contrary he seemed at complete ease with the world. Was this strange girl a sorceress to discover what was hidden deep in only two men's minds? I had a sense that Vernon and Miss Arabin, with nothing on earth in common, had yet a certain affinity. Each had a strain of romance in them—romance and the unpredictable.

Vernon had motored over to Wirlesdon and proposed to walk back, so I accompanied him for part of the road. I was glad of a chance for a talk, for I was miserably conscious that we were slipping away from each other. I didn't see how I could help it, for I was immersed in practical affairs, while he would persist in living for a dream. Before the war I had been half under the spell of that dream, but four years' campaigning had given me a distaste for the fantastic and set my feet very solidly on the rock of facts. Our two circles of comprehension, which used to intersect, had now become self-contained.

I asked him what he was doing with himself, and he said hunting and shooting and dabbling in books. He was writing something—I think about primitive Greek religion, in consequence of some notions he had picked up during his service in the Ægean.

" Seriously, old fellow," I said, " isn't it time you settled down to business ? You are twenty-five, you have first-class brains, and you are quite fit now. I can't have you turning into a *flâneur*."

" There is no fear of that," he replied rather coldly. " I am eager for work, but I haven't found it yet. My training isn't finished. I must wait till after next April."

" But what is going to happen after that ? "

" I don't know. I must see what happens *then*."

" Vernon," I cried, " we are old friends and I am going to speak bluntly. You really must face up to facts. What is going to happen next April ? What *can* happen ? Put it at its highest. You may pass through some strange mental experience. I can't conceive what it may be, but suppose the last door does open and you see something strange and beautiful or even terrible—I don't know what. It will all happen inside your mind. It will round off the recurring experiences you have had from childhood, but it can't do anything more."

" It will do much more," he said. " It will be the crisis of my life. . . . Why have you become so sceptical, Ned ? You used to think as I do about it."

" It will only be a crisis if you make it so, and it's too risky. Supposing on the other hand that nothing happens. You will have keyed your whole being up to an expectation which fails. You will be derelict, cut clean from your moorings. It's too risky, I tell you."

He shook his head. "We have fallen out of understanding each other. Your second alternative is impossible. I know it in my bones. Something will happen—must happen—and then I shall know what I have to do with my life. It will be the pistol-shot for the start."

"But, my dear old man, think of the hazard. You are staking everything on a wild chance. Heaven knows, I'm not unsympathetic. I believe in you—I believe in a way in the reality of the dream. But life is a prosaic thing, and if you are to have marvels in it you should take them in your stride. I want to see you with some sort of policy for the future, and letting the last stage of your dream drop in naturally into a strategic plan. You can't at twenty-six sit waiting on a revelation. You must shape your own course, and take the revelation when it comes. If you don't, you'll find yourself derelict. Damn it, you're far too good to be a waif."

He smiled a little sadly. "We're pretty far apart now, I'm afraid. Can't you see that the thing is too big a part of me to be treated as a side-show? It's what I've been sent into the world for. I'm waiting for my marching orders."

"Then you're waiting for a miracle," I said testily.

"True. I am waiting for a miracle," he replied. "We needn't argue about it, Ned, for miracles are outside argument. In less than six months

I will know. Till then I am content to live by faith."

After leaving him, I walked back to the house in an uncomfortable frame of mind. I realised that the affection between us was as deep as ever, but I had a guilty sense of having left him in the lurch. He was alone now, whereas once I had been with him, and I hated to think of his loneliness.

As I crossed the bridge between the lakes I met Miss Arabin sauntering bareheaded in the autumn sunlight. I would have passed on, with a curt greeting, for I was in no mood to talk trivialities to a girl I disliked, but to my surprise she stopped and turned with me up the long grassy aisle which led to the gardens.

" I came out to meet you," she said. " I want to talk to you."

My response cannot have been encouraging, but she took no notice of that.

" You're a lawyer, aren't you ? " she went on. " Mollie says you are very clever. You look clever."

I dare say I grinned. I was being comprehensively patronised.

" Well, I want you to help me. I have some tiresome legal complications to disentangle, and my solicitor is a sheep. I mean to sack him."

I explained the etiquette of my profession.

" Oh, then you can tell him what to do. You'll understand his silly talk, which I don't. You make him obey you."

" My dear young lady," I said, " I cannot undertake private business. You see I'm in the employ of the Government."

" Don't be afraid, I can pay you all right."
The words were too naïve to be insulting.

I said nothing, and she darted before me and
looked me in the face.

" You mean that you won't help me ? " she
asked.

" I mean that I'm not allowed," I replied.

Without another word she swung round and
disappeared up a side glade. As she vanished
among the beech-trees, a figure as russet as the
drift of leaves, I thought I had never seen anything
more quick and slender, and I fervently hoped
that I should never see her again.

In that hope I was mistaken. A fortnight later the Treasury Solicitor sent me the papers in one of those intricate international cases which were the debris of the war. It was a claim by a resident abroad, who had not lost his British nationality, for compensation for some oppressive act of one of the transient Greek Governments. I left the thing to my " devil," and just skimmed his note before the necessary conference with the plaintiff's solicitors. To my surprise I saw that it had to do with the island of Plakos and the name of Arabin.

Mr Mower, of the reputable firm of Mower & Lidderdale, was not unlike a sheep in appearance —a Leicester ewe for choice. He had a large pale high-boned face, rimless spectacles, a crop of nice fleecy white hair, and the bedside manner of the good family solicitor. My hasty study of the papers showed me that the oppressive acts were not denied, but that the title of the plaintiff was questioned.

" This is a matter of domestic law," I said— " the *lex loci rei sitœ*. If the title to the land is disputed, it is a case for the Greek courts."

" We have reason to believe that the defence is not seriously put forward, for the title is beyond dispute, and we are at a loss to understand the attitude of the Greek Government. The docu-

ments are all in our possession, and we took Mr
Blakeney's advice on them.   His opinion is among
the papers left with you—and you will see that he
has no doubt on the matter."

Mr Blakeney certainly had not, as I saw from
his opinion, nor had my " devil."   The latter
characterised the defence as " monstrous."   It
seemed to be based on an arbitrary act of the old
Greek National Assembly of 1830.   My note said
that   the title   was   complete   in   every   respect,
and   that   the attempt   to question   it seemed to
be   a species   of insanity.   A name caught my
attention.

" What is Koré ? " I asked.

" It is Miss Arabin's Christian name.   Greek, I
presume," said Mr Mower, very much in the tone
in which Mr Pecksniff observed, " Pagan, I regret
to say."

I read the note again, and Blakeney's opinion.
Blakeney was an authority from whom I was not
disposed to differ, and the facts seemed too patent
for argument.   As I turned over the papers I saw
the name of another solicitor on them.

" You   have   not   always   acted   for   the   Arabin
family ? " I asked.

" Only within the last few months.   Derwents
were the family solicitors, but Miss Arabin was
dissatisfied with them and withdrew her business.
Curiously enough, they advised that the claim of
the Greek Government was good, and should not
be opposed."

" What ! " I exclaimed.   Derwents are one of
the best firms in England, and the senior partner,
Sebastian Derwent, was my oldest client.   He was
not only a sound lawyer, but a good scholar and

a good fellow. What on earth had induced him to give such paradoxical advice ?

I told Mr Mower that the matter seemed plain enough, but that for my own satisfaction I proposed to give further consideration to the papers. I took them home with me that evening, and the more I studied them the less I could understand Derwent's action. The thing seemed a bluff so impudent as to be beyond argument. The abstract of title was explicit enough, and Blakeney, who had had the original documents, was emphatic on the point. But the firm of Derwents was not in the habit of acting without good cause. . . . I found myself becoming interested in the affair. Plakos was still a disquieting memory, and the outrageous girl at Wirlesdon was of a piece with its strangeness.

A day or two later I was dining at the Athenæum before going down to the House, and I saw Sebastian Derwent eating a solitary meal at an adjacent table. I moved over beside him, and after some casual conversation I ventured to sound him on the subject. With another man it might have been a delicate task, but we were old and confidential friends.

I told him I had had the Plakos case before me. " You used to act for the Arabins ? " I said.

He nodded, and a slight embarrassment entered his manner. " My father and grandfather too before me. The firm had a difficult time with old Tom Arabin. He had a habit of coming down to the office with a horsewhip, and on one occasion my grandfather was compelled to wrest it from him, break it over his knee and pitch it into the fire."

" I can imagine easier clients. But I am
puzzled about that preposterous Greek claim. I
can't think how it came to be raised, for it is sheer
bluff."

He reddened a little and crumbled his bread.

" I advised Miss Arabin not to dispute it," he
said.

" I know, and I can't imagine why. You advised her to sit down under a piece of infamous
extortion."

" I advised her to settle it."

" But how can you settle a dispute when all the
rights are on one side ? Do you maintain that
there was any law or equity in the Greek case ? "

He hesitated for a second. " No," he said, " the
claim was bad in law. But its acceptance would
have had certain advantages for Miss Arabin."

I suppose I looked dumbfounded. " It's a long
story," he said, " and I'm not sure that I have the
right to tell it to you."

" Let us leave it at that, then. Of course it's
no business of mine." I did not want to embarrass
an old friend.

But he seemed disinclined to leave it. " You
think I have acted unprofessionally ? " he ventured.

" God forbid ! I know you too well, and I
don't want to poke my nose into private affairs."

" I can tell you this much. Miss Arabin is in a
position of extreme difficulty. She is alone in the
world without a near relation. She is very young
and not quite the person to manage a troublesome
estate."

" But surely that is no reason why she should
surrender her patrimony to a bogus demand ? "

" It would not have been exactly surrender. I advised her not to submit but to settle. Full compensation would have been paid if she had given up Plakos."

" Oh, come now," I cried. " Who ever heard of voluntary compensation being paid by a little stony-broke Government in Eastern Europe ? "

" It would have been arranged," he said. " Miss Arabin had friends—a friend—who had great influence. The compensation was privately settled and it was on a generous scale. Miss Arabin has fortunately other sources of income than Plakos : indeed I do not think she draws any serious revenue from the island. She would have received a sum of money in payment, the interest on which would have added substantially to her income."

" But I still don't see the motive. If the lady is not worried about money, why should her friends be so anxious to increase her income ? "

Mr Derwent shook his head. " Money is not the motive. The fact is that Plakos is a troublesome property. The Arabin family have never been popular, and the inhabitants are turbulent and barely civilised. The thing is weighing on her mind. It is not the sort of possession for a young girl."

" I see. In order to rid Miss Arabin of a *damnosa hœreditas* you entered into a friendly conspiracy. I gather that she saw through it."

He nodded. " She is very quick-witted, and was furious at the questioning of her title. That was my mistake. I underrated her intelligence. I should have had the thing more ingeniously framed. I can assure you that my last interview with her was very painful. I was forced to admit the thinness of the Greek claim, and after that I had a taste of Tom Arabin's temper. She is an extraordinary child, but there is wonderful quality in her, wonderful courage. I confess I am thankful as a lawyer to be rid of her affairs, but as a friend of the family I cannot help being anxious. . . . She is so terribly alone in the world."

" That is a queer story," I said. " Of course you behaved as I should have expected, but I fancy that paternal kindliness is thrown away on that young woman. I met her a few weeks ago in a country house, and she struck me as peculiarly able to look after herself. One last question. Who is the friend who is so all-powerful at Athens ? "

"That I fear I am not at liberty to tell you," was the answer.

This tale whetted my curiosity. From old Folliot I had learned something of the record of the Arabins, and I had my own impression of Plakos as clear as a cameo. Now I had further details in my picture. Koré Arabin (odd name ! I remembered from my distant schooldays that Koré was Greek for a " maiden "—it had nothing to do with Corisande of the circus) was the mistress of that sinister island and that brooding house of a people who detested her race. There was danger in the place, danger so great that some friend unknown was prepared to pay a large price to get her out of it, and had involved in the plot the most decorous solicitor in England. Who was this friend ? I wanted to meet him and to hear more of Plakos, for I realised that he and not Derwent was the authority.

Speculation as to his identity occupied a good

deal of my leisure, till suddenly I remembered what Lady Nantley had told me. Miss Arabin had been living in London with the Ertzbergers before she came to Wirlesdon. The friend could only be Theodore Ertzberger. He had endless Greek connections, was one of the chief supporters of Venizelos, and it was through his house that the new Greek loan was to be issued. I had met him, of course, and my recollection was of a small bright-eyed man with a peaked grey beard and the self-contained manner of the high financier. I had liked him and found nothing of the *rastaquou-ère* in him to which Mollie objected. His wife was another matter. She was a large flamboyant Belgian Jewess, a determined social climber and a great patron of art and music, who ran a salon and whose portraits were to be found in every exhibition of the young school of painters. It was borne in on me that my curiosity would not be satisfied till I had had a talk with Ertzberger.

Lady Amysfort arranged the meeting at a Sunday luncheon when Madame Ertzberger was mercifully stricken with influenza.

Except for the hostess, it was a man's party, and afterwards she manœuvred that Ertzberger and I should be left alone in a corner of the big drawing-room.

I did not waste time beating about the bush, for I judged from his face that this man would appreci-ate plain dealing. There was something simple and fine about his small regular features and the steady regard of his dark eyes.

" I am glad to have this chance of a talk with you," I said. " I have lately been consulted about Plakos and Miss Arabin's claim against the Greek

Government. Also a few weeks ago I had the
pleasure of meeting Miss Arabin. The whole
business interests me strongly—not as a lawyer
but as a human being. You see, just before the
war I happened to visit Plakos and I can't quite
get the place out of my head. You are a friend
of hers, and I should like to know something more
about the island. I gather that it's not the most
comfortable kind of estate."

He looked me straight in the face. " I think you
know Mr Sebastian Derwent," he said.

" I do. And he gave me a hint of Miss Arabin's
difficulties and the solution proposed. His con-
duct may not have been strictly professional, but
it was extraordinarily kind. But let me make it
quite clear that he never mentioned your name,
or gave me any sort of clue to it. I guessed that
you were the friend, because I knew that Miss
Arabin had been staying in your house."

" You guessed rightly. It is not a thing that I
naturally want made public, but I am not in the
least ashamed of the part I played. I welcome
the opportunity of discussing it with you. It is
a curious thing, but Miss Arabin has already
spoken of you to me."

" She asked me to advise her, and I'm afraid
was rather annoyed when I told her that I couldn't
take private practice."

" But she has not given up the notion. She
never gives up any notion. She has somehow
acquired a strong belief in your wisdom."

" I am obliged to her, but I am not in a position
to help."

He laid his hand on my arm. " Do not
refuse her," he said earnestly. " Believe me, no

woman ever stood in more desperate need of friends."

His seriousness impressed me. "She has a loyal one in you, at any rate. And she seems to be popular and to have a retinue of young men."

He looked at me sharply. "You think she is a light-headed girl, devoted to pleasure—rather second-rate pleasure—a little ill-bred perhaps. But you are wrong, Sir Edward. Here in England she is a butterfly—dancing till all hours, a madcap in town and in the hunting-field, a bewitcher of foolish boys. Oh, bad form I grant you—the worst of bad form. But that is because she comes here for an anodyne. She is feverishly gay because she is trying to forget—trying not to remember that there is tragedy waiting behind her."

"Where?" I asked.

"In the island of Plakos."

Tragedy—that was the word he used. It had an incongruous sound to me, sitting in a warm London drawing-room after an excellent luncheon, with the sound of chatter and light laughter coming from the group around my hostess. But he had meant it—his grave voice and burdened face showed it—and the four walls seemed to fade into another picture—a twilight by a spring sea, and under a shadowy house two men with up-lifted hands and hate and fear in their eyes.

"If you will do me the honour to listen," Ertzberger was speaking, "I should like to tell you more about Miss Arabin's case."

"Have you known her long?" I asked. A sudden disinclination had come over me to go further in this affair. I felt dimly that if I became the recipient of confidences I might find myself involved in some distasteful course of action.

"Since she was a child. I had dealings with her father—business dealings—he was no friend of mine—but there was a time when I often visited Plakos. I can claim that I have known Miss Arabin for nearly fifteen years."

"Her father was a bit of a blackguard?"

"None of the words we use glibly to describe evil are quite adequate to Shelley Arabin. The man was rotten to the very core. His father—I remember him too—was unscrupulous and violent, but he had a heart. And he had a kind of burning courage. Shelley was as hard and cold as a stone, and he was also a coward. But he had genius— a genius for wickedness. He was beyond all comparison the worst man I have ever known."

"What did he do?" I asked. "I should have thought the opportunities for wrong-doing in a remote island were limited."

"He was a student of evil. He had excellent brains and much learning and he devoted it all to researches in devilry. He had his friends—people of his own tastes who acknowledged him as their master. Some of the gatherings at Plakos would have made Nero vomit. Men and women both. . . . The place stank of corruption. I have only heard the orgies hinted at—heathenish remnants from the backstairs of the Middle Ages. And on the fringes of that hell the poor child grew up."

"Unsmirched?"

"Unsmirched! I will stake my soul on that. A Muse, a Grace, a nymph among satyrs. Her innocence kept her from understanding. And then as she grew older and began to have an ink-

ling of horrors she was in flaming revolt. . . . I
managed to get her sent away, first to school,
then to my wife's charge. Otherwise I think
there would have been a tragedy."

" But surely with her father's death the danger
is gone."

He shook his head. " Plakos is a strange place,
for the tides of civilisation and progress seem to
have left it high and dry. It is a relic of old
days, full of wild beliefs and pagan habits. That
was why Shelley could work his will with it. He
did not confine his evil-doing to his friends and
the four walls of his house. He laid a spell of
terror on the island. There are horrid tales—I
won't trouble you with them—about his dealings
with the peasants, for he revelled in corrupting
youth. And terror grew soon into hate, till in
his last days the man's nerve broke. He lived his
last months in gibbering fear. There is something
to be said after all for mediæval methods. Shelley
was the kind of scoundrel whom an outraged people
should have treated with boiling oil."

" Does the hatred pursue his daughter ? " I
asked.

" Most certainly. It took years for Plakos to
recognise Shelley's enormities, and now the realisation has become cumulative, growing with every
month. I have had inquiries made—it is easy for
me since I have agents everywhere in the Ægean
—and I can tell you the thing has become a mania.
The war brought the island pretty near starvation,
for the fishing was crippled and a succession of
bad seasons spoiled the wretched crops. Also
there was a deadly epidemic of influenza. Well,
the unsettlement of men's minds, which is found

all over the world to-day, has become in Plakos sheer madness. Remember, the people are primitive, and have savagery in their blood and odd faiths in their hearts. I do not know much about these things, but scholars have told me that in the islands the old gods are not altogether dead. The people have suffered and they blame their sufferings on the Arabins, till they have made a monstrous legend of it. Shelley is in hell and beyond their reach, but Shelley's daughter is there. She is the witch who has wronged them, and they are the kind of folk who are capable of witch-burning."

" Good God ! " I cried. " Then the girl ought never to be allowed to return."

" So I thought, and hence my little conspiracy which failed. I may tell you in confidence that it was I who prompted the action of the Greek Government and was prepared to find the compensation. But I was met by a stone wall. She insists on holding on to the place. Worse, she insists on going back. She went there last spring, and the spring is a perilous time, for the people have had the winter to brood over their hatred. I do not know whether she is fully conscious of the risk, for sometimes I think she is still only a child. But last year she was in very real danger, and she must have felt it. Behind all her bravado I could see that she was afraid."

It was an odd tale to hear in a commonplace drawing-room, and it was odder to hear it from such a narrator. There was nothing romantic about Ertzberger. I dare say he had the imaginative quickness of his race, but the dominant impression was of solid good sense. He looked

at the thing from a business man's point of view,
and the cold facts made him shudder.

" What on earth is her reason ? " I asked. " Has
she any affection for Plakos ? "

" She hates it. But there is some stubborn
point of honour which forbids her to let it go.
She has her grandfather's fierce obstinacy. Fate
has dared her to defend her own, and she has
accepted the challenge. . . . It is not merely the
sense of property. I think she feels that she has
a duty—that she cannot run away from the
consequences of her father's devilry. Her presence
there at the mercy of the people is a kind of atonement."

" Has she any friends in the island ? "

" An old steward is the only man in the house.
She may have her well-wishers outside, but they
cannot be many, for she has not lived continuously
there for years. Last spring I tried to have her
guarded, but she saw through my plan and forbade
it. All I could do was to have the place watched
on my own account. This winter my information
is that things are worse. There is famine in the
hills, and the hillmen are looking with jealous
eyes towards the house by the sea. The stories
grow wilder, too."

" What kind ? "

" Oh, witchcraft. That the Arabins are sor-
cerers and that she herself is a witch. Every
misfortune in the island is laid to her account.
God knows what may happen this spring, if she
persists in going back ! My hope was that she
might find some lover who would make her forget
the obsession, but on the contrary the obsession
has made her blind to lovers. Perhaps you have

noticed it. . . . She seems to flirt outrageously, but she keeps every man at a distance. . . . Now, do you understand Miss Arabin a little better ? "

I was beginning to. A picture was growing up in my mind of something infinitely pathetic, and terribly alone. A child terrified by a nightmare life which she did not understand—carried off to a new environment from which she extracted what was more feverish and vulgar, for she had no canons, yet keeping through it all a pitiful innocence—returning to a half-comprehension which revolted her soul—resolute to face the consequences of the past with an illogical gallantry. I did not know when I had heard a tale that so moved me.

" You will not refuse her if she asks your help ? " Ertzberger pleaded.

" But what can I do ? " I said. " I'm a lawyer and she doesn't want legal advice, even if I were free to give it her."

" She has got the notion that you can help her. Don't ask me why or how. Call it a girl's fancy and make the best of it. I cannot influence her, Derwent couldn't, but you may, because for some reason or other she believes that you are wise. . . . I think . . . I think that she thinks that you can tell her what precisely she has to fear in Plakos. There is a mass of papers, you know."

" What to fear ! " I exclaimed. " Surely you have just made that plain. A famished and half-civilised peasantry with a long record of ill treatment. Isn't that enough ? "

" There may be something more," Ertzberger said slowly. " She has an idea that there is something more . . . and she is terrified of that something. If you can get rid of her terrors you will be doing a humane act, Sir Edward. The trouble, as I have told you, is that she will take so few into her confidence."

"Look here, Mr Ertzberger," I said. "I will be quite frank with you. Miss Arabin did not attract me—indeed I have not often been more repelled by a young woman. But what you have said puts a new complexion on her behaviour. Tell her I am willing to do my best for her, to advise her, to help her in any way I can. But if she wouldn't listen to you, you may be certain she won't listen to me."

"That's very good of you," he said, rising. "She proposes to go to Plakos in March. Pray God we can put some sanity into her in the next three months."

Two days later I had to go north by an early
train from Euston, and opposite my platform a
special was waiting, to take a hunting party
down to somewhere in the Shires. Around the
doors of the carriages stood a number of expensive-
looking young people, among whom I recognised
Miss Arabin. She wore a long fur coat and sniffed
at a bunch of violets, while in her high clear
voice she exchanged badinage with two young men.
As she stood with one foot on the carriage step,
her small head tilted backward, her red lips
parted in laughter, it was hard to connect her with
the stricken lady of Ertzberger's story. Just as
the special was leaving I saw Vernon hurry up,
also in hunting-kit. He cast one glance at Miss
Arabin, and found a seat in another carriage. I
hoped the Pytchley would have a fast day, for I
did not see these two fraternising during waits
at covert-side.

Curiously enough I saw the girl again the
same week, also in a railway train. I was returning
from Liverpool, and our trains halted beside each
other at Rugby. She was alone in her carriage,
the winter dusk was falling but the lights were not
yet lit, and I saw her only faintly, silhouetted
against the farther window. She was not asleep,
but her head was sunk as if in a dream. In the
few seconds during which I watched I had a

strong impression of loneliness, almost of dejec-
tion. She was alone with her thoughts, and they
were heavy.

That evening on my return to my flat I found
a big parcel of papers. Characteristically there
was no covering letter or identification of any sort,
but a glance showed me what they were. My time
after dinner that night was at my own disposal,
and I devoted it to reading them. I believe I
would have put aside work of whatever urgency
for that purpose, for Plakos had begun to dominate
my thoughts.

The papers were a curious jumble—no legal
documents, but a mass of family archives and
notes on the island. I observed that there was
nothing concerned with Shelley. Most of the
things had to do with old Tom Arabin—corre-
spondence, original and copied, which had passed
between him and his friends or enemies. There
were letters from Byron and Shelley and Tre-
lawny, one from no less a person than Sir Walter
Scott, many from John Cam Hobhouse, official
dispatches from the British Foreign Office, a
formal note or two from Castlereagh, and several
long and interesting epistles from Canning, who
seemed to have had some friendship for the old
fellow. There was a quantity, too, of corre-
spondence with Continental statesmen, and I
observed several famous names. All this I put on
one side, for it did not concern my purpose.

Then there was old Tom Arabin's diary, which
I skimmed. It was a very human and explosive
document, but there was little about Plakos
in it. Tom was more interested in the high
politics of Europe than in the little domain he had

acquired. Next I turned up a manuscript history of the island in French, written apparently about 1860 by a Greek of the name of Karapanos. This was a dull work, being merely a summary of the island's record under Venetian and Turkish rule, and the doings of its people in the War of Liberation. Then came a bundle of early nineteenth-century maps and charts, and some notes on olive culture. There was a batch, too, of verses in Greek and English, probably Tom's work and not very good. There was a pedigree of the Arabin family in the old Irtling days, and a great deal more junk which had not even an antiquarian interest. I shoved away the papers with a sense of failure. There was nothing here to throw light on Plakos ; if such material existed it must have been in Shelley's papers, of which his daughter had doubtless made a bonfire.

Then I noticed something among the notes on olive culture, and drew out a thick old-fashioned envelope heavily sealed with green wax, which bore the Arabin device of a Turk's head. I opened it and extracted a sheet of yellowish parchment, covered closely with Greek characters. I was taught Greek at school, though I have forgotten most of it, but I never professed to be able to read even the printed Greek of the fifteenth and sixteenth centuries. This document seemed to be of that date, and its insane ligatures and contractions completely defeated me. But there might be something in these hieroglyphics, so I bundled up the rest of the papers and locked the envelope in a dispatch box.

Next day I paid a visit to a Chancery barrister of my acquaintance whose hobby was mediæval

Greek and who had written a monograph on Aldus
Manutius. He examined the thing with delight,
pronounced the calligraphy fifteenth century and
promised to write out the contents for me in decent
Greek script.

It was not till early in the New Year that I got
the manuscript back from him. The task, he said,
had been very difficult, and though he was pretty
certain that he had got the transliteration correct,
he did not profess to be able to construe it. " I'm
a typographer," he wrote, " not a scholar. The
thing, too, is obviously corrupt, and I should call
it the work of an uneducated man who copied
what he did not understand. But it is very
curious. It seems to be an account of a place
called Kynætho. Better show it to——" and he
mentioned several names.

I did not happen to know any of the people he
cited, and it occurred to me that I might consult
Vernon. He was, I knew, a fine scholar, and he
had kept up his interest in Greek literature. So
I sent the original and the modern version to him,
saying that the document had come into my hands
professionally and I should like to know if he could
make anything of it.

Next day I had Vernon on the telephone and he
seemed to be excited. " Where on earth did you
pick up that thing ? " he asked. " I suppose it
isn't a fake ? "

" Genuine enough," I replied, " but I can't tell
you its story yet. Can you make sense of it ? "

" I wouldn't say exactly ' sense,' but I can
translate it after a fashion. I worked at it last
night till the small hours. If I knew the *prove-
nance* of the manuscript, I might be able to under-

stand it better. Come and dine to-night, and we'll talk about it."

Vernon had taken a flat in Cleveland Row, and it was a proof of our gradual estrangement that till that evening I had never been inside its doors. Indeed we had not met since that Sunday at Wirlesdon.

"I saw you at Euston one morning before Christmas," I said. "Miss Arabin was going to hunt in the same train."

"Miss Arabin?" he puzzled. "I don't think I know——"

"The queer girl who was at Wirlesdon."

"Is that her name? I didn't know it. She rides well, but her manners are atrocious. Lord, how I dislike these *déracinés!* Let's get dinner over, for I've a lot to say to you about your jig-saw puzzle. It's extremely interesting, you know."

Later in the evening he put before me several sheets of foolscap on which he had written the translation in his small beautiful hand.

"The thing is headed *Ta Exotika,*" he said. "That puzzled me at first, till I remembered the phrase in Basil of Cæsarea. It was the word used by the early Christians to describe the old divinities. Whoever wrote this—I don't mean the fifteenth-century scribe, but the original author—was no doubt a Christian, and he is describing a belief and a rite which existed in his time at a place called Kynætho."

"Where is that?"

"I'm hanged if I know. It's a fairly common place name in Greece. There's one in Arcadia."

I read his translation and could not make much

of it. It reminded me of a schoolboy's version of
a bit of Herodotus. " In Kynætho," said the
writer, " there is a custom at the Spring Festival
of welcoming the Queen (*Despoina* was the word)
with the rites of the tympanon and the kestos,
such as they use in the Mysteries. There is a
certain sacred place, a well beside a white cypress,
from which all save the purified are excluded. In
Kynætho the Queen is known as Fairborn (Kalli-
genia). In winter the Queen is asleep but she
wakes in Spring, wherefore the Spring month is
called by her name. . . . " After this came a fuller
description of the rites and a lot of talk about
" mantic birds."

" There's nothing much in the first part," said
Vernon. " It's the ordinary ceremony of the re-
birth of Demeter. But notice that she is called
' Lady of the Wild Things.' There was a mighty
unpleasant side to Demeter as well as an idyllic
one, and it didn't do to take liberties with the
Queen of the Shades. But read on."

The writer went on to say that in time of great
distress at Kynætho there was a different ceremony.
It then became necessary to invite not only the
Mistress but the Master. For this purpose a
virgin and a youth must be chosen and set apart
in a hallowed place, and fed upon sacred food.
The choosing was done by the victor in a race,
who was given the name of King. Then on the
appointed day, after the purification, when the
dithyramb had been sung, Bromios would be born
from Semele in the fire, and with him would come
the Mistress. After that the place would be loved
by the Gods and corn and oil and wine would be
multiplied.

That was the gist of the story. The manuscript must have been imperfect, for there were gaps and some obvious nonsense, and there were fragments of verse quoted which I took to be part of the dithyramb. One ran like this :

" Io, Kouros most great. I give thee hail.
  Come, O Dithyrambos, Bromios come, and bring with thee
  Holy hours of thy most holy Spring. . . .
  Then will be flung over earth immortal a garland of flowers,
  Voices of song will rise among the pipes,
  The Dancing Floor will be loud with the calling of crowned
    Semele."

I laid the paper down. Vernon was watching me with bright eyes.

" Do you see what it is ? Some of those lines I recognise. They come from the Hymn of the Kouretes, which was discovered the other day in Crete, and from the Pæan to Dionysos found at Delphi, and there is a fragment of Pindar in them too. We know Koré, the Maiden, and we know the Kouros, who might be any male god—Dionysos or Zeus or Apollo—but this is the only case I ever heard of where both Koré and Kouros are found in the same ceremony. Kynætho, wherever it was, must have fairly gone on the bust. . . . It's amazingly interesting and that's why I want to know the story of the manuscript. I tell you it's a find of the first importance to scholarship. Look at the other things too—the sacred race and the winner called the King, just like the Basileus at the Olympic games.

" And there's more," he went on. " Look at the passage about the hallowing of the maiden and the youth. How does it go ? " He picked up the paper and read : " ' Then the Consecrator shall set aside a youth and a virgin, who shall remain consecrate in a sanctity which for all others shall be a place unapproachable. For seven days they shall be fed with pure food, eggs and cheese and barley-cakes and dried figs and water from the well by the white cypress.' Do you see what that means ? It was a human sacrifice. The fellow who wrote this skates lightly over the facts—I don't believe he was a Christian after all, or he wouldn't have taken it so calmly. The boy and the girl had to die before the Gods could be re-born. You see, it was a last resource —not an annual rite, but one reserved for a desperate need. All the words are ritual words— *horkos*, the sanctuary, and *abatos*, the tabu place, and *hosioter*, the consecrator. If we knew exactly what *hosiotheis* meant we should know a good deal about Greek religion. There were ugly patches in it. People try to gloss over the human sacrifice side, and of course civilised Greeks like the Athenians soon got rid of it ; but I haven't a doubt the thing went on all through classical times in Thessaly and Epirus and Arcadia and some of the islands. Indeed in the islands it survived till almost the other day. There was a case not so long ago in Santorini."

He pressed me to tell him the origin of the paper, but I felt reluctant to mention Miss Arabin. He was so deeply prejudiced against the girl, that it seemed unfair to reveal to him even the most trivial of her private affairs. I put him off by saying it was the property of a client, and that I would find out its history and tell him later.

" I have made a copy of the Greek text," he said. " May I keep it ? "

I told him, certainly. And that was all that happened during the evening. Formerly we would have sat up talking and smoking till all hours, but now I felt that the curtain was too heavy between us to allow of ordinary conversation. We would get at once into difficult topics. Besides I did not want to talk. The fact was that I was acquiring an obsession of my own—a tragic defiant girl moving between mirthless gaiety and menaced solitude. She might be innocent of the witchcraft in which Plakos believed, but she had cast some outlandish spell over me.

Before the end of the week Miss Arabin rang me up.

" You're Sir Edward Leithen ? I sent you some papers. Have you looked at them ? "

I told her I had.

" Then you had better come and talk to me. Come on Saturday and I'll give you luncheon. Half-past one."

There was no word of thanks for my trouble, but I obeyed the summons as if it had been a royal command. She had taken a flat in a block off Berkeley Square, and I wondered what sort of environment she had made for herself. I think I expected a slovenly place full of cushions and French novels and hot-house flowers. Instead I found a large room wholly without frippery—a big bare writing-table, leather arm-chairs like a man's smoking-room, and on the walls one or two hunting prints and some water-colour sketches of English landscape. There were few books, and those I looked at were county history. It was a mild frosty day and the windows were wide open. The only decorations were some dogwood branches and hedgerow berries—the spoil which townsfolk bring back in winter from country week-ends.

She was in tweeds, for she was off to Wirlesdon that afternoon, and—perhaps in my honour—she had forborne to powder her face. Once again I was struck by the free vigour of her movements, and the quick vitality of her eyes. The cabaret atmosphere was clearly no part of the real woman ; rather, as I now saw her, she seemed to carry with her a breath of the fields and hills.

At luncheon we talked stiltedly of the Nantleys and hunting, but no sooner was coffee served than she came to business.

" Theodore has told you about me ? You see the kind of fence I'm up against. What I want to know is just exactly how high and thick it is, and that no one can tell me. I liked your looks the first time I saw you, and everyone says you are clever. Now, understand one thing about me. I'm not going to show the white feather. Whatever it is, I'm going to stick it out. Have you that clear in your head ? "

As I looked at the firm little chin I believed her.

" Well, can you enlighten me about the fence ? You've heard all that Theodore has to say, and you know the cheerful sort of family I belong to. Did you find anything in the papers ? "

" You've read them yourself ? " I asked.

" I tried to, but I'm not clever, you see. I thought my grandfather's journal great nonsense. I had never heard of most of the names. But you're good at these things. Did you make nothing of them ? "

" Nothing." I ran over the items in the bundle, not mentioning the Greek manuscript, which seemed to me to have nothing to do with the subject. " But there must be other papers."

She flushed slightly. " There were many others, but I burned them. Perhaps you can guess why."

" Miss Arabin," I said ," I want to help you, but I don't think we need bother about the papers. Let's go back to the beginning. I suppose it's no use my urging you to get out of Plakos, settle in England and wipe all the past out of your memory ? "

" Not the slightest."

" I wonder why. After all it's only common sense."

" Common cowardice," she retorted, with a toss of her head. " I have known Theodore all my life and I have forbidden him to raise that question. I have known you about a month and I forbid *you*."

There was something so flat-footed and final about her that I laughed. She stared at me haughtily for a moment, and then laughed also.

" Go on with what you were saying," she said. " I stay at Plakos, and you must make your book for that. Now then."

" Your family was unpopular—I understand, justly unpopular. All sorts of wild beliefs grew up about them among the peasants and they have been transferred to you. The people are half savages, and half starved, and their mood is dangerous. They are coming to see in you the cause of their misfortunes. You go there alone and unprotected and you have no friends in the island. The danger is that, after a winter of brooding, they may try in some horrible way to wreak their vengeance on you. That is what I learned from Mr Ertzberger."

The summary, as I made it, sounded unpleasant enough, but the girl did not seem to feel it so. She nodded briskly. " That, at any rate, is what Theodore says. He thinks they may make me a sacrifice. Stuff and nonsense, *I* say."

The word " sacrifice " disquieted me. It reminded me of the Greek which Vernon had translated.

" Some risk there must be," I went on, " but what I cannot tell is the exact amount of it. Even among a savage people unpopularity need not involve tragedy. You were in Plakos last spring. Tell me what happened."

She fitted a cigarette into a long amber holder, and blew a cloud of smoke which she watched till it disappeared.

" Nothing much. I was left entirely to myself. There was only one servant in the house, old Mitri the steward, and I had also my maid. The whole establishment was sent to Coventry. We had to get our food from the mainland, for we could buy nothing, except now and then a little milk through Mitri's married daughter. It wasn't pleasant, I can tell you. But the worst was when I went for a walk. If I met a man he would make the sign of the evil eye and spit. If I spoke to a child its mother would snatch it up and race indoors with it. The girls and women all wore blue beads as a charm against me and carried garlic. I could smell it wherever I went. Sometimes I wanted to cry and sometimes I wanted to swear, but you can do nothing with a silent boycott. I could have shaken the fools."

" What had they against you ? Did you ever find out ? "

" Oh, Mitri used to tell us gossip that he had heard through his daughter, but Mitri isn't too popular himself, and he is old and can go about very little. It seemed they called me Basilissa. That means Queen and sounds friendly enough, but I think the word they really used was *diabolissa*, which means a she-devil. The better disposed ones thought I was a Nereid—that's what they call fairies—but some said I was a *strigla*—that's a horrible kind of harpy, and some thought I was a *vrykolakas*, which is a vampire. They used to light little fires in the graveyards to keep me away. Oh, I got very sick of my reputation. It was a hideous bore not to be able to go anywhere without seeing scared people dodging up by-ways, and making the sign of the cross and screaming for their children—simply damnable."

" It must have been damnable. I should have thought it rather terrifying too."

" Don't imagine that they frightened me. I was really more sorry than angry. They were only foolish people scared half out of their minds, and, after all, my family has done a good deal to scare them. It is folly—nothing but folly, and the only way to beat folly is to live it down. I don't blame the poor devils, but I'm going to bring them to a better mind. I refuse to run away because of a pack of fairy tales."

" There were no hostile acts ? " I asked.

She seemed to reflect. " No," she answered. " One morning we found a splash of blood on the house door, which sent old Mitri to his prayers. But that was only a silly joke."

" Mr Ertzberger hinted that there might be trouble this year from the people in the hills ? "

Her face hardened.

" I wish to Heaven I knew that for certain. It would be the best news I ever got. Those hill-men are not my people, and if they interfere I will have them whipped off the place. I will not have any protection against my own peasantry —Theodore is always pressing me, but I won't have it—it would spoil everything—it wouldn't be the game. But if those filthy mountaineers come within a mile of Plakos I will hire a regiment to shoot them down. Pray God they come. We of the coast have always hated the mountains, and I believe I could rally my people."

" But I thought you owned the whole island ? "

" No one owns the hills. My grandfather obtained the seigneury of Plakos, but he never claimed more than the good land by the sea. The hills have always been a no-man's-land full of bandits. We paid them dues—I still pay them— and we did not quarrel, but there was no coming and going between us. They are a different race from our pure Greek stock—mongrels of Slav and Turk, I believe."

The spirit of the girl comforted me. If Ertz-berger's news was true, it might save the situation, and bring the problem out of the realm of groping mystery to a straightforward defence of property. . . . But after all the hills were distant, and the scared tenants were at the house door. We must face the nearer peril.

" Is there no one in the village," I said, " whom you can have it out with ? No big farmer ? What about the priests ? "

She shook her head. " No one. The priests do not love my family, for they call themselves Christians, while we are Catholics."

Twenty years spent in examining witnesses has given me an acute instinct about candour. There was that in the girl's eyes and voice as she spoke which told me that she was keeping something back, something which made her uneasy.

" Tell me everything," I said. " Has no priest talked to you ? "

" Yes, there was one. I will tell you. He is an old man, and very timid. He came to me at night, after swearing Mitri to tell no one. He urged me to go away for ever."

Her eyes were troubled now, and had that abstracted look which I had noted before.

" What was his reason ? "

" Oh, care for his precious church. He was alarmed about what had happened at Easter."

She stopped suddenly.

" Have you ever been in Greece at Easter— during the Great Week ? No ? Then you cannot imagine how queer it is. The people have been starved all Lent, living only on cuttle-fish soup and bread and water. Everyone is pale and thin and ill-tempered. It is like a nightmare."

Then in rapid staccato sentences she sketched the ritual. She described the night of Good Friday, when the bier with the figure of the crucified Christ on it stands below the chancel step, and the priests chant their solemn hymn, and the women kiss the dead face, and the body is borne out to burial. With torches and candles flickering in the night wind, it is carried through the village streets, while dirges are sung, and the tense crowd breaks now and then into a moan or a sigh. Next day there is no work done, but the people wander about miserably, waiting on something which may be either death or deliverance. That night the church is again crowded, and at midnight the curtains which screen the chancel are opened, and the bier is revealed—empty, but for a shroud. " Christ is risen," the priest cries, as a second curtain is drawn back, and in the sanctuary in an ineffable radiance stands the figure of the risen Lord. The people go mad with joy, they light their tapers at the priest's candle, and like a procession of Bacchanals stream out, shouting ' He is risen indeed.' Then to the accompaniment of the firing of guns and the waving of torches the famished peasants, maddened by the miracle they have witnessed, feast till morning on wine and lamb's flesh in the joy of their redemption.

She drew the picture for me so that I saw it as if with my own eyes, and my imagination quickened under the spell of her emotion. For here was no longer the cool matter-of-fact young woman of the world, with no more than tolerance for the folly of superstition. It was someone who could enter into that very mood, and feel its quivering nerves and alternate despair and exultation.

" What had the priest to complain of ? " I asked.

" He said that the people were becoming careless of the Easter holiness. He said that last year the attendance at the rite was poor. He feared that they were beginning to think of something else."

" Something else ! " Two of the most common-

place words in the language. She spoke them in
an even voice in an ordinary London dining-room,
with outside the wholesome bustle of London and
the tonic freshness of an English winter day.
She was about to go off to a conventional English
week-end party at a prosaic country house. But
the words affected me strangely, for they seemed
to suggest a peril far more deadly than any turbulence of wild men from the hills—a peril, too,
of which she was aware.

For she was conscious of it—that was now
perfectly clear to me—acutely conscious. She had
magnificent self-command, but fear showed out
from behind it, like light through the crack of a
shutter. Her courage was assuredly not the valour
of ignorance. She was terrified, and still resolute
to go on.

It was not my business to add to that terror.
Suddenly I had come to feel an immense pity
and reverence for this girl. Ertzberger was right.
Her hardness, her lack of delicacy and repose,
her loud frivolity, were only on the surface—a
protective sheathing for a tormented soul. Out
of a miserable childhood and a ramshackle education she had made for herself a code of honour
as fine and as hard as steel. It was wildly foolish,
of course, but so perhaps to our dull eyes the
innocent and the heroic must always be.

Perhaps she guessed my thoughts. For when
she spoke again it was gently, almost hesitatingly.

" I scarcely hoped that you could tell me anything about Plakos. But I rather hoped you
would say I am right in what I am doing. Theodore
has been so discouraging . . . I rather hoped from
your face that you would take a different view.

You wouldn't advise me to run away from my job—— ? "

" God forbid that I should advise you at all," I said. " I see your argument, and, if you will let me say so, I profoundly respect it. But I think you are trying yourself—and your friends also—too high. You must agree to some protection."

" Only if the hill folk give trouble. Don't you see, protection would ruin everything if I accepted it against my own people ? I must trust myself to them—and—and stick it out myself. It is a sort of atonement."

Then she got up briskly and held out her hand. " Thank you very much, Sir Edward. It has done me good to talk to you. I must be off now or I'll miss my train. I'll give your love to Mollie and Tom."

" We shall meet again. When do you leave England ? "

" Not till March. Of course we'll meet again. Let me know if you have any bright idea. . . . Élise, Élise ! Where's that fool woman ? "

Her maid appeared.

" Get a taxi at once," she ordered. " We haven't any time to waste, for I promised to pick up Lord Cheviot at his flat."

I asked one question as I left. " Have you ever heard of a place called Kynætho ? "

" Rather. It's the big village in Plakos close to the house."

I ONCE read in some book about Cleopatra that that astonishing lady owed her charm to the fact that she was the last of an ancient and disreputable race. The writer cited other cases—Mary of Scots, I think, was one. It seemed, he said, that the quality of high-coloured ancestors flowered in the ultimate child of the race into something like witchcraft. Whether they were good or evil, they laid a spell on men's hearts. Their position, fragile and forlorn, without the wardenship of male kinsfolk, set them on a romantic pinnacle. They were more feminine and capricious than other women, but they seemed, like Viola, to be all the brothers as well as all the daughters of their father's house, for their soft grace covered steel and fire. They were the true sorceresses of history, said my author, and sober men, not knowing why, followed blindly in their service.

Perhaps Koré Arabin was of this sisterhood. At any rate one sober man was beginning to admit her compelling power. I could not get the girl from my thoughts. For one thing I had awakened to a comprehension of her beauty. Her face was rarely out of my mind, with its arrogant innocence, its sudden brilliancies and its as sudden languors. Her movements delighted me, her darting grace, the insolent assurance of her carriage, and then, without warning, the relapse into the child or the hoyden. Even her bad manners soon ceased to annoy me, for in my eyes they had lost all vulgarity. They were the harshnesses of a creature staving off tragedy. Indeed it was her very extravagances that allured, for they made me see her as a solitary little figure set in a patch of light on a great stage among shadows, defying of her own choice the terrors of the unknown.

What made my capture complete was the way she treated me. She seemed to have chosen me as her friend, and to find comfort and security in being with me. To others she might be rude and petulant, but never to me. Whenever she saw me she would make straight for me, like a docile child waiting for orders. She would dance or sit out with me till her retinue of youth was goaded to fury. She seemed to guess at the points in her behaviour which I did not like and to strive to amend them. We had become the closest friends, and friendship with Koré Arabin was a dangerous pastime.

The result was that I was in a fair way of making a fool of myself. No . . . I don't think I was in love with her. I had never been in love in my life, so I was not an expert on the subject, but I fancied that love took people in a different way. But I was within measurable distance of asking her to be my wife. My feeling was a mixture of affection and pity and anxiety. She had appealed to me, and I had become her champion. I wanted to protect her, but how was a middle-aged lawyer to protect a determined girl from far-away perils which he did not comprehend ? The desperate expedient of marriage occurred to me, but I did not believe she would accept me, and, if she did, would not the mating of age and youth be an out-

rage and a folly ?   Nevertheless I was in a mood to
venture even on that.

I must have presented a strange spectacle to
my friends.   There were other men of forty in
London at the time who behaved as if they were
twenty-five—one buxom Cabinet Minister was to
be seen at every dance—but none, I am certain,
cut an odder figure than I.   The dancing Cabinet
Minister sought the ball-room for exercise, because
he preferred dancing to golf.   I had no such excuse,
for I danced comparatively little ;   my object was
patently the society of one particular lady.   In
Koré's train I found myself in strange haunts.   I
followed her into the Bohemian *coulisses* to which
Shelley Arabin's daughter had an entrée—queer
studio parties in Chelsea where the women were
shorn and the men left shaggy :   the feverish
literary and artistic salons of the emancipated
and rather derelict middle-class :   dances given
at extravagant restaurants by the English and
foreign new-rich, where I did not know or wish to
know one single soul.   Also we appeared together
at houses which I had frequented all my life, and
there my friends saw me.   Of course they talked.
I fancy that for about two months I was the prime
subject of London gossip.   I didn't care a hang,
for I was in a queer obstinate excitable mood.   We
hunted together, too, and there is no such nursery
of scandal as the hunting-field.   With a great deal
of work on hand I found this new life a considerable
strain, and I was perfectly conscious that I was
playing the fool.   But, though I don't think I
was in love with her, I simply could not let the girl
out of my sight.

Now and then my conscience awoke and I

realised with a shock that the time was slipping
past, and that the real problem was still unsolved.
I knew that I could not shake Koré in her resolution, and I suppose I hoped blindly that something
would occur to prevent her acting on it. That
something could only be a love affair. I was
perfectly certain that she was not in love with me,
but she might accept me, and at the back of my
head I had the intention of putting it to the test.
Ertzberger had divined what was going on and
seemed to approve. " A boy is no use to her," he
said more than once. " Besides she wouldn't
look at one. She must marry a grown man."
He implied that I filled the bill, and the man's
assumption gave me an absurd pleasure. If anyone had told me that I would one day go out of
my way to cultivate a little Jew financier, I would
have given him the lie, yet the truth is that, when
I was not with Koré, I hungered for Ertzberger's
company. He alone understood what was in my
mind, and shared my anxieties. " She must not
go back," he kept declaring; " at all costs she must
be kept away from Plakos—at any rate during this
spring. I get disquieting reports. There is mischief brewing in the hills, and the people of the
coast have had a bitter winter of famine. There
has been a lot of sickness too, and in the village at
the house gates the mortality among the children
has been heavy."

" You mean Kynætho ? " I asked.

" Kynætho." He looked at me curiously.
" You seem to have been getting up the subject. . . .
Well, I don't like it. If she goes there in April
there may be a disaster. Upon my soul, we should
be justified in having her kidnapped and shut

up in some safe place till the summer. So far as
I can learn, the danger is only in the spring. Once
let the people see the crops springing and the
caiques bringing in fish, and they will forget their
grievances."

Early in March I was dining with the Nantleys,
and after dinner Mollie took me aside for a talk.
As I have told you, she is one of my oldest friends,
for when I was a grubby little private schoolboy
and she was a girl of thirteen we used to scamper
about together. I had had her son Hugo in my
chambers, before he went into Parliament, and
Wirlesdon had always been a sort of home to me.
Mollie was entitled to say anything she liked, but
when she spoke it was rather timidly.

" I hear a good deal of talk about you," she said,
"and I can't help noticing too. Do you think it
is quite fair, Ned ? "

" Fair to whom ? " I asked.

" To Koré Arabin. You're different from the
boys who run after her. You're a distinguished
man with a great reputation. Is it fair to her to
turn her head ? "

" Is that very likely ? What if she has turned
mine ? "

" Do you really mean that ? " she cried. " I
never thought of it in that way. Do you honestly
want to marry her ? "

" I don't know . . . I don't know what I want
except that I must stand by her. She's in an
appallingly difficult position, and badly needs a
friend."

" Yes. But there's only one way in which a
man can protect a young woman. Do you mean to
marry her ? "

" She wouldn't accept me."

" But you mean to ask her ? "

" It may come to that," I said.

" But, Ned dear, can't you see it wouldn't do ? Koré is not the right sort of wife for you. She's—she's too—— Well, you've a career before you. Is she the woman to share it with you ? "

" It's not many months since at Wirlesdon you implored my charity for Miss Arabin."

" Oh, I don't want to say a word against her, and if you were really desperately in love I would say nothing and wish you luck. But I don't believe you are. I believe it's what you say—charity, and that's a most rotten foundation to build on."

Mollie in such affairs is an incurable romantic.

" I promise never to ask her to marry me unless I am in love," I said.

" Well, that means you are not quite in love yet. Hadn't you better draw back before it is too late ? I can't bear to see you making a bad blunder, and Koré, dear child, would be a bad blunder for you. She's adorably pretty, and she has wonderful qualities, but she is a little savage, and very young, and quite unformed. Really, really it wouldn't do."

" I admit the difficulties, my dear Mollie. But never mind me, and think of Miss Arabin. You said yourself that she was English at heart and would be very happy settled in England."

" But not with you."

" She wouldn't accept me, and I may never propose. But if I did, and she accepted me, why not with me ? "

" Because you're you—because you're too good
for a rash experiment."

" I'm not good enough for her, for I'm too old,
as you've just told me. But anyhow your argument thinks principally of me, not of Miss Arabin.
It is she who matters."

Mollie rose with a gesture of impatience. " You
are hopeless, Ned. I'm sick of you hard, unsus-
ceptible, ambitious people. You never fall in
love in your youth, but wait till after forty and
then make idiots of yourselves."

I had a different kind of remonstrance from
Vernon. We saw little of each other in these
days beyond a chance word in the street or a casual
wave of the hand in the club smoking-room. When
I thought of him it was with a sense of shame that
I had let him slip so hopelessly out of my life.
Time had been when he was my closest friend, and
when his problem was also my problem. Now
the whole story of his dream seemed a childish
fancy.

One night in March I found him waiting for me
in my rooms.

" I came round to say good-bye," he said. " I
shall probably leave London very soon."

It shows how completely I had forgotten his
affairs that I did not remember that his particular
crisis was drawing near, that, as he believed, the
last door in his dream-world would soon be
opened.

Then, before I could ask about his plans, he
suddenly broke out :

" Look here, I hope there's no truth in what
people tell me."

His tone had the roughness of one very little

at his ease, and it annoyed me. I asked coldly what he meant.

"You know what I mean—that you're in love with Miss What's-her-name—the girl I met at Wirlesdon."

"I don't know that you've any right to ask the question, and I'm certainly not going to answer it."

"That means that you are in love," he cried. "Good God, man, don't tell me that you want to marry that—that tawdry girl!"

I must have reddened, for he saw that he had gone too far.

"I don't mean that—I apologise. I have no reason to say anything against her."

Then his tone changed.

"Ned, old man, we have been friends for a long time and you must forgive me if I take liberties. We have never had any secrets from each other. My own affairs give me a good deal to think about just now, but I can't go away with an easy mind till I know the truth about you. For God's sake, old fellow, don't do anything rash. Promise me you won't propose to her till I come back in April."

His change of manner had softened me, and as I saw the trouble in his honest eyes I felt a return of the old affection.

"Why are you anxious on my account?"

"Because," he said solemnly, "I know that if you married that girl our friendship would be over. I feel it in my bones. She would always come between us."

"I can't make any promises of that kind. But one thing I can promise—that no woman will ever break our friendship."

" You don't understand. Some women wouldn't, but that girl——! Well, I can say no more. Good-bye, Ned. I'll hunt you up when I come back."

He left me with a feeling of mingled regret and irritation. I hated to go against Vernon's wishes, but his manner when he had spoken of Koré, the look in his eyes, the inflection of his voice, conveyed an utter distaste which made me angry. I pictured him at Severns nursing his unreasoning dislike of the poor child. Vernon, as my nephew Charles had said, was a prig, and his narrow world had room only for blameless and vapid virginity. The promise he had asked of me was an outrage.

.   .   .   .   .

Yet I kept a promise which I had never made. For suddenly Cinderella disappeared from the ball. After a country-house dance I drove her back to town in my car, and left her at the door of her flat. During the long drive she had talked more seriously than I had ever known her to talk before, had spoken of herself and her affairs with a kind of valiant simplicity. The only sophisticated thing about her was her complexion. All day afterwards my conviction was growing that she was the woman for me, that I could make her not only secure but happy. We were by way of dining with the Lamanchas, and I think if we had met that night I should have asked her to marry me. . . . But we did not meet, for by the evening she was gone.

I looked for her in vain in the Lamanchas' drawing-room and my hostess guessed what I sought. " I'm so sorry about Koré Arabin," she whispered to me. " She was coming to-night,

but she telephoned this afternoon that she was
unexpectedly called out of town." I did not
enjoy my dinner, and as soon as I could decently
leave I hurried off to her flat. It was shut up, and
from the porter on the ground floor I learned that
she and her maid had left with a quantity of
luggage to catch the night boat to France. He was
positive that she had gone abroad, for he had seen
the foreign labels, and Miss Arabin had told him
she would not be back for months. The keys of
the flat had been sent to her solicitors.

With a very uneasy mind I drove to the Ertzbergers' house in Belgrave Square. Ertzberger
had just come in from a City dinner, and his wife
seemed to be giving some kind of musical party,
for the hall was full of coats and hats and extra
footmen, and the jigging of fiddles drifted down the
staircase. He took me to his study at the back
of the house, and when he heard my news his face
grew as solemn as my own. There was nothing
to be done that night, for the Continental mail had
long since gone, so I went back to my chambers
with a pretty anxious mind. I felt that I had let
something rare and precious slip out of my hand,
but far more that this preciousness was in instant
danger. Honestly I don't think that I was much
concerned about myself. I wanted Koré Arabin
saved—for me—for everyone—for the world. If
I was in love with her it was with an affection more
impersonal than usually goes by that name. It
was as if an adored child had gone amissing.

Regardless of our many engagements, Ertzberger and I appeared on the doorstep of Messrs
Mower & Lidderdale, the solicitors, at the hour
when according to the information given me by

telephone the senior partner usually arrived. Mr Mower confirmed our fears. Miss Arabin had returned to Plakos ; she had been preparing for some weeks for the journey ; he had not advised it—indeed he had not been asked his advice nor would he have dared to volunteer it. "A very strong-minded young lady," he repeated—"I might almost say strong-headed." She had sold the lease of her flat, and had left no instructions about her return. Yes, she was well supplied with money. Miss Arabin was her own mistress absolutely, for her father had created no trust. He had nothing more to tell us, and Ertzberger departed for the City and I for the Temple.

In the afternoon I was rung up by Ertzberger in my room in the House of Commons. He had been making inquiries, he said—he had his own ways of doing that sort of thing—and he had discovered that Koré had recently sold large parcels of stocks. She had been selling out steadily throughout the winter, and now had practically no investments left. The proceeds had been deposited on current account in her bank. There his information stopped, but he was profoundly disquieted. "That child has all her fortune in cash under her hand," he said, "and God knows what she means to do with it. Any moment she may beggar herself, and no one can prevent her."

That night I understood that my infatuation was over, if indeed it had ever existed. I wanted the girl safe, and I did not care who saved her, but I wanted it so much that at the moment nothing in heaven or earth seemed to matter in comparison.

It was now near the end of March, the Courts had just risen and Parliament was about to adjourn for the Easter vacation. I had a good deal of important work on hand, but I was entitled to a holiday, and I thought I could arrange for at any rate a fortnight's absence from town. But whether I could arrange it or not I meant to go, for I could no more settle to my tasks than a boy can settle to Tacitus on the day he is playing for his school. When Ertzberger according to our arrangement turned up at my chambers that night after dinner, he found me busy with an atlas and a Continental Bradshaw.

" I am going to Plakos," I said.

" That is good. You are still a young man, and you have been a soldier. It is very good. But if you had not gone, I had decided to go myself."

" This is Wednesday. Miss Arabin left last night. She will get there—when ? "

He made some calculations. " Not before Tuesday. You might overtake her, but I do not think that is necessary. Easter is the danger point and the Greek Easter is still a fortnight off. Besides you must stop a day in Athens."

" I shall want help. Can you get me half-a-dozen handy fellows I can trust ? "

" I had thought of that. Indeed I telegraphed about it this afternoon. I can find you the men—and money, of course, if you want it. I will find you a lieutenant, too, and make all arrangements about transport. That at least I can do. You realise, Sir Edward, that there is a certain danger in this enterprise ? "

" I realise that Miss Arabin in a week's time will

be in deadly danger. . . . I must have a day or two
to wind up my work here. I think I can leave
on Saturday morning."

As a matter of fact I left London on the Friday
night.

PART II

I CAME to Plakos in a blind sea-fog. After a day and a night of storm the wind died utterly, and we made the isle on a compass course, feeling our way in by constant soundings. A thick salt dew hung on every stay and hawser, the deck and bulwarks swam with moisture, and our coats were in an instant drenched as if we had been out in a hurricane. Sea and land alike were invisible. The air was thick and oppressive to the breath, and every muscle in the body felt weak and flaccid. Also there was a strange quiet—only the ripple caused by our slow movement and the creak of sodden cordage. I might have been a shade looking on an island of the dead.

I had reached Athens in record time, but there I found a weariful delay. In spite of Ertzberger's influence the wheels were clogged. I was met at the Piræus by his agent, one Constantine Maris, whose instructions were to hold himself at my disposal. I took to Maris at once—a young fellow of thirty, who had been in the Greek regular army and had been the right-hand man of Zimbrakis when at Salonika his troops declared for Venizelos. He had been all through the war till it ended in Bulgaria's submission, had been twice wounded and once in prison, and had been chosen by Ertzberger to represent him in Athens because of his truculent honesty and tireless energy. Both

in character and appearance he was more like a
Frenchman than a Greek—a Norman, for choice,
for he had reddish-brown hair and a high-bridged
northern nose. He had the additional merit of
being well educated, having put in two years at
the Sorbonne : and he talked excellent French.
His family were of Athens, but his mother, I
think, was from one of the islands. He had the
looks and manners of a soldier.

But Maris had found the task set him almost
impossible. Ertzberger had bidden him get together a batch of reliable fellows who would obey
orders and ask no questions, but as we rumbled
Athens-ward from the Piræus in the little train
he confessed that such men were not to be found.
In the war it was otherwise, but the best had all
gone back to the country villages. He had collected a dozen but he was not enthusiastic about
them, except a certain Janni, who had been a
corporal in his old battalion. When he paraded
them for my inspection I was inclined to agree
with him. They were an odd mixture—every
kind of clothes from the dirty blue jeans of the
stoker to the black coat and pointed yellow shoes
of the clerk—ages from nineteen to sixty—physique
from prize-fighter to sneak-thief. All had served
in the war, however, and the best of them, Janni,
had an empty left sleeve. After much consultation
we dismissed two and were left with ten who at any
rate looked honest. Whether they would be
efficient was another matter. Maris proposed to
arm them with revolvers, but not till we got to
Plakos, in case they started shooting up the town.
They were told that they were wanted as guards
for an estate which was threatened by brigands,

but I doubt if they believed it. The younger ones seemed to think that our object was piracy.

Transport was another problem. I had hoped to be able to hire a small steam yacht, but such a thing was not to be had, and the best we could do was to induce a dissolute-looking little Leghorn freighter, named the *Santa Lucia*, to go out of its way and touch at Plakos. Maris told the captain a yarn about men being needed there for making a new sea-wall. The boat was bound for the Dodecanese, and would pick us up on her return a fortnight later.

Before we rounded Cape Sunium we got into foul weather, a heavy north-easter and violent scurries of rain. Our ruffians were all sea-sick and lay about like logs, getting well cursed by the Italian sailors, while Maris and I in the one frowsy little cabin tried to make a plan of campaign. I found out at once that Maris was well informed about the situation in Plakos, partly from Ertzberger and partly from his own knowledge. He knew about Shelley Arabin's career, which seemed to be the common talk of the Ægean. Of Koré he had heard nothing save from Ertzberger, but he had much to tell me of Plakos and its people. They had a name for backwardness and turbulence, and the Government seemed to leave them very much to themselves. There were gendarmes, of course, in the island, but he fancied they didn't function. But the place had sent good soldiers to Venizelos, and its people were true Hellenes. After an interval when he expatiated on that Hellenic empire of the islands which was the dream of good Venizelists, he returned to their superstition. " That is the curse of my countrymen," he cried.

" They are priest-ridden." He was himself, he told me, a free-thinker and despised all mumbo-jumbo.

I told him that the trouble was not with the priests, but he did not seem to understand, and I did not attempt to explain.

Our task as he saw it was straightforward enough—to protect the House during the Easter season when fear of the girl as a witch and the memory of Shelley's misdeeds might induce some act of violence. There was also the trouble with the hill folk, and this seemed to him the greater danger. The dwellers in the stony mountains which filled the centre and south of the island had always been out of hand, and, since the winter had been cruel and the war had unsettled the whole earth, he thought it likely that they might have a try at looting the House, which they no doubt held to be full of treasure, since the Arabins had a name for wealth. I could see that he didn't quite believe in danger from the coast folk, however beastly their superstitions might be. He had the Greek respect for a mountaineer and contempt for the ordinary peasant.

We studied the map—a very good one prepared for the British Navy—and on Maris's advice I decided to begin by dividing our forces. My first business was to get into the House and discover how things were going. But with danger threatening from the hills it would be unwise for all of us to concentrate in a place from which egress might be difficult. Now the House stood at the north-west corner of the island, and the hill country began about ten miles to the south-east. He proposed to send five of our men, under Corporal

Janni, to a little port called Vano on the west coast some miles south of the House. They would take supplies with them—we were well provided with these—and reconnoitre towards the hills, giving out that they were a Government survey party. The rest of us would land at the House, and, after satisfying ourselves about the position, would get in touch with Janni by the overland route. Our first business was strictly reconnaissance ; Janni could not hope to prevent mischief from the hills if it were really on its way, but he could satisfy himself as to its extent and character, and then join us in the defence of the House, which was our main task. Maris was confident about this. He did not see how a dozen armed men in a strong place could fail to hold off a mob of undisciplined peasants.

For an extra payment the captain of the *Santa Lucia* was induced to carry Janni and his men to Vano. Weapons were served out to all, and I gave Janni a map which he professed to be able to read. Then in the shrouding fog Maris and I and our five got into the ship's one boat and were rowed ashore. We had our supplies both of food and ammunition in half-a-dozen wooden cases, and the wretched cockle was pretty low in the water. I knew from my former visit that the landing-place was just below the House, and the fog seemed to me a godsend, for it would enable us to get indoors unobserved. My only doubt was the kind of reception we might get from Koré.

As it turned out, the mist was our undoing. We were landed at a stone jetty in a dead white blanket which made it difficult to see a yard ahead. Our baggage was put on shore, the boat started back, and in a moment both sound and sight of it were swallowed up. It was an eerie business, and I felt the craziness of our errand as I stood blinking on the wet cobbles. There was no human being about, but the dim shapes of several caiques and some kind of lugger seemed to show below us as we started along the jetty. Our five ruffians had recovered from their sea-sickness, and, feeling solid ground beneath them, were inclined to be jolly. One of them started a song, which I promptly checked. Maris ordered them to wait behind with the boxes, and to keep dead quiet, while he and I prospected inland.

My recollection of that visit in 1914 was hazy, for I had only seen the landing-place from the causeway above it, and at the time I had been too preoccupied to observe accurately. But I was pretty certain that at the shore end of the jetty there were some rough stone steps which led to the causeway. I groped for them in the mist but could not find them. Instead I came on a broad track which bore the mark of wheels and which led away to the left. I waited for the steep to begin, but found no sign of it. The land was dead flat for a long way, and then I came on a rough boundary wall.

It was an orchard with blossoming trees—that much I could see through the brume—and at the end was a cottage. My first thought was to retrace my steps and try a cast to the right, for I still believed that we had found the proper landing-place, and had somehow missed the causeway. But, as I hesitated, there came one of those sudden clearings in the air which happen in the densest fogs, and I had a prospect of some hundreds of yards around me. We were on the edge of a village, the cottage we had reached was at the extreme seaward end a little detached from the rest ; beyond lay what seemed to be a shallow valley with no sign of the House and its embattled hill.

It would have been well for us if there and then we had turned and gone back to the jetty, even at the risk of relinquishing our supplies and having to scramble for miles along a difficult shore. For, of course, we had come in that infernal fog to the wrong place. The skipper had landed us at Kynætho instead of below the House, and though I knew from the map that Kynætho was at the House's gates, yet it was on the east side, distant at least two miles by coast from the spot which Vernon and I had visited.

It was Maris who decided me. The cottage seemed a solitary place where discreet inquiries might be made without rousing attention. He had little stomach for wandering around Plakos in fog, and we had our five men and the baggage to think of. I followed him into the rough court-yard, paved with cobbles, and strewn with refuse. The low walls were washed with red ochre and above the lintel a great black pentacle was painted. Also over the door was hung a bunch of garlic.

There was a woman standing in the entry watching us. Maris took off his hat with a flourish, and poured out a torrent of soft-sounding dialect. She replied in a harsher accent, speaking with the back of her throat. She seemed to be inviting us to enter, but her face was curiously without expression, though her eyebrows worked nervously. She was a middle-aged woman, terribly

disfigured by smallpox; her features were regular,
and she had large, prominent, vacant black eyes.
She was not in the least repulsive, but somehow
she was not reassuring.

As we entered the cottage she called out to someone at the back. A second later I heard footsteps
as of a child running.

Maris, as I learned afterwards, told her the
story we had agreed on—that we were a Government survey party sent from Athens to make a
map of the island. Then he felt his way to more
delicate subjects. This was Kynætho, he understood ? There was a large house near which
belonged to some foreigners ? English, weren't
they ? Where, exactly, did it lie from the village,
for, if he might venture to explain what madam
no doubt knew, one must have a starting-point
for a survey, and the Government had chosen
that house ?

The woman's eyebrows twitched, and she crossed
herself. She flung a hand over her left shoulder.
" The place is there," she said. " I know nothing
of it. I do not speak of it."

All the time she was looking at us with her
staring empty eyes, and I realised that she was
in an extreme fright. There was certainly nothing
in our appearance to discompose her, and I had
the uneasy feeling which one has in the presence
of a human being who is suffering from an emotion
that one cannot fathom. Maris whispered to me
that he did not like the look of things. " She has
not offered us food," he said.

Her ear must have caught some sound from
out-of-doors, for her face suddenly showed relief.
She walked to a window and cried to someone

outside. Then she turned to us. " There are
men now to speak with you." She had found
her tongue, for as she hustled us out she kept
muttering, with sidelong glances at us, what
seemed to be an invocation to Saint Nicolas. Also
she gripped Maris violently by the shoulder and
spat words into his ear. He told me afterwards
that she was advising him not to be a fool and
to go home.

The little courtyard had filled with people, most
of them men, but with two or three old crones
in the forefront. Their aspect was not threatening,
but rather puzzled and timid. The men took off
their hats in response to Maris's bow, and politely
waited for him to speak. I noticed that they
were a well-made, upstanding lot, but with the
same flat expressionlessness as the woman of the
cottage, and I guessed that that was a mask to
hide fear.

Maris told them the same story of our errand.
He said—I repeat what he told me later—that
our men and baggage were still down by the
beach, and that he wanted to be directed to the
inn. There was dead silence. The little crowd
stared at us as if their lives depended on it, but
not a syllable came in reply.

This made Maris angry. " Are you dumb
mules," he asked, " not to answer a simple question ? I have heard that you of the islands
boasted of your hospitality. Is this the way to
treat strangers ? "

Still no answer. His taunts were as futile as
his exposition. But, since I had nothing to do
but to look on, I saw something which made me
uneasy. The crowd was drawing together, and

each was covertly touching the other's sleeve.
There was a purpose in this mob, a purpose of
action, and I don't like that kind of purpose
when it is accompanied by fear.

" Since you will not speak," Maris cried, " I
will go to your priest. Where is his dwelling ?
Or do you treat your church as you treat your
visitors ? "

This time he got a reply. A dozen voices spoke,
and a dozen hands pointed towards the village.

" It seems you are not dumb after all ? We will
seek a lodging from the priest, who doubtless has
some regard for his country's Government. We
have baggage with us—boxes of instruments and
food—and they are now at the jetty. I want
two able-bodied fellows to help carry them, and
I will pay them well. Who offers ? "

But no one offered. Once again they were
like gaping cattle. And then an old beldam in
the foreground, who had been crossing herself
vigorously, cried out a monosyllable and instantly it was taken up in a shout.

Maris turned to me with an angry smile. " They
are advising us to go home. I can mention an
island, my friend, in which there is going to be
trouble. Let us go back to the shore. Perhaps
the sight of our belongings will change their mind."

They did not obstruct us, but opened a lane
for us to pass—opened it with feverish haste, as
if they were afraid of coming too near us. The
fog had now thinned to a light haze, through
which I already felt the glow of the sun. As we
moved shorewards they trailed after us, keeping
always a respectful distance, and halted fifty
yards from the jetty.

Our five fellows were sitting smoking on the boxes, and since we could get no help from the villagers there was nothing for it but to carry the baggage ourselves. My first notion was to go straight to the House, of which by this time I could judge the whereabouts, and it would have been well for us perhaps if I had acted on that impulse. But, until I had prepared the way, I was shy of facing Koré Arabin with a defence force which would make her furious, and I had a notion too that if I marched in broad daylight to the House gates there might be trouble with these scared and sullen natives. So I decided to go first to the inn, where we could leave our stuff, and then to interview the priest. After all, I knew from Koré that the priest was alarmed about the local situation, and from him I might get some counsel. It seemed to me a case for wary walking.

I could have laughed at that progress village-wards, if I hadn't been so anxious. The mob in front of us had doubled in size, and retreated mechanically before us till we were in the village street. The sun was now bright in the sky, and I had a view of the straggling houses, grouped thickly in the centre where there seemed to be a kind of *place*, and thinning out into farms and enclosures on the slopes of the green hills. It was a wide, shallow vale bounded on the south by low ridges ; but on the west rose a higher tree-clad hill, and there were glimpses of white masonry which I took to be the House. Once we were in the village the crowd was enlarged by women and children. They kept a good distance, retiring a pace for every step we took, and when we entered the untidy square they huddled against the house doors as if they were forming guard. They were perfectly silent, even the children. It was an eerie business, I can assure you, promenading before that speechless, staring gallery. They were not an ill-looking race, as I have said, for the men were mostly well-built and upstanding, and though the old wives looked like the Witch of Endor the young ones were often comely. But you could see that they were bitter poor, for their cheeks were thin and their eyes hollow. And beyond doubt they were in the throes of some nervous terror. I felt as if at any moment something might snap and the air be filled with a wild screaming.

The inn was easy enough to find. A big plane tree grew before it, and in the yard behind the low whitewashed walls grew a second, beside a stone fountain which had not been erected within these last five hundred years. The place was only a wine-shop, with no guest-rooms for travellers, but there were ample outbuildings where our men could encamp. But there was no sign of any landlord. Maris and I pushed indoors and found no trace of life in the big drinking-room with its sanded floor, or in the purlieus beyond. The inn folk must have gone to swell the crowd in the street. But we found a reasonably clean barn at the back of the yard, and there Maris bade our fellows make their quarters, get ready their breakfast and await our return. Then the two of us set out to find the priest.

The villagers had not pressed nearer. When we emerged into the street they were standing as we had left them, patiently staring. Maris cried out, asking to be shown the priest's house, and at that the spell seemed to be broken, for there was a shout in reply. A visit to the priest seemed to be in the popular view the right course for us to take. We were directed to a house a hundred yards on, next door to a squat church, and to my surprise we were not followed. Once they had seen us enter, the crowd remained to watch the inn door.

The priest had evidently been apprised of our coming. His dwelling was only a bigger cottage, but in the furnishing of it there were a few signs of a class above the peasantry—a shelf of books, one or two gaudy religious pictures, a Swiss cuckoo clock, and, incongruously enough, two of the cheap copies of Tanagra statuettes which they sell in the Athens shops. I dare say he imagined that they were figures of saints. He was an old man, nearer eighty than seventy to my eye, and much bent in the shoulders. An unkempt beard fell over his chest, and his white hair was long and brushed back from his forehead like a recent fashion among young men in England. The skin was waxen white, and the lines on his face were like the grey shadows in a snowdrift. His eyes were mild, benevolent and fanatical. He looked stupid but kind and, like everybody else in that mad place, horribly frightened.

With him Maris went straight to the point.

" We are a Government survey party, Pappa," he said. " But that story is for the peasants. To you we open our hearts. This gentleman is a colonel in the army of Britain, and likewise a member of the British Government. He is also a friend of the lady in the House of Plakos. What gadfly has bitten the people of this island ? Come !

We know much already but we would hear your tale."

The priest—his venerable name was Hieronymos—was ready enough to tell. With a wealth of gesticulation remarkable in one so ancient, but always with a lowered voice, he repeated crudely what we already knew. The people of Plakos had suffered much and long, and were now resolved to make an end of their incubus. The girl was a witch and they had determined that she must die. They were only waiting till the convenient season. All this he said in the most matter-of-fact tone, as if it were a natural sequence of cause and effect.

" But you would not consent to such barbarity ? " Maris asked.

" My consent is not asked," he replied. " Beyond doubt the woman is evil and comes of an evil stock. But the Scriptures teach mercy, and, though doubtless death is deserved, I would not counsel it. For if she is evil she is also witless. Why else did she return here, when she knew that the whole island desired her death ? Did I not go to her secretly, as Nicodemus went to our Lord, and besought her never to return ? And she has given immense sums of money to her enemies. Me she gave gold for the Church and that I have secure, but she has given it to others who have bought guns. The men from the hills, who are most bitter against her, carry rifles bought with her money."

Now I knew why the foolish child had realised her investments.

The priest was gaining confidence.

" The death of a witch may be a righteous

deed," he said, "but the hearts of this people
are not righteous. They are dabbling in a blacker
magic than hers, for they are following the Outland Things. And that is heresy and blasphemy,
which in the eyes of Holy Church are sins not
less mortal than witchcraft."

Real anger, the jealous anger of a priest for his
own prerogatives, blazed in his old eyes. He used
for "outland things" the word *exotika*, the very
word which had puzzled Vernon in the manuscript
I gave him, till he found help from Basil of Cæsarea.
The word caught my ear and I made Maris translate
for me. He had clearly no compassion for poor
Koré, but he was up in arms for his Church. Maris
tried to probe the trouble, but he got the vaguest
answers. The man seemed eager to unburden his
soul and yet terrified to speak, and his eyes were
always turning to the window and the closed
street door.

Last Eastertide there had been a lamentable
neglect of sacred rites. This year the carelessness
was complete. Holy Week had begun, but the
minds of the people were not on its solemnities.
"They fast indeed," he said, "but they do not
pray." They had gone a-whoring after other
gods, and what those other gods were it did not
become a Christian man to consider. They medi-
tated a sacrifice, but they had forgotten the sacrifice on which their salvation hung. "There is
a madness which surges up at times in these
islands. It happened so in my grandfather's day
in Santorini, and there is no quelling it till some
black deed has been done and the people come to
their right minds in a bitter repentance." He,
their priest, had become less regarded than a cur

dog. Men stopped talking in the streets when he drew near, and would not meet his eyes. If he spoke, they moved off. They were conscious of a guilty purpose, and yet resolved on it, and he was powerless to check them. " They will come back, doubtless, and bemoan their folly, but in the meantime they are breaking the hearts of the saints and loading their miserable souls with sin."

Then he broke off and his face took an expression of shrewdness.

" You have brought men with you. How many ? "

Maris told him ten stout fellows all armed.

" What foolishness ! " he cried. " The Government should have sent a regiment—a regiment with cannons. The madmen in Plakos are fifty times your number, and they have the hill folk at their back, and that is a thousand more."

" Nevertheless," said Maris, " we may be sufficient to garrison the House, and protect the lady. I have heard that it is a strong place."

He looked at us queerly. " No garrison is sufficient against fire. They will burn the House and all that is in it. . . . Listen to me, sirs. I do not think as you think. I have no care for the woman nor for any of her accursed race, but I have much care for the souls of this wayward people, and would save them from mortal sin. There are no two ways about it—the woman must burn or she must depart. Can you carry her off ? "

Maris translated to me rapidly. " Things look ugly," he said, " and I rather think this old one talks sense. But to carry off the lady we must

have a ship, and God knows where we shall find
one. At Vano perhaps ? Maybe we did wrong
to separate our forces. It strikes me that the
sooner we get into touch with friend Janni the
better. It is indicated that one of us must presently make his way into the House, and that
one had better be you. Let us interrogate the
old one about the topography of this damned
village."

"You must enter the House," said the priest,
in reply to Maris's question, "but it will be a task,
I promise you, for Digenes the Cyprian. The place
is guarded at all hours, and no one enters or leaves
it without the knowledge of the warders. But it
might be achieved by bold men under cover of
dark. The moon is nearing its full, and when it
has set in the small hours there might be a chance."

I got out the map of the island, and tried to
get him to give me my bearings. But he was
hopeless with a map, and instead on the white
hearth-stone he drew a plan of his own. The
main road to the House from Kynætho ran west
from the village square, up a lane lined with crofts
and past a big olive grove, till it reached the wood
of chestnuts which was the beginning of the
demesne. All the ground on this side rose steeply,
and there were dwellings almost to the gates, so
that it would be hard to escape detection. To the
left the slopes curved in a shallow vale, bounded
on the east by the main road to the hills and to
Vano, and to south and west by a rim of upland
beyond which lay the rugged coastline and the
sea. This vale was broad and flat, and tilted up
gently towards the west, and it bore the curious
name of the Dancing Floor. In the old days,

said the priest, the Panegyria were held in it, the island festivals before poverty and madness came to Plakos. The Dancing Floor bordered on the demesne, and he thought that a way of entry might be found there.

I made Maris ask about the shore road, but the priest was emphatic against it. There was no way into the House on that side except by the staircases from the jetty, which Vernon and I had seen in 1914, and there it was certain the watchers would be most vigilant. Besides the staircases were disused, and he believed that the postern doors had been walled up. The cliffs could not be climbed, and if the coast was followed towards the south the difficulties increased. From my recollection of the place, I thought he exaggerated, but I was not prepared to bank on a dim memory.

"There is no time to lose," he said, with an earnestness which convinced me that, though our motives might be different, our purposes were alike. "In two days it will be Good Friday, and the night after comes the solemn hour when our Lord breaks the bonds of death. I grievously fear that that is the hour which my foolish folk have fixed for this sacrilege. If great sin is to be averted, the woman must be gone by then and the House given to the flames. The flames, I say, for whatever happens, there will be no peace in Plakos till it is in ashes. But let it be burned honestly and religiously, and not made an altar to the outland devils whom Holy Church has long ago cast into the darkness."

The problem seemed to me to be clarifying itself. I was inclined to think that the priest was

too badly scared to take a balanced view of things,
and also too wrapped up in his religious anxieties.
I agreed that we must somehow induce Koré to
come away, and that for this purpose we must get
all our ten men together and beg, borrow or steal
some kind of boat. It was also plain that the
sooner I got inside the House the better, for Koré
would need some persuading. I was not able to
view the black magic of the villagers quite seriously. It was obviously a real peril, but it was so
wholly outside the range of my mental conception
that I took it as a straightforward risk, like that
from a wild animal or a thunderstorm.

Maris and I had a short talk in French and
settled our plans. He would go back to the inn
and see our fellows fixed up for the night. Then he
would make his way on foot towards Vano and get
into touch with Janni. We fixed a point on his
map, on the edge of the cliffs about two miles
south of the House, where he was to bring Janni
and his posse, and where next morning I was to
take out the others to join him. There seemed no
risk in leaving the five men in the inn for the night.
The villagers would scarcely interfere with
strangers who purported to be a Government
survey party and had no desire to move. Nor was
it likely that any obstacle would be set in the way
of Maris's own journey. After all he was moving
towards Vano and away from the prohibited area.

My own case was more intricate. If I went back
to the inn, it would be harder to make my way
from it to the Dancing Floor, for I should have the
village street to go through. We put this to the
priest, and he proved unexpectedly helpful. Why
should I not stay on in his house till the evening?

The church was adjacent, and behind the church lay the grave-yard, by which a road could be found to the Dancing Floor. He would give me food, if I cared to share his humble meal. The old fellow might be a bigot, but he was honest and friendly and patently on our side. I beamed on him and thanked him in dumb show, while Maris made ready to start.

" Get into the House somehow and fix up a plan with the lady," he said. " That is the first job. You are quite clear about the rendezvous on the cliffs ? You had better get back to the inn somehow, and to-morrow morning bring the men to join me there. The village will think we've started on our surveying—and a long way off the danger-point. You will have to open the boxes and make each man carry his own supplies. You have your gun ? "

I patted my pocket. " Yes, but there isn't going to be any shooting. We haven't a dog's chance at that game, with Miss Arabin arming the natives with Mauser rifles."

MANY times that day I wished that my education had included modern Greek. Through the hot afternoon and evening I remained in the little room, bored and anxious and mystified, while the priest sat opposite me, a storehouse of vital knowledge which I could not unlock. I raked up my recollection of classical Greek and tried him with a sentence or two, but he only shook his head. Most of the time he read in a little book, a breviary no doubt, and his lips muttered. An old woman came in and made ready a meal. We lunched off onion soup and black bread and a very odd-tasting cheese, and I was given a glass of some wine which smacked of turpentine. I smoked one of the two cigarettes left in my case, and afterwards fell asleep. When I woke the old man was sitting just as I had left him, but he had laid down his book and seemed to be praying. There was no reserve now in the old face; I saw the age of it, and the innocence, and also the blind fear. He seemed to be pleading fiercely with his God, and his mouth worked like a child's in a passion of disquiet.

Of course I might have strolled out-of-doors, and gone back to the inn, where I could have seen our five men and retrieved my pipe and pouch. It struck me that we were behaving like fools;

we had come to visit the House, and we ought to lose no time in getting there. My nap had put our previous talk out of my head, and I found myself on my feet in a sudden impulse. Then I remembered how Maris had enjoined the utmost caution, and I remembered, too, the look of those queer people in the street. The House was *tabu*, and if I was seen going towards it I should be stopped, and I might even precipitate some wild mischief without Maris to help me. There in the priest's homely kitchen, with a belt of golden light on the floor and the hum of flies in the window, I had an acute sense of being among shadows which might suddenly turn into monstrous forms of life. The whole island seemed to me like a snake still numb from the winter cold but thawing fast into a malignant activity. And meantime Koré was all alone in that ill-omened House with the circle of hate closing around her, and I, who had come there to protect her, was still outside the cordon. I cursed the infernal fog which had brought us so fatally out of our course; and I resolved that no power on earth would hinder me, when the dark came, from piercing the barrier.

The presbytery opened into a narrow lane with outbuildings in front of it, but from the window I could see a corner of the main street. The sun poured into the lane, and I watched the little green lizards on the wall beyond. There was scarcely a sign of life in the segment I saw of the main street ; indeed there was a silence strange in a village, so that every tiny natural noise—the chirping of grasshoppers, the slow flight of a dove —came with a startling clearness. Once a woman with a shawl over her head hurried past the opening. There should have been children playing at the corner, but there were no children nor any sound of them. Never a cart rumbled by, nor mule nor horse crossed my line of vision. The village seemed to be keeping an eerie fast.

One man indeed I saw—a big fellow with a white blouse and long boots of untanned leather. He stood staring down the alley, and I noticed that he carried a rifle. I beckoned to the priest and we watched him together out of a corner of the window. The old man shook his head violently and muttered something which ended in "bounos." Then he added between his teeth a word which sounded like "Callicantzari." I had heard that word from Maris as a term of abuse—he had said, I remember, that it meant men who become beasts, like the ancient Centaurs. I guessed that this fellow must be one of the mountain-men, who were now in league with their old enemies of the coast. If they were among the besiegers, Koré could no longer refuse our help. " I will hire a regiment to shoot them down," she had furiously told me. But what good was *our* help likely to be ?

The sight of that fellow put an edge to my discomfort, and before the shadows had begun to fall I was roaming about the little room like a cat in a cage. The priest left me, and presently I heard the ringing of a bell. In the quiet, now deepened by the hush of twilight, the homely sound seemed a mockery—like the striking of the bells of a naval battery I once heard on the Yser. Then, in the midst of mud and death, it had incongruously suggested tea on the cool deck of a liner ; now this tintinnabulation with its call to a meek worship had the same grotesque note of parody. Clearly there were no worshippers. I went to the back of the cottage, and from the window of the bare little bedroom had a view of the church in that amethyst gloaming. It was a baroque edifice, probably five centuries old, but renovated during the last fifty years, and in part painted a violent red. Beside it was a tiny bell-tower, obviously far more ancient. I could see a faint light in the window, and beyond that a dark clump of ilex above which the evening star was rising.

When the priest returned it was almost dark. He lit a lamp and carefully locked the door and shuttered the window. His barren service seemed to weigh heavily on him, for he moved wearily and did not raise his long-lidded eyes. It was borne in on me that at any price I must find some means of communicating with him, for my hour of action was approaching.

I tried him in French, but he never lifted his head.

Then it occurred to me that even a priest of the Greek church must know a little Latin. I used the English pronunciation, and though he did not understand me, he seemed to realise what tongue I was talking, for he replied in a slow broad Latin. I could not follow it, but at any rate we had found a common speech. I tore a page from my note-book and was about to write, when he snatched it and the pencil from my hand. There was something he badly wanted to say to me. He hesitated a good deal, and then in laborious capitals he wrote:

" *Si populus aliquid periculi tibi minatur, in-*

venies refugium in ecclesia." Then he scored out
" *refugium* " and wrote in " *sanctuarium.*"

" *Quid periculi ?* " I wrote.

He looked at me helplessly, and spread out his
hands. Danger, he seemed to suggest, lay in every
quarter of the compass.

We used up five pages in a conversation in the
doggiest kind of style. My Latin was chiefly of
the legal type, and I often used a word that
puzzled him, while he also set me guessing with
phrases which I suppose were ecclesiastical. But
the result was that he repeated the instructions
he had given me through Maris. If I was to enter
the House, the only way was by the Dancing Floor
—it took me some time to identify " *locus salta-
torum* "—and to climb the great wall which
separated it from the demesne. But it would be
guarded, probably by the " *incolæ montium,*" and
I must go warily, and not attempt it till the moon
was down. Also I must be back before the first
light of dawn.

I showed him my pistol, but he shook his head
violently and went through a pantomime, the
meaning of which was clear enough. I was not
to shoot, because, though the guards were armed,
there would be no shooting. But all the same
I was in some deadly danger. He scribbled
in abusive Latin that the people I had to fear
were " *pagani, nefasti, mysteriorum abominabilium
cultores.*" If I were seen and pursued my only
hope was to reach the church. Not his house—
that was no use—but the church. Twice he printed
in emphatic capitals : " *Pete sanctuarium ecclesiæ.*"

Then he took me into his little bedroom, and
showed me the lie of the land. The moon was now

up, the fog of the morning had gone out of the air, and the outline of the church and the bell-tower and the ilex grove beyond might have been cut in amber and jet. Through the trees there appeared a faint reddish glow as if fires were burning. I asked what this might be, and after a good deal of biting the stump of my pencil he wrote that there lay the graveyard, and the lights were burning " *ut vrykolakes absint.*" He seemed to doubt whether I could follow his meaning, but I did, for I knew about this from Koré—how the peasants kept lamps at the grave-heads to ward off vampires.

He was clear that I must traverse the valley of the Dancing Floor while the moon was up, for otherwise I should miss my way. He looked at me appraisingly and wrote " You are a soldier," implying, as I took it, that there was cover for a man accustomed to use cover. Then he drew a plan on which he marked my road. If I skirted the graveyard I should find myself on a hillside which sloped towards the Dancing Floor. I must keep this ridge, which was the northern containing wall of the place, till I reached the boundaries of the House. On no account must I go down into the valley, and when I asked why, he said that it was " *nefasta.*" That could not mean merely that it was well-guarded, but that it was held in dread by the people of Kynætho, a dread which their priest shared.

I left the house just after eleven o'clock. Our long silent sederunt had made the two of us good friends, for he wept at parting and insisted on blessing me and kissing me on the forehead. I was on his side, on the side of his Church, a

crusader going into peril in a strife with heathenish
evil.

It was a marvellous night for scent and colour,
but as silent as the deeps of the sea. I got with
all speed into the shade of the ilexes, and climbed
up a rocky slope so that I looked down on the
village graveyard beyond the trees. Dozens of
little lights twinkled in it like fireflies, those un-
dying lamps which were lit to preserve the inmates from outrage by the terrible demons that
enter into the bodies of the dead. Suddenly I
remembered with horror that it was Koré against
whom these precautions were taken—Koré, now
because of her crazy gallantry alone in a doomed
House, dreaming perhaps that she was winning
back the hearts of her people, and knowing little
of the dark forces massing against her out of the
ancientry of time. There was that in this mania
of superstition which both infuriated and awed
me ; it was a thing against which a man could
find no weapon. And I had the ironic recollection
of how little more than a week earlier, in a case
before the Judicial Committee of the Privy Council,
I had been defending the legalisation of certain
African rites, on the ground that what to one
man was superstition might to another be an
honest faith. I had struck a belief which had
the compelling power of a fanatical religion,
though it was born of the blackness of night.

The hillside was a mass of scrub and boulder,
giving excellent cover, and, since the ridge shut
me off from the village, I could move with reasonable speed and safety. My spirits were rising
with the exercise, and the depression which had
overwhelmed me in the priest's house was lifting.

Then suddenly I topped a rise and found myself looking down on the Dancing Floor.

It was not a valley so much as an upland meadow, for there was no stream in it nor had there ever been one, and, though tilted up gently towards the west, most of it was as flat as a cricket-field. There it lay in the moonlight, yellow as corn in its cincture of broken ridges, a place plainly hallowed and set apart. All my life I have cherished certain pictures of landscape, of which I have caught glimpses in my travels, as broken hints of a beauty of which I hoped some day to find the archetype. One is a mountain stream running in broad shallows and coming down through a flat stretch of heather from a confusion of blue mountains. Another is a green meadow, cut off like a garden from neighbouring wildernesses, secret and yet offering a wide horizon, a place at once a sanctuary and a watch-tower. This type I have found in the Scottish Borders, in the Cotswolds, once in New Hampshire, and plentifully in the Piedmont country of Virginia. But in the Dancing Floor I had stumbled upon its archetype. The moonlight made the farther hills look low and near, and doubtless lessened the size of the level ground, but the constriction only served to increase its preciousness.

I sat down and stared at the scene, and in that moment I underwent a great lightening of spirit. For this meadow was a happy place, the home of gentle and kindly and honourable things. Mildness and peace brooded over it. The priest had said that it was " *nefasta*," but he could only have meant that it was sacred. Sacred indeed it must be, what the Greeks of old called a *temenos*, for the

dullest could not be blind to the divinity that
dwelt here. I had a moment of wonder why the
Arabins, lords of the island, had not included
a spot so gracious in their demesne, until I saw
that that could not be. The Dancing Floor must
be open to the winds and the starry influences
and the spirits of earth ; no human master
could own or enclose it.

You will call me fantastic, but, dull dog as I
am, I felt a sort of poet's rapture as I looked
at those shining spaces, and at the sky above,
flooded with the amber moon except on the
horizon's edge where a pale blue took the place
of gold and faint stars were pricking. The place
was quivering with magic drawn out of all the
ages since the world was made, but it was good
magic. I had felt the oppression of Kynætho,
the furtive frightened people, the fiasco of Easter-
tide, the necromantic lamps beside the graves.
These all smacked evilly of panic and death. But
now I was looking on the Valley of the Shadow
of Life. It was the shadow only, for it was mute
and still and elusive. But the presage of life
was in it, the clean life of fruits and flocks, and
children and happy winged things, and that spring
purity of the earth which is the purity of God.

The moon was declining, but it would be at
least two hours before I could safely approach
the House. The cover was good, I was protected
by the ridge from the side of the village, and
no human being was likely to be abroad on the
Dancing Floor. I decided that I must get within
sight of my destination before the light failed and
spy out the land. It was rough going among
the ribs of rock and stone-falls and dense thickets

of thorn and arbutus, but sometimes I would
come on a patch of turf drenched with dew and
scented with thyme. All the myrrh of Arabia
was in the place, for every foot of sward I trod
on and every patch of scrub I brushed through
was aromatic, and in the open places there was
the clean savour of night and the sea. Also
at my left hand and below lay the Dancing Floor,
lambent under the moon like the cool tides of a
river.

By and by I came to the end of the ridge, and
had a view of the crest where the House stood.
There was a blur of ebony which must be the
wood that surrounded it, and bounding it a ribbon
of silver-grey. I puzzled at this, till I realised
that it was the wall of which the priest had spoken
—a huge thing, it seemed, of an even height,
curving from the dip where the village lay and
running to what seemed to be the seaward scarp
of the island. I was now in the danger zone, and
it behoved me to go warily, so I found a shelter
where the cover of the ridge ended and studied
the details of the scene. The wall could not be
less than fifteen feet in height, and it appeared to
be regularly masoned and as smooth as the side
of a house. In that landscape it was a startling
intrusion of something crude and human, a defiance
of nature. Shelley Arabin had built it for the
sake of his sinister privacy, but why had he built
it so high ? And then I guessed the reason. He
wanted to shut out the Dancing Floor from his
life. That blessed place would have been a mute
protest against his infamies.

There was a black patch in the even sheen of
the wall. I wormed my way a little nearer and

saw that for perhaps a dozen yards the wall had
been broken down. I could see the ragged edges
and the inky darkness of the shrubberies beyond.
This had been done recently, perhaps within the
last month. And then I saw something more.
There were men—guards—stationed at the gap.
I made out their figures, and they seemed to have
the baggy white shirts of the mountaineer I had
seen in the village. Also they were armed. One
stood in the gap, and the two others patrolled the
sides, and I could see that they carried rifles
at the trail. It seemed absurd that three men
were needed for that tiny entrance, and I concluded that they wanted each other's company.
There must be something in the task which put a
heavy strain on their courage. I noticed, too,
that they kept their faces resolutely averted from
the Dancing Floor. When one moved he walked
with his head screwed round facing the House.
The shining meadow might be *nefastus,* as the
priest had said, or it might be too sacred at this
solemn hour of night for the profane gaze.

When I had watched them for a little it seemed
to me that, though the moon had not set, these
fellows were too preoccupied to be dangerous, and
that I might safely continue my reconnaissance.
There was not much cover, but the declining moon
made an olive shadow at the upper end of the
Dancing Floor, and I proceeded to crawl across
it like a gillie after deer. I went very cautiously,
stopping every now and then to prospect, but I
found the wall now beyond my range and I had
to chance the immobility of the sentries. My
breeches were sopping with dew before I reached
the point which I judged to be out of sight of the

gap. The wall, as I had observed, curved at the sea end, and once there—unless there were further guards—I should be at liberty to test my climbing powers. The thing looked a most formidable barrier, but I was in hopes that it might be turned where it abutted on the cliffs.

Before I realised it I was looking down on the sea.

The coast bent inward in a little bight, and a hundred feet below me the water lapped on a white beach. It was such a revelation of loveliness as comes to a man only once or twice in his lifetime. I fancy that the short commons on which I had subsisted all day and the sense of dwelling among portents had keyed me up to a special receptiveness. Behind me was the Dancing Floor, and in front a flood of translucent colour, the shimmer of gold, the rarest tints of sapphire and amethyst, fading into the pale infinity of the sky. I had come again into a world which spoke. From below came the sound of dreamily moving water, of sleepy pigeons in the rocks. Recollections of poetry fleeted through my mind :

> " where Helicon breaks down
> In cliff to the sea . . .
>
> Where the moon-silver'd inlets
> Send far their light voice——"

Yes, but something was wanting. There should have been white flocks on the sward, something to link up nature with the homely uses of man, in order to produce the idyllic. This place was not idyllic, it was magical and unearthly. Above me was a walled mystery, within which evil had once been followed and a greater evil might soon be

done, and there were men with quaking hearts
bent upon ancient devilries.

I followed the edge of the scarp as it rose to
the highest point where the wall ended. There
I had a sharp disappointment. The wall ran
sheer to the edge of the cliff, and a steep buttress
descended to the face of the limestone crag. The
stone was as smooth as a water-worn pebble.
I have been a rock-climber since I was an undergraduate, and have faced in my time some awkward
problems, but this was starkly impossible. Even
with a companion and a rope I do not believe it
could have been done, and to attempt it alone
meant the certainty of a broken neck.

I prospected eastward along the wall and found
no better hope there. The thing was simply not
to be climbed except by a lizard. If I had had
Maris with me I might have stood on his shoulders
and made a jump for the coping; as it was it
might have been a hundred feet high instead of
fifteen for all the good it was to me. There were
no branches about to make a ladder, or loose
stones to make a cairn—nothing but the short
downland turf.

The sight of this insuperable obstacle effectively
put a stop to my brief exhilaration of spirit. I
felt small and feeble and futile. It was impera-
tive that I should get into the House without
further delay and see Koré, and yet the House
was as impracticable as the moon, now swiftly
setting. The rapid darkening of the world pointed
out the only road. I must dodge the sentries
and get through the breach in the wall. It was
a wild notion, but my growing ill-temper made me
heedless of risks. The men had no pistols, only

rifles, and were probably not too ready in the use of them.   After all I had played this game before with success.   In the first winter of the war, when I was a subaltern, I used to be rather good at wriggling across No-man's-land and eavesdropping beside the German trenches.

I didn't give my resolution time to weaken, but in the shadow of the wall made the best pace I could towards the gap.   It was now really dark, with only a faint glow from the stars, and I moved in what seemed to my eyes impenetrable shade after the brightness of the moon.   I was wearing rubber-soled boots and cloth gaiters, my garments were subfusc in colour, and I have always been pretty light on my feet.   I halted many times to get my bearings, and presently I heard the sound of a man's tread.   So far as I could judge before, two of the sentries had their patrol well away from the wall, and I might escape their notice if I hugged the stones.   But one had had his stand right in the breach, and with him I would have difficulty. My hope was to dart through into the shelter of the thick shrubbery.   Even if they fired on me they would be likely to miss, and I believed that they would not follow me into the demesne.

I edged my way nearer, a foot at a time, till I guessed by the sound that I was inside the beat of the patrols.   I had no white about me, for my shirt and collar were drab, and I kept my face to the wall.   Suddenly my hands felt the ragged edge of the gap and I almost stumbled over a fallen stone.   Here it was very dark and I had the shadow of the trees inside to help me.   I held my breath and listened, but I could not hear any noise from within the breach. Had the sentry there deserted his post?

I waited for a minute or so, trying to reckon up the chances. The tread of the man on my right was clear, and presently I could make out also the movement of the man on my left. Where was the third? Suddenly I heard to the right the sound of human speech. The third must be there. There was a sparkle of fire, too. The third sentry had gone to get a light for his cigarette.

Now was my opportunity, and I darted into the darkness of the gap. I was brought up sharp and almost stunned by a blow on the forehead. There was a gate in the gap, a stout thing of wattles with a pole across. I strained at it with my hands, but it would not move.

There was nothing for it but to bolt. The sentries had been alarmed—probably horribly alarmed—by the noise, and were drawing together. The only safety lay in violent action, for they had a means of getting light and would find me if I tried to lurk in the shadows. I raised my arms in the orthodox ghostly fashion, howled like a banshee, and broke for the open.

I was past them before they could stop me and plunging down the slope towards the Dancing Floor. I think that for the first moments they were too scared to shoot, for they must have believed that I had come out of the forbidden House, and when they recovered their nerve I was beyond their range. The upper slope was steep, and I went down it as Pate-in-Peril in *Redgauntlet* went down Errickstane-brae. I rolled over and over, found my feet, lost them again, and did not come to rest till I was in the flats of the meadow. I looked

back and saw a light twinkling at the gap. The
guards there must have been amazed to find the
gate intact and were now doubtless at their
prayers.

I did not think that, even if they believed me
flesh and blood, they would dare to follow me to
the Dancing Floor. So I made my way down it
at a reasonable pace, feeling rather tired, rather
empty and very thirsty. On the road up I had
decided that there was no stream in it, but almost
at once I came to a spring. It was a yard across,
bubbling up strongly, and sending forth a tiny
rill which presently disappeared in some fissure
of the limestone. The water was deliciously cold
and I drank pints of it. Then it occurred to me
that I must put my best foot forwards, for there
was that trembling in the eastern sky which is the
presage of dawn. My intention was to join my
fellows in the inn courtyard, and meet Maris there
in the morning. After all the inhabitants of
Kynætho had nothing as yet against me. All they
knew of me was that I was a surveyor from the
Government at Athens, whose presence no doubt
was unwelcome but who could hardly be treated
as an enemy.

I reached the eastern bounds of the Dancing
Floor, and scrambled up on the ridge above the
ilexes of the graveyard. The lamps were still
twinkling like glow-worms among the graves. From
there it was easy to get into the lane where stood
the priest's house, and in a few minutes I was in
the main village street. The chilly dawn was
very near and I thought lovingly of the good food
in our boxes. My first desire was a meal which
should be both supper and breakfast.

The door of the courtyard stood open, and I pushed through it to the barn beyond. The place was empty—not a sign of men or baggage. For a moment I thought they might have been given quarters in the inn, till I remembered that the inn had no guest-room. I tried the other outbuildings —a stable, a very dirty byre, a place which looked like a granary. One and all were empty.

It was no use waking the landlord, for he probably would not answer, and in any case I did not understand his tongue. There was nothing for it but to go back to the priest. My temper was thoroughly embittered, and I strode out of the courtyard as if I were at home in my own village.

But my entrance had been observed, and the street was full of people. I doubt if Kynætho slept much these days, and now it seemed that from every door men and women were emerging. There was something uncanny in that violent vigilance in the cold grey light of dawn. And the crowd was no longer inert. In a second I saw that it was actively hostile, that it wanted to do me a mischief, or at any rate to lay hands on me. It closed in on me from every side, and yet made no sound.

It was now that I had my first real taste of fear. Before I had been troubled and mystified, but now I was downright afraid. Automatically I broke into a run, for I remembered the priest's advice about the church.

My action took them by surprise. Shouts arose, meaningless shouts to me, and I broke through the immediate circle with ease. Two fellows who moved to intercept me I handed off in the best Rugby football style. The street was empty before me and I sprinted up it at a pace which I doubt if I ever equalled in my old running days.

But I had one determined pursuer. I caught a glimpse of him out of a corner of my eye, one of the young men from the hills, a fellow with a dark hawk-like face and a powerful raking stride. In my then form he would have beaten me easily if the course had been longer, but it was too short to let him develop his speed. Yet he was not a yard behind me when I shot through the open door of the church.

I flung myself gasping on the floor behind one of the squat pillars. As I recovered my breath I wondered why no shot had been fired. A man with a gun could have brought me down with the utmost ease, for I had been running straight in the open. My second thought was that the priest had been right. The peasant had stopped in his tracks at the church door. I had found safety for the moment—a sanctuary or, it might be, a prison.

THE morning light was filtering through the windows, and since the glass was a dirty yellow, the place seemed still to be full of moonshine. As my eyes grew accustomed to it, I made out the features of the interior. A heavy curtain separated the sanctuary from the chancel; the floor was of rough stone, worn with the feet and knees of generations of worshippers; there were none of the statues and images which one is accustomed to in a Roman church, not even a crucifix, though there may have been one above the hidden altar. From a pillar hung an assortment of votive offerings, crutches, oar-blades, rudders of ships, old-fashioned horn spectacles. The walls were studded with little ikons of saints, each one with its guttering lamp before it. The place smelt dank and unused and mouldy, like a kirk in winter-time in some Highland glen. Behind me the open door showed an oval of pure pale light.

I was in a mood of profound despondency which was very near despair. The men had gone and with them our stores of food and ammunition. God knew where Maris was or how I should find him again. The village was actively hostile, and I was shut up in the church as in a penitentiary. I was no nearer Koré than when we landed— farther away indeed, for I had taken the wrong turning, and she was shut off from me by mountainous barriers. I could have laughed bitterly when I thought of the futility of the help which I had been so confident of giving her. And her danger was far more deadly than I had dreamed. She was the mark of a wild hate which had borrowed some wilder madness out of the deeps of the past. She had spoken of a " sacrifice." That was the naked truth of it ; any moment tragedy might be done, some hideous rite consummated, and youth and gallantry laid on a dark altar.

The thought drove me half crazy. I fancy the lack of food and sleep had made me rather light-headed, for I sat in a stupor which was as much anger as pity—anger at those blinded islanders, at my own feebleness, at Koré's obstinacy. This was succeeded by an extreme restlessness. I could not stay still, but roamed about examining the ill-favoured ikons. There was a little recess on the right of the chancel which was evidently the treasury, for I found a big chest full of dusty vestments and church plate. Sacrilege must have been an unknown crime in Kynætho, for the thing was unlocked.

Then I noticed a strange object below the chancel step. It seemed to be a bier with a shrouded figure laid on it. The sight gave me a shock, for I thought it a dead body. Reluctantly I approached it and drew back the shroud, expecting to see the corpse of a peasant.

To my amazement it was a figure of Christ—a wooden image, rudely carved but with a strange similitude of life. It reminded me of a John the Baptist by Donatello which I once saw in Venice. The emaciated body was naked but for the loin cloth, the eyes were closed, the cheeks sunken. It was garishly painted, and the stigmata were done in a crude scarlet. But there was power in it, and dignity and a terrible pitifulness. I remembered Koré's story. This was the figure which on the night of Good Friday, after the women had kissed and wailed over it, was borne in procession among the village lanes and then restored to its sepulchre. This was the figure which at the Easter Resurrection stood in a blaze of candles before the altar, the Crucified and Risen Lord.

That sight worked a miracle with me. I suddenly felt that I was not alone, but had august allies. The Faith was behind me, that faith which was deep in the heart of Kynætho though for the moment it was overlaid. The shabby church, the mazed and ignorant priest took on suddenly a tremendous significance. . . . They were the visible sign and warrant of that creed which we all hold dumbly, even those who call themselves unbelievers —the belief in the ultimate omnipotence of purity and meekness.

I reverently laid the shroud again over the figure, and must have stood in a muse before it, till I found that the priest had joined me. He knelt beside the bier, and said his prayers, and never have I heard such an agony of supplication in a man's voice. I drew back a little, and waited. When he had finished he came to me and his eyes asked a question.

I shook my head and got out my notebook.

He asked me if I had breakfasted, and when I wrote the most emphatic negative which my Latin could compass, he hobbled off and returned with

some food under his cassock. It was only cheese
and black bread, but I ate it wolfishly and felt
better for it. I looked on the old man now with a
sincere liking, for he was my host and my ally,
and I think he had changed his attitude towards
me. Those minutes beside the bier had established
a bond between us.

In the recess I have mentioned there was a door
which I had not hitherto noticed. This opened
into a kind of sacristy, where the priest kept his
odds and ends. There was a well in the floor of
it, covered by an immense oaken lid, a well of cold
water of which I had a long drink. The old man
drew several buckets, and set about cleaning the
chancel, and I was glad to lend a hand. I spent
the better part of the morning like a housemaid
on my knees scrubbing the floor and the chancel
step, while he was occupied inside the sanctuary.
The physical exertion was an anodyne to my
thoughts, which in any case were without purpose. I could do nothing till the night came
again.

On one of my journeys to the sacristy to fetch
water I saw a face at the little window, which
opened on the yard of the priest's house. To my
immense relief it was Maris, very dirty and dis-
hevelled, but grinning cheerfully. That window
was a tight fit, but he managed to wriggle half
through and a strong pull from me did the rest.
He drank like a thirsty dog out of my bucket, and
then observed that a church had its drawbacks
as a resort, since one couldn't smoke.

" I have much to tell you, my friend," he said,
" but first I must interview his Holiness. By
God, but he has the mischievous flock."

I do not know what he said to the priest,
but he got answers which seemed to give him
a melancholy satisfaction. The old man spoke
without ever looking up, and his voice was flat
with despair. Often he shook his head, and
sometimes he held up his hand as if to avert
a blasphemy. Maris turned to me with a shrug
of the shoulders. " This madness is beyond him,
as it is beyond me. It is a general breaking
down of wits. What can you and I, soldiers
though we be, do against insanity ? Presently
I must sleep, and you too, my friend, to
judge by your heavy eyes. But first I make
my report."

" I suppose we are safe here ? " I said.

" Safe enough, but impotent. We can take
our sleep confidently, but it is hard to see that
we can do much else. We are in quarantine, if
you understand. But to report——"

He had gone to the inn the night before, and
found our five men supping and playing cards
like Christians. They seemed to understand what
was required of them—to wait for me and then
join Janni and the others at the rendezvous on
the western cliffs. So far as he could judge they
had had no communication of any kind with the
people of the village. Then he had set out with
an easy mind on the road to Vano. No one had
hindered him ; the few villagers he met had
stared but had not attempted even to accost
him. So over the moonlit downs he went,
expecting to find Janni and the other five in
bivouac in the open country towards the skirts
of the hills.

He found Janni alone—on the roadside some

miles east of Vano, squatted imperturbably by a
fire, in possession of five revolvers and ample
stores, but without a single follower. From the
one-armed corporal he heard a strange tale. The
party had made Vano before midday in the *Santa
Lucia,* had landed, and marched inland from the
little port, without apparently attracting much
attention. He himself had explained to the
harbour-master that they had been sent to do
survey work, and the wineshop, where they stopped
for a drink, heard the same story. They had then
tramped up the road from Vano to the hills, stopping at the little farms to pass the time of day
and pick up news. They heard nothing till night-
fall, when they encamped beside a village among
the foothills. There Janni talked to sundry
villagers and heard queer stories of Kynætho.
There was a witch there who by her spells had
blighted the crops and sent strange diseases among
the people, and the cup of her abominations was
now full. St Dionysios had appeared to many
in a dream summoning them to Kynætho in the
Great Week, and the best of the young men had
already gone thither.

That was all that Janni heard, for being the man
in authority he spoke only with the elders, and
they were wary in their talk. But the others,
gossiping with the women, heard a fuller version
which scared them to the bone. Your Greek
townsman is not a whit less superstitious than the
peasant, and he lacks the peasant's stolidity,
and is prone to more speedy excitement. Janni
did not know exactly what the women had told
his men, except that Kynætho was the abode
of vampires and harpies for whom a surprising

judgment was preparing, and that no stranger could enter the place without dire misfortune. There might be throat-cutting, it was hinted, on the part of the young men now engaged in a holy war, and there would for certain be disaster at the hand of the *striglas* and *vrykolakes* in the House, for to them a stranger would be easy prey.

Whatever it was, it brought the men back to Janni gibbering with terror and determined to return forthwith to Vano. The island was accursed and the abode of devils innumerable, and there was nothing for honest men to do but to flee. They would go back to Vano and wait on a boat, the *Santa Lucia* or some other. To do the rascals justice, Janni thought that they might have faced the throat-cutting, but the horrors of the unseen and the occult were more than they could stomach. Janni, who was a rigid disciplinarian, had fortunately possessed himself of their pistols when they encamped for the night, and he was now in two minds whether he should attempt to detain them by force. But the sight of their scared eyes and twitching lips decided him that he could do nothing in their present mood, and he resolved to let them go back to Vano till he had seen Maris and received instructions. They had already had wages in advance, and could fend for themselves till he made a plan. So he doled out to each man a share of the supplies and watched them scurry off in the direction of the coast, while he smoked his pipe and considered the situation. There about two in the morning Maris found him.

The defection of these five men suggested to Maris that the same kind of trouble might be expected with the batch in Kynætho. So he and Janni humped the stores and started off across the downs to the rendezvous on the cliffs which he had settled with me. That occupied a couple of hours, and there Janni was left with orders not to stir till he was summoned. The place was a hollow on the very edge of the sea, far removed from a road or a dwelling—a lucky choice, for it had been made at haphazard from the map without any local knowledge. Then Maris set off at his best pace for Kynætho, skirting the Dancing Floor on the south, and striking the road to Vano a mile or so from the village.

There he met the rest of our posse, and a more dilapidated set of mountebanks he declared he had never seen. So far as he could gather from their babble, they had been visited in the small hours by a deputation of villagers, who had peremptorily ordered them to depart. The deputation backed its plea not by threats but by a plain statement of facts. Kynætho was labouring under a curse which was about to be removed. No doubt the villagers expounded the nature of the curse with details which started goose-flesh on their hearers. What was about to be done was Kynætho's own affair, and no stranger could meddle with it and live. They may have enforced their argument with a sight of their rifles, but probably they did not need any mundane arguments to barb the terror which their tale inspired. For they succeeded in so putting a fear of unknown horrors into these five Athens guttersnipes that they decamped without a protest. They did not even stay to collect some provender, but fled for their lives along the Vano road.

When Maris met them they were padding along in abject panic. One man still carried unconsciously a tin from which he had been feeding, another clutched a crumpled pack of cards. They had their pistols, but they had no thought of using them. Pantingly they told their story, irking to be gone, and when Maris seemed to be about to detain them they splayed away from him like frightened sheep. Like Janni, he decided that it was no good to try to stop them—indeed he was pretty clear by now that even if they stayed they would be useless for the job we had in hand. He cursed their female relatives for several generations and speeded the hindmost on his way with a kick.

His next business was to find me, and he concluded that I would probably be still in the neighbourhood of the House. So, as the moon was down, he retraced his steps by the south side of the Dancing Floor and reached the edge where the wall abutted on the cliffs probably an hour after I had been there. He shared my view about the impracticality of an entrance to the demesne at that point. As it was now almost daylight he did not dare to follow the wall, but returned to Janni on the cliffs, who gave him breakfast. He was getting anxious about my doings, for he argued that if I returned to the inn to look for the men there would probably be trouble. It seemed to him important that the village should still believe him to have gone off, so he was determined not to show himself. But he must get

in touch with me, and for that purpose he decided
first to draw the priest's house. He had a difficult
journey in the broad daylight by way of the graveyard. It would have been impossible, he said, if
the village had been living its normal life, for he
had to pass through a maze of little fields and
barns. But all farm work seemed to have been
relinquished, and not a soul was to be seen at
the lower end of the Dancing Floor. Everybody,
except the guards round the House, seemed to
be huddling in the village street. In the end he
got into the priest's house, found it empty and
followed on to the church.

I told him briefly my doings of the night. I
could see that he was completely in the dark as
to what was happening, except that Kynætho,
under the goad of some crazy superstition, intended very resolute mischief to the House and
its chatelaine. You see he had not talked to
Koré—had indeed never seen her, nor had he
read the disquieting manuscript which Vernon
had translated for me. I did not see how I
could enlighten him, for on that side he was
no scholar, and was too rooted in his brand
of minor rationalism to take my tale seriously.
It was sufficient that we were both agreed that
the House must be entered, and Koré willy-nilly
removed.

" But we have no ship," he cried. " The lady
would be no safer in the open than in the House,
for they mean most certainly that she shall die.
I think it may come to putting our backs to the
wall, and the odds are unpleasant. We cannot
telegraph for help, for the office is in the village and
it has been destroyed. I have ascertained that

there is no wire at Vano, or elsewhere in the island."

Things looked pretty ugly, as I was bound to admit. But there was one clear and urgent duty, to get into the House and find Koré. Before we lay down to snatch a little sleep, we made a rough plan. Maris would try the coast to the north and see if an entrance could be effected by a postern above the jetty where Vernon and I had first landed. He thought that he had better undertake this job, for it meant skirting the village, and he believed he might pass in the darkness as one of the men from the hills. He could talk the language, you see, and, if accosted, could put up some kind of camouflage. I was to make for Janni, and then the two of us would try along the shore under the cliffs in the hope that some gully might give us access to the demesne north of the point where the wall ended. We were to rendezvous about breakfast time at Janni's camp, and from the results of the night frame a further programme.

I slept without a break till after eight o'clock in the evening, when the priest woke us and gave us another ration of the eternal bread and cheese. I felt frowsy and dingy and would have given much for a bath. The priest reported that the day in the village had passed without incident, except that there had been a great gathering in the central square and some kind of debate. He had not been present, but the thing seemed to have deepened his uneasiness. " There is no time to lose," he told Maris, " for to-morrow is Good Friday, and to-morrow I fear that unhallowed deeds may be done." Maris discussed his route with him very carefully, and several more pages of my notebook were used up in plans. It was going to be a ticklish business to reach the jetty—principally, I gathered, because of the guards who watched all the sides of the demesne which were not bounded by the cliffs or the great wall. But the priest seemed to think it possible, and Maris's Gascon soul had illimitable confidence.

My road was plain—up the ridge on the south side of the Dancing Floor till it ended at the sea, a matter of not more than four miles. I skirted as before the little graveyard with its flickering lamps, and then made a cautious traverse of a number of small fields each with its straw-covered barn. Presently I was out on the downs, with the yellow levels of the Dancing Floor below me on the right. I was in a different mood from the previous night, for I was now miserably conscious of the shortness of our time and the bigness of our task. Anxiety was putting me into a fever of impatience and self-contempt. Here was I, a man who was reckoned pretty competent by the world, who had had a creditable record in the war, who was considered an expert at getting other people out of difficulties—and yet I was so far utterly foiled by a batch of barbarian peasants. I simply dared not allow my mind to dwell on Koré and her perils, for that way lay madness. I had to try to think of the thing objectively as a problem to be solved, but flashes of acute fear for the girl kept breaking through to set my heart beating.

I found Janni cooking supper by his little fire in a nook of the downs, and the homely sight for

the moment comforted me. The one-armed corporal was, I dare say, by nature and upbringing as
superstitious as any other Greek peasant, but his
military training had canalised his imagination,
and he would take no notice of a legend till he was
ordered to by his superior officer. He reminded
me of the policeman Javert in *Les Misérables* :
his whole soul was in the ritual of his profession,
and it must have been a black day for Janni when
the war stopped. Maris, whom he worshipped
blindly, had bidden him take instructions from
me, and he was ready to follow me into the sea.
Mercifully his service at Salonika had taught
him a few English words and a certain amount
of bad French, so we could more or less com-
municate.

He had supplies with him, so I had a second
supper—biscuits and sardines and coffee, which
after two days of starvation tasted like nectar and
ambrosia. Also he had a quantity of caporal
cigarettes with which I filled my pockets. Our
first business was to get down to the beach, and
fortunately he had already discovered a route a
few hundred yards to the south, where a gully with
a stone shoot led to the water's edge. Presently
we stood on the pebbly shore looking out to the
luminous west over a sea as calm as a mill-
pond. I would have liked to bathe, but decided
that I must first get the immediate business
over.

That shore was rough going, for it was a succession of limestone reefs encumbered with great
boulders which had come down from the rocks
during past winters. The strip of beach was very
narrow and the overhang of the cliffs protected

us from observation from above, even had any
peasant been daring enough to patrol the Dancing
Floor by night. We kept close to the water where
the way was easiest, but even there our progress
was slow. It took us the better part of an hour to
get abreast of the point where the wall ended.
There the cliffs were at least two hundred feet high
and smooth as the side of a cut loaf. Crowning
them we could see the dark woodlands of the
demesne.

My object was to find a route up them, and
never in all my mountaineering experience had I
seen a more hopeless proposition. The limestone
seemed to have no fissures, and the faces had
weathered smooth. In the Dolomites you can
often climb a perpendicular cliff by the countless
little cracks in the hard stone, but here there were
no cracks, only a surface glassy like marble. At
one point I took off my boots and managed to
ascend about twenty yards, when I was brought up
sharp by an overhang, could find no way to
traverse, and had my work cut out getting down
again. Janni was no cragsman, and in any case his
one arm made him useless.

Our outlook ahead was barred by a little cape,
and I was in hopes that on the other side of that
the ground might become easier. We had a bad
time turning it, for the beach stopped and the
rock fell sheer to the water. Happily the water
at the point was shallow, and, partly wading and
partly scrambling, we managed to make the passage. In the moonlight everything was clear as
day, and once round we had a prospect of a narrow
bay, backed by the same high perpendicular
cliffs and bounded to the north by a still higher

bluff which ended to seaward in a sheer preci-
pice.

I sat down on a boulder with a sinking heart to
consider the prospect. It was more hopeless than
the part we had already prospected. There was
no gully or chimney in the whole glimmering semi-
circle, nothing but a rim of unscalable stone
crowned with a sharp-cut fringe of trees. Beyond
the bluff lay the oliveyards which I had seen
six years before when I landed from the yacht, but
I was pretty certain that we would never get
round the bluff. For the margin of shore had now
disappeared, and the cliffs dropped sheer into deep
water.

Suddenly Janni by my side grunted and pointed
to the middle of the little bay. There, riding at
anchor, was a boat.

At first it was not easy to distinguish it from a
rock, for there was no riding light shown. But, as
I stared at it, I saw that it was indeed a boat—
a yawl-rigged craft of, I judged, about twenty
tons. It lay there motionless in the moonlight,
a beautiful thing which had no part in that setting
of stone and sea—a foreign thing, an intruder.
I watched it for five minutes and nothing moved
aboard.

The sight filled me with both hope and mysti-
fication. Here was the " ship " which Maris had
postulated. But who owned it and what was it
doing in this outlandish spot, where there was no
landing ? It could not belong to Kynætho, or it
would have been lying at the jetty below the House
or in the usual harbour. Indeed it could not
belong to Plakos at all, for, though I knew little
about boats, I could see that the cut of this one

spoke of Western Europe. Was anyone on board?
It behoved me forthwith to find that out.

I spoke to Janni, and he whistled shrilly. But
there was no answer from the sleeping bay. He
tried again several times without result. If we
were to make inquiries, it could only be by swim-
ming out. Janni of course was no swimmer, and
besides the responsibility was on me. I can't say
I liked the prospect, but in three minutes I had
stripped and was striking out in the moon-silvered
water.

The fresh cold aromatic sea gave me new vigour
of body and mind. I realised that I must proceed
warily. Supposing there was someone on board,
someone hostile, I would be completely at his
mercy. So I swam very softly up to the stern and
tried to read the name on it. There was a name,
but that side was in shadow and I could not make
it out. I swam to the bows and there again saw
a name of which I could make nothing, except
that the characters did not seem to me to be
Greek.

I trod water and took stock of the situation. It
was the kind of craft of which you will see hundreds
at Harwich and Southampton and Plymouth—a
pleasure boat, obviously meant for cruising, but
with something of the delicate lines of a racer. I
was beginning to feel chilly, and felt that I must
do something more than prospect from the water.
I must get on board and chance the boat being
empty or the owner asleep.

There was a fender amidships hanging over the
port side. I clutched this, got a grip of the gunwale, and was just about to pull myself up, when
a face suddenly appeared above me, a scared, hairy

face, surmounted by a sort of blue nightcap. Its owner objected to my appearance, for he swung a boathook and brought it down heavily on the knuckles of my left hand. That is to say, such was his intention, but he missed his aim and only grazed my little finger.

I dropped off and dived, for I was afraid that he might start shooting. When I came up a dozen yards off and shook the water out of my eyes, I saw him staring at me as if I was a merman, with the boathook still in his hand.

" What the devil do you mean by that ? " I shouted, when I had ascertained that he had no pistol. " What boat is it ? Who are you ? "

My voice seemed to work some change in the situation, for he dropped the boathook, and replied in what sounded like Greek. I caught one word " Ingleez " several times repeated.

" I'm English," I cried, " English . . . philos . . . philhellene—damn it, what's the Greek for a friend ? "

" Friend," he repeated, " Ingleez," and I swam nearer.

He was a tough-looking fellow, dressed in a blue jersey and what appeared to be old flannel bags, and he looked honest, though puzzled. I was now just under him, and smiling for all I was worth. I put a hand on the fender again, and repeated the word " English." I also said that my intentions were of the best, and I only wanted to come aboard and have a chat. If he was well disposed toward England, I thought he might recognise the sound of the language.

Evidently he did, for he made no protest when I

got both hands on the gunwale again.   He allowed
me to get my knee up on it, so I took my chance
and swung myself over.   He retreated a step and
lifted the boathook, but he did not attempt to hit
me as I arose like Proteus out of the sea and stood
dripping on his deck.

I held out my hand, and with a moment's hesitation he took it.   " English . . . friend," I said,
grinning amicably at him, and to my relief he
grinned back.

I was aboard a small yacht, which was occi-
dental in every line of her, the clean decks, the
general tidy workmanlike air.   A man is not at
his most confident standing stark naked at midnight in a strange boat, confronting somebody of
whose speech he comprehends not one word.   But
I felt that I had stumbled upon a priceless asset
if I could only use it, and I was determined not
to let the chance slip.   He poured out a flow of
Greek, at which I could only shake my head and
murmur " English."   Then I tried the language
of signs, and went through a vigorous pantomime
to explain that, though I could not speak his
tongue, I had a friend on shore who could.   The
yacht had a dinghy.   Would he row me ashore and
meet my friend ?

It took me the devil of a time to make this clear
to him, and I had to lead him to where the dinghy
lay astern, point to it, point to the shore, point
to my dumb mouth and generally behave like a
maniac.   But he got it at last.   He seemed to
consider, then he dived below and returned with a
thing like an iron mace which he brandished round
his head as if to give me to understand that if I
misbehaved he could brain me.   I smiled and

nodded and put my hand on my heart, and he smiled back.

Then his whole manner changed. He brought me a coat and an ancient felt hat and made signs that I should put them on. He dived below again and brought up a bowl of hot cocoa which did me good, for my teeth were beginning to chatter. Finally he motioned me to get into the dinghy and set his mace beside him, took the sculls and pulled in the direction I indicated.

Janni was sitting smoking on a stone, the image of innocent peace. I cried out to him before we reached shore, and told him that this was the skipper and that he must talk to him. The two began their conversation before we landed, and presently it seemed that Janni had convinced my host that we were respectable. As soon as we landed I started to put on my clothes, but first I took the pistol from my coat pocket and presented the butt-end to my new friend. He saw my intention, bowed ceremoniously, and handed it back to me. He also pitched the mace back into the dinghy, as if he regarded it as no longer necessary.

He and Janni talked volubly and with many gesticulations, and the latter now and then broke off to translate for my benefit. I noticed that as time went on the seaman's face, though it remained friendly, grew also obstinate.

" He says he awaits his master here," said Janni, " but who his master is and where he is gone he will not tell. He says also that this island is full of devils and bad men and that on no account will he stay on it."

I put suggestions to Janni, which he translated, but we could get nothing out of the fellow, except

the repeated opinion—with which I agreed—that
the island was full of devils and that the only
place for an honest man was the water. About
his master he remained stubbornly silent. I
wanted him to take me in his boat round the
farther bluff so that we could land on the oliveyard slopes and possibly get in touch with Maris,
but he peremptorily refused. He would not leave
the bay, which was the only safe place. Elsewhere were the men and women of Plakos, who
were devils.

After about an hour's fruitless talk I gave it up.
But one thing I settled. I told him through
Janni that there were others besides ourselves and
himself who were in danger from the devils of the
island. There was a lady—an English lady—
who was even now in dire peril. If we could
bring her to the spot would he be on the watch
and take her on board ?

He considered this for a little and then agreed.
He would not leave the island without his master,
but he would receive the lady if necessary, and if
the devils followed he would resist them. He was
obviously a fighting man, and I concluded he would
be as good as his word. Asked if in case of pursuit
he would put to sea, he said, " No, not till his
master returned." That was the best I could
make of him, but of that precious master he refused
to speak a syllable. His own name he said was
George—known at home as Black George, to
distinguish him from a cousin, George of the Hare-
lip.

We parted in obscure friendliness. I presented
him with my empty cigarette-case, and he kissed
me on both cheeks. As I handed him back the

garments which he had lent me to cover my nakedness, I noticed a curious thing. The coat was an aquascutum so old that the maker's tab had long since gone from it. But inside the disreputable felt hat I saw the name of a well-known shop in Jermyn Street.

JANNI and I returned to the camp before dawn.
For some unknown reason a heavy weariness over-
came me on the way back, and I could scarcely
drag my limbs over the last half-mile of shore and
up the stone-shoot to the edge of the downs. I
dropped on the ground beside the ashes of the fire,
and slept like a drugged man.

When I woke it was high forenoon. The sun
was beating full on the little hollow, and Janni
was cooking breakfast. My lethargy had gone
and I woke to a violent anxious energy. Where
was Maris ? He ought to have rejoined us, according to plan, before sunrise. But Janni had seen
no sign of him. Had he got into the House ?
Well, in that case he would find means to send us
a message, and to send it soon, for this was Good
Friday, the day which the priest feared. I was in
a fever of impatience, for I had found a boat, a
means of escape of which Maris did not know. If
he was in the House, I must get that knowledge
to him, and he in turn must get in touch as soon
as possible with me. Our forces were divided,
with no link of communication.

I did my best to possess my soul in that hot
scented forenoon, but it was a hard job, for the
sense of shortening time had got on my nerves.
The place was cooled by light winds from the sea,
and for Janni, who lay on his back and consumed

cigarettes, it was doubtless a pleasant habitation.
Rivers of narcissus and iris and anemone flooded
over the crest and spilled into the hollow. The
ground was warm under the short herbage, and
from it came the rich clean savour of earth quickening after its winter sleep under the spell of the sun.
The pigeons were cooing in the cliffs below me and
the air was full of the soft tideless swaying of the
sea. But for all the comfort it gave me I might
have been stretched on frozen bricks in a dungeon.
I was constantly getting up and crawling to a high
point which gave me a view of the rim of the downs
up to the wall, and eastwards towards the Vano
road. But there was no sign of Maris in the wide
landscape.

About one o'clock the thing became unbearable.
If Maris was in the House I must find touch with
him ; if he had failed, I must make the attempt
myself. It was a crazy thing to contemplate in
broad daylight, but my anxiety would not let me
stay still. I bade Janni wait for me, and set off
towards the Vano road, with the intention of
trying Maris's route of the previous night and
making a circuit by the east side of the village
toward the jetty.

I had the sense to keep on the south side of the
ridge out of sight of the Dancing Floor and the
high ground beyond it. There was not a soul to
be seen in all that grassy place ; the winding high-
way showed no figure as far as the eye could reach ;
even the closes and barns clustered about the foot
of the Dancing Floor seemed untenanted of man or
beast. I gave the village a wide berth, and after
crossing some patches of cultivation and scrambling
through several ragged thickets found myself due

east of Kynætho and some three hundred feet
above it.

There I had the prospect of the church rising
above a line of hovels, a bit of the main street,
the rear of the inn, and the houses which straggled
seaward toward the jetty. The place had undergone another transformation, for it seemed to be
deserted. Not one solitary figure appeared in the
blinding white street. Everyone must be indoors
engaged in some solemn preparation against the
coming night. That gave me a hope that the
northern approaches to the House might be un-
guarded. So great was my anxiety that I set off
at a run, and presently had reached the high
ground which overlooked the road from the village
to the harbour. Here I had to go circumspectly,
for once I descended to the road I would be in
view of anyone on the jetty, and probably, too, of
the northernmost houses in the village.

I scanned the foreground long and carefully
with my glass, and decided that no one was
about, so I slipped down from the heights, crossed
the road a hundred yards above the harbour, and
dived into the scrub which bordered the beach
on the farther side. Here I was completely
sheltered, and made good going till I rounded a
little point and came into a scene which was
familiar. It was the place where six years before
Vernon and I had landed from Lamancha's yacht.
There were the closes of fruit blossom, the thickets,
the long scrubby ravine where we had listened
to the Spring Song. I had a sudden sense of
things being predestined, of the ironical fore-
ordination of life.

I knew what to expect. Round the horn of the

little bay where I stood lay the House with its
jetty and the causeway and the steep stairs to the
postern gates. My success thus far had made me
confident and I covered the next half-mile as if
I were walking on my own estate. But I had the
wit to move cautiously before I passed the containing ridge, and crept up to the skyline.

It was well that I did so, for this was what I
saw. On the jetty there were guards, and there
were posts along the causeway. More, some
change had been wrought in the seaward wall of
the House. The huge place rose, blank and white,
in its cincture of greenery, but at the points where
the steps ended in postern doors there seemed to
be a great accumulation of brushwood which
was not the work of nature. My glass told me
what it was. The entrance was piled high with
faggots. The place had been transformed into a
pyre.

But it was not that sight which sent my heart
to my boots—I had been prepared for that or any
other devilry; it was the utter impossibility of
effecting an entrance. The fabric rose stark and
silent like a prison, and round it stood the wardens.

I didn't wait long, for the spectacle made me
mad. I turned and retraced my steps, as fast as
I could drag my legs, for every ounce of vigour had
gone out of me. It was a dull listless automaton
that recrossed the harbour road, made the long
circuit east of the village, and regained the downs
beyond the Dancing Floor. When I staggered
into camp, where the placid Janni was playing
dice, it was close on five o'clock.

I made myself a cup of tea and tried to piece the
situation together. Maris could not have entered

the House—the thing was flatly impossible, and what had happened to him I could only guess. Where he had failed I certainly could not succeed, for the cliffs, the wall and the guards shut it off impenetrably from the world. Inside was Koré alone—I wondered if the old servant whom she had called Mitri was with her, or the French maid she had had in London—and that night would see the beginning of the end. The remembrance of the faggots piled about the door sent a horrid chill to my heart. The situation had marched clean outside human power to control it. I thought with scorn of my self-confidence. I had grievously muddled every detail, and was of as little value as if I had remained in my Temple chambers. Pity and fear for the girl made me clench my hands and gnaw my lips. I could not stay still. I decided once more to prospect the line of the cliffs.

One-armed Janni was no use, so I left him behind. I slid down the stone-shoot and in the first cool of evening scrambled along that arduous shore. When I had passed the abutment of the wall I scanned with my glass every crack in the cliffs, but in daylight they looked even more hopeless than under the moon. At one place a shallow gully permitted me to reach a shelf, but there I stuck fast, for the rock above could only have been climbed by a hanging rope. The most desperate man—and by that time I was pretty desperate—could not find a way where the Almighty had decided that there should be none. I think that if there had been the faintest chance I would have taken it, in spite of the risks ; I would have ventured on a course which at Chamonix or Cortina would have been pronounced suicidal ; but here

there was not even the rudiments of a course—
nothing but that maddening glassy wall.

By and by I reached the cape beyond which lay
the hidden bay and Black George with his boat.
It occurred to me that I had not prospected very
carefully the cliffs in this bay, and in any case I
wanted to look again at the boat, that single frail
link we had with the outer world. But first I
stripped and had a bathe, which did something
to cool the fret of my nerves. Then I waded
round the point to the place where Janni and I had
talked with the seaman.

Black George had gone. There was not a trace
of him or the boat in the shining inlet into which
the westering sun was pouring its yellow light.
What on earth had happened ? Had his mysterious
master returned ? Or had he been driven off by
the islanders ? Or had he simply grown bored
and sailed away ? The last solution I dismissed :
Black George, I was convinced, was no quitter.

The loss of him was the last straw to my hope-
lessness. I was faced with a situation with which
no ingenuity or fortitude could grapple—only
some inhuman skill in acrobatics or some Berserker
physical powers which I did not possess. I
turned my glass listlessly on the cliffs which
lined the bay. There was nothing to be done
there. They were as sheer as those I had already
prospected, and, although more rugged and broken,
it was by means of great noses of smooth rock on
which only a fly could move.

I was sitting on the very boulder which Janni
had occupied the night before, and I saw on the
shingle one or two of his cigarette stumps. And
then I saw something else.

It was a cigarette end, but not one of Janni's caporals. Moreover it had been dropped there during the past day. Janni's stumps, having been exposed to the night dews, were crumpled and withered ; this was intact, the butt end of an Egyptian cigarette of a good English brand. Black George must have been here in the course of the day. But I remembered that Black George had smoked a peculiarly evil type of Greek tobacco. Perhaps he had been pilfering his master's cigarettes ? Or perhaps his master had come back ?

I remembered that he had refused to utter one word about that master of his. Who could he be ? Was he an Englishman ? He might well be, judging from Black George's reverence for the word "English." If so, what was he doing in Plakos, and how had he reached this spot, unless he had the wings of a bird ? If he had come along the downs and the shore Janni would have seen him. . . . Anyhow, he was gone now, and our one bridge with a sane world was broken.

I made my way back to Janni with a feeling that I had come to the edge of things and would presently be required to go over the brink. I was now quite alone—as much alone as Koré—and fate might soon link these lonelinesses. I had had this feeling once or twice in the war— that I was faced with something so insane that insanity was the only course for me, but I had no notion what form the insanity would take, for I still saw nothing before me but helplessness. I was determined somehow to break the barrier, regardless of the issue. Every scrap of manhood in me revolted against my futility. In that moment I became primitive man again. Even if the woman were not my woman she was of my own totem, and whatever her fate she should not meet it alone.

Janni had food ready for me, but I could not eat it. I took out my pistol, cleaned and reloaded it, and told Janni to look to his. I am not much of a pistol shot, but Janni, as I knew from Maris, was an expert. There would be something astir when the moon rose, and I had an intuition that the scene would be the Dancing Floor. The seaward end of the House might be the vital point in the last stage of the drama, but I was convinced that the Dancing Ground would see the first act. It was the holy ground, and I had gathered from the priest that some dark ritual would take the place of the Good Friday solemnity.

There was only one spot where Janni and I might safely lie hidden, and at the same time look down on the Dancing Floor, and that was in the shadow of the wall between the guarded breach and the cliffs. There were large trees there and the progress of the moon would not light it up, whereas everywhere else would be clear as noonday. Moreover it was the strategic point, for whatever mischief was intended against the House would pass through the breach and therefore under our eyes. But it was necessary to get there before the moon was fully risen, for otherwise to men coming from the village we should be silhouetted against the cliff edge. I cut Janni's supper short and we started out, using every crinkle of the ground as cover, much as stalkers do when they are fetching a circuit and know that the deer are alarmed and watchful.

We had not much more than a mile to go, and

by the route we chose we managed, as it happened, to keep wholly out of sight of the Dancing Floor. Janni—no mountaineer—grumbled at my pace, for I had acquired an extraordinary lightness of limb so that I felt as if I could have flown. I was puzzled to explain this, after my listlessness of the day, but I think it was due partly to tense nerves and partly to the magic of the evening. The air was cool and exhilarating, and when the moon rose with a sudden glory above the House it was as tonic as if one had plunged into water. . . . Soon we were on the edge of the inky belt of shadow and moving eastward to get nearer the breach. But now I noticed something I had forgotten. The wall curved outward, and beyond that bulge—a couple of hundred yards from the breach—the light flooded to the very edge of the stone. We came to a halt at the apex of the curve, flat on our faces, and I turned to reconnoitre the Dancing Floor.

I wish to Heaven that I had the gift of words. It is too much to ask a man whose life has been spent in drawing pleadings and in writing dull legal opinions to describe a scene which needs the tongue or pen of a poet. For the Dancing Floor was transfigured. Its lonely beauty had been decked and adorned, as an altar is draped for high festival. On both slopes people clustered, men, women and children, all so silent that I thought I could hear them breathe. I thought, too, that they mostly wore white—at any rate the moonlight gave me the impression of an immense white multitude, all Kynætho and doubtless half the hills. The valley was marked out like a race-course. There seemed to be posts at regular intervals in

a broad oval, and at each post was a red flicker
which meant torches. The desert had become
populous, and the solitary places blossomed with
roses of fire.

The people were clustered toward the upper
end, making an amphitheatre of which the arena
was the Dancing Floor, and the entrance to the
stage the breach in the wall of the House. I saw
that this entrance was guarded, not as before by
three sentries, but by a double line of men who
kept an avenue open between them. Beyond the
spectators and round the arena was the circle of
posts, and between them lay the Dancing Floor,
golden in the moon, and flanked at its circum-
ference by the angry crimson of the torches. I
noticed another thing. Not quite in the centre
but well within the arena was a solitary figure
waiting. He was in white—gleaming white, and,
so far as I could judge, he was standing beside
the spring from which I had drunk the night
before.

I have set out the details of what I saw, but
they are only the beggarly elements, for I cannot
hope to reproduce the strangeness which caught
at the heart and laid a spell on the mind. The
place was no more the Valley of the Shadow of
Life, but Life itself—a surge of dæmonic energy
out of the deeps of the past. It was wild and
yet ordered, savage and yet sacramental, the
home of an ancient knowledge which shattered
for me the modern world and left me gasping like
a cave-man before his mysteries. The magic
smote on my brain, though I struggled against it.
The passionless moonlight and the passionate
torches—that, I think, was the final miracle—a

marrying of the eternal cycle of nature with the fantasies of man.

The effect on Janni was overwhelming. He lay and gibbered prayers with eyes as terrified as a deer's, and I realised that I need not look for help in that quarter. But I scarcely thought of him, for my trouble was with myself. Most people would call me a solid fellow, with a hard head and a close-texture mind, but if they had seen me then they would have changed their view. I was struggling with something which I had never known before, a mixture of fear, abasement and a crazy desire to worship. Yes—to worship. There was that in the scene which wakened some ancient instinct, so that I felt it in me to join the votaries.

It took me a little time to pull myself together. I looked up at the dome of the sky, where on the horizon pale stars were showing. The whole world seemed hard and gem-like and unrelenting. There was no help there. Nature approved this ritual. And then a picture flashed into my mind which enabled me to recover my wits. It was the carven Christ lying in its shroud in the bier in the deserted church. I am not a religious man in the ordinary sense—only a half-believer in the creed in which I was born. But in that moment I realised that there was that in me which was stronger than the pagan, an instinct which had come down to me from believing generations. I understood then what were my gods. I think I prayed. I know that I clung to the memory of that rude image as a Christian martyr may have clung to his crucifix. It stood for all the broken lights which were in me as against this ancient charméd darkness.

I was steadier now and with returning sanity came the power of practical thought. Something, someone, was to be brought from the House. Was there to be a trial in that arena? Or a sacrifice? No—I was clear that to-night was only the preparation, and that the great day was the morrow. There was no sound from the gathering. I could not see the faces, but I knew that everyone, down to the smallest child, was awed and rapt and expectant. No crowd, hushing its breath in the decisive moments of a great match, was ever more rigidly on the stretch. The very air quivered with expectation.

Then a movement began. Figures entered the arena at the end farthest from me—men, young men, naked I thought at first, till my glass showed me that each wore a sort of loin-cloth or it may have been short drawers. . . . They aligned themselves, like runners at the start of a race, and still there was no sound. The figure who had been standing by the well was now beside them and seemed to be speaking softly. Each held himself tense, with clenched hands, and his eyes on the ground. Then came some kind of signal and they sprang forward.

It was a race—such a race as few men can have witnessed. The slim youths kept outside the torches, and circled the arena of the Dancing Floor. Over the moonlit sward they flew, glimmering like ghosts—once round, a second time round. And all the while the crowd kept utter silence.

I ran the mile myself at school and college, and know something about pace. I could see that it was going to be a close finish. One man I noted,

I think the very fellow who had hunted me into the church—he ran superbly and won a lead at the start. But the second time round I fancied another, a taller and leaner man who had kept well back in the first round, and was slowly creeping ahead. I liked his style, which was oddly like the kind of thing we cultivate at home, and he ran with judgment too. Soon he was abreast of the first man, and then he sprinted and took the lead. I was wondering where the finish would be, when he snatched a torch from one of the posts, ran strongly up the centre of the Dancing Floor and plunged the flame in the spring.

Still there was no sound from the crowd. The winner stood with his head bent, a noble figure of youth who might have stepped from a Parthenon frieze. The others had gone ; he stood close beside the well with the white-clad figure who had acted as master of ceremonies—only now the victor in the race seemed to be the true master, on whom all eyes waited.

The sight was so strange and beautiful that I watched it half in a trance. I seemed to have seen it all before, and to know the stages that would follow. . . . Yes, I was right. There was a movement from the crowd and a man was brought forward. I knew the man, though he wore nothing but pants and a torn shirt. One could not mistake the trim figure of Maris, or his alert bird-like head.

He stood confronting the beautiful young barbarian beside the spring, looking very much as if he would like to make a fight of it. And then the latter seemed to speak to him, and to lay a hand on his head. Maris submitted, and the next I saw was that the runner had drawn a jar of

water from the well and was pouring it over him.
He held it high in his arms and the water wavered
and glittered in the moonshine ; I could see Maris
spluttering and wringing out his wet shirt-sleeves.

With that recollection flooded in on me. This
was the ceremonial of which Vernon had read to
me from Koré's manuscript. A virgin and a
youth were chosen and set apart in a hallowed
place, and the choser was he who was victor in
a race and was called the King. The victims were
hallowed with water from the well by the white
cypress. I was looking at the well, though the
cypress had long since disappeared. I was looking
at the King, and at one of those dedicated to the
sacrifice. The other was the girl in the House. . . .
Vernon had said that if we knew what the word
hosiotheis meant we should know a good deal about
Greek religion. That awful knowledge was now
mine.

It was as I expected. The consecrator and the
consecrated were moving, still in the same hushed
silence, towards the *horkos*—the sanctuary. The
torches had been extinguished as soon as the victor
plunged his in the spring, and the pure light of
the moon seemed to have waxed to an unearthly
brightness. The two men walked up the slope
of the Dancing Floor to the line of guards which
led to the breach in the wall. I could not hold
my glass because of the trembling of my hands,
but I could see the figures plainly—the tall runner,
his figure poised like some young Apollo of the
great age of art, his face dark with the sun but
the skin of his body curiously white. Some youth
of the hills, doubtless—his crisp hair seemed in
the moonlight to be flaxen. Beside him went the

shorter Maris, flushed and truculent. He must have been captured by the guards in his attempt on the House, and as a stranger and also a Greek had been put forward as the male victim.

I was roused by the behaviour of Janni. He had realised that his beloved *capitaine* was a prisoner, towards whom some evil was doubtless intended, and this understanding had driven out his fear and revived his military instincts. He was cursing fiercely and had got out his pistol.

" Sir," he whispered to me, " I can crawl within shot, for the shadow is lengthening, and put a bullet into yon bandit. Then in the confusion my *capitaine* will escape and join us and break for the cliffs. These people are sheep and may not follow."

For a second it appeared to me the only thing to do. This evil Adonis was about to enter the House and on the morrow Koré and Maris would find death at his hands, for he was the sacrificer. I seemed to see in his arrogant beauty the cruelty of an elder world. His death would at any rate shatter the ritual.

And then I hesitated and gripped Janni firmly by his one arm. For, as the two men passed out of my sight towards the breach in the wall, I had caught a glimpse of Maris's face. He was speaking to his companion, and his expression was not of despair and terror, but confident, almost cheerful. For an instant the life of the young runner hung on a thread, for I do not think that Janni would have missed. Then I decided against the shot, for I felt that it was a counsel of despair. There was something which I did not comprehend, for Maris's face had given me a glimmer of hope.

I signed to Janni and we started crawling back towards the cliffs. In that hour the one thing that kept me sane was the image of the dead Christ below the chancel step. It was my only link with the reasonable and kindly world I had lost.

I HAD only one impulse at that moment—an overwhelming desire to get back to the church and look again at the figure on the bier. It seemed to me the sole anchor in the confusion of uncharted tides, the solitary hope in a desert of perplexities. I had seen ancient magic revive and carry captive the hearts of a people. I had myself felt its compelling power. A girl whom I loved and a man who was my companion were imprisoned and at the mercy of a maddened populace. Maris was, like Ulysses, an old campaigner and a fellow of many wiles, but what could Maris do in the face of multitudes? An unhallowed epiphany was looked for, but first must come the sacrifice. There was no help in the arm of flesh, and the shallow sophistication of the modern world fell from me like a useless cloak. I was back in my childhood's faith, and wanted to be at my childhood's prayers.

As for Janni he had a single idea in his head, to follow his captain into the House and strike a blow for him, and as he padded along the seaward cliffs he doubtless thought we were bent on attacking the place from another side. We took pretty much the road I had taken in the morning, skirting the Dancing Floor on its southern edge. One strange thing I saw. The Dancing Floor was still thronged, though a space was kept clear in the centre round the well. Clearly it was no longer *tabu*, but a place of holiday. Moreover the people seemed to intend to remain there, for they had lit fires and were squatting round them, while some had already stretched themselves to sleep. Kynætho had moved in a body to the scene of the sacrament.

When we reached the fringe of the village I saw that I had guessed correctly. There was not a sign of life in the streets. We walked boldly into the central square, and it might have been a graveyard. Moreover, in the graveyard itself the lamps by the graves had not been lit. Vampires were apparently no longer to be feared, and that struck me as an ill omen. Keats's lines came into my head about the " little town by river or sea shore " which is " emptied of its folk this pious morn." Pious morn !

And then above us, from the squat campanile, a bell began to toll—raggedly, feebly, like the plaint of a child. Yet to me it was also a challenge.

The church was bright with moonshine. The curtains still shrouded the sanctuary, and there were no candles lit, nothing but the flickering lamps before the ikons. Below the chancel step lay the dark mass which contained the shrouded Christ. Janni, like myself, seemed to find comfort in being here. He knelt at a respectful distance from the bier and began to mutter prayers. I went forward and lifted the shroud. The moon coming through one of the windows gave the carved wood a ghastly semblance of real flesh, and I could not bear to look on it. I followed Janni's example and breathed incoherent prayers. I was bred a Calvinist, but in that moment I was not worshipping any graven image. My prayer was to be delivered from the idolatry of the heathen.

Suddenly the priest was beside me. In one hand he held a lighted candle, and the other carried a censer. He seemed in no way surprised to see us, but there was that about him which made me catch my breath. The man had suddenly become enlarged and ennobled. All the weakness had gone out of the old face, all the languor and bewilderment out of the eyes, the shoulders had straightened, his beard was no longer like a goat's, but like a prophet's. He was as one possessed, a fanatic, a martyr.

He had forgotten that I knew no Greek, for he spoke rapidly words which sounded like a command. But Janni understood, and went forward obediently to the bier. Then I saw what he meant us to do. We were to take the place of the absent hierophants and carry the image of the dead Christ through the bounds of the village. The bier was light enough even for one-armed Janni to manage his share. The shroud was removed, he took the fore-end, and I the back, and behind the priest we marched out into the night.

The streets were deathly still, the cool night air was unruffled by wind, so that the candle burned steadily ; the golden dome of the sky was almost as bright as day. Along the white beaten road we went, and then into the rough cobbles of the main street. I noticed that though the houses were empty every house door was wide open. We passed the inn and came into the road to the harbour and to the cottage among fruit trees where I had first made inquiries. Then we turned up the hill where lay the main entrance to the House, past little silent untenanted crofts and oliveyards which were all gleaming grey and silver. The old man moved slowly, swinging his censer, and intoning what I took to be a dirge in a voice no longer tremulous, but masterful and strong, and behind him Janni and I stumbled along bearing the symbol of man's salvation.

I had never been present at a Greek Good Friday celebration, but Koré had described it to me— the following crowds tortured with suspense, the awed kneeling women, the torches, the tears, the universal lamentation. Then the people sorrowed not without hope, for their dead Saviour. But the ordinary ceremonial can never have been so marvellous as was our broken ritual that night. We were celebrating, but there were no votaries. The torches had gone to redden the Dancing Floor, sorrow had been exchanged for a guilty ecstasy, the worshippers were seeking another Saviour. Our rite was more than a commemoration, it was a defiance, and I felt like a man who carries a challenge to the enemy.

The moon had set and darkness had begun before we returned to the church. Both Janni and I were very weary before we laid down our burden in the vault below the nave, a place hewn out of the dry limestone rock. By the last flickering light of the candle I saw the priest standing at the head of the bier, his hands raised in supplication, his eyes bright and rapt and unseeing. He was repeating a litany in which a phrase constantly recurred. I could guess its meaning. It must have been " He will yet arise."

I slept till broad daylight in the priest's house

on the priest's bed, while Janni snored on a pile of sheepskins. Since Kynætho was deserted, there was no reason now for secrecy, for the whole place, and not the church only, had become a sanctuary. The aged woman who kept house for the priest gave us a breakfast of milk and bread, but we saw no sign of him, and I did not wish to return to the church and disturb his devotions. I wondered if I should ever see him again; it was a toss-up if I should ever see anybody again after this day of destiny. We had been partners in strange events and I could not leave him without some farewell, so I took the book of his which seemed to be most in use, put two English five-pound notes inside, and did my best in laboriously printed Latin to explain that this was a gift for the Church and to thank him and wish him well.

I did another thing, for I wrote out a short account of the position, saying that further information might be obtained from Ertzberger and Vernon Milburne. Anything might happen to-day, and I wanted to leave some record for my friends. I addressed the document under cover to the priest, and—again in Latin—begged him, should anything happen to me, to see that it reached the British Minister in Athens. That was about all I could do in the way of preparation, and I had a moment of grim amusement in thinking how strangely I, who since the war had seemed to be so secure and cosseted, had moved back to the razor-edge of life.

I have said that there was no need for secrecy, so we walked straight through the village towards the harbour. Janni had made a preliminary survey beyond the graveyard in the early morning, and had reported that the people of Kynætho were still encamped around the Dancing Floor. The trouble would not begin till we approached the House, for it was certain that on that day of all days the guards would be vigilant. We were both of us wholly desperate. We simply had to get in, and to get in before the evening ; for that purpose anything, even wholesale homicide, was legitimate. But at the same time it would do no good to get caught, even if we succeeded in killing several of our captors.

I think I had a faint unreasonable hope that we should find the situation at the causeway more promising than it had appeared on the day before. But when—after a walk where we had seen no trace of man or beast—we came to the crest of the little cape beyond which lay the jetty and the House, I had a sad disillusionment. The place was thick with sentries. I saw the line of them along the causeway and at the head of the jetty ; moreover there seemed to be men working to the left of the House where there was a cluster of outbuildings descending to the shallow vale up which ran the road from the sea. My glass showed me what they were doing. They were piling more straw and brushwood, so that from the outbuildings, which were probably of wood and would burn like tinder, the flames might have easy access to the windows of the House. The altar was being duly prepared for the victim.

Long and carefully I prospected the ground. There was cover enough to take us down to within a few yards of the jetty. If I tried to cross it I should be within view of the people on the causeway, and even if I got across unobserved there

was the more or less open beach between the causeway and the sea. It was true that directly under
the wall I should be out of sight of the causeway
guards, but then again, though I could get shelter
behind some of the boulders, I could not move
far without being noticed by whoever chose to
patrol the jetty. Nevertheless that was the only
road for me, for my object was to get to the far
end of the causeway, where before the cliffs began
there were oliveyards and orchards, through which
some route must be possible to the House.

I considered the left side of the picture, where
the valley led upwards past the outbuildings.
That way I could see no hope, for if I succeeded
in passing the faggot-stackers I would only reach
the confines of the main entrance to the demesne
from Kynætho, which was certain to be the best
warded of all.

I had also to consider what to do with Janni.
He would be a useful ally if it came to a scrap, but
a scrap would be futile against such numbers, and
in stalking or climbing his lack of an arm would be a
serious handicap. Besides, if our business was to
escape observation, one man would be better than
two. . . . But it was possible that he might create
a diversion. Supposing he tried the road on the
left up the valley and made himself conspicuous,
he might draw off attention while I crossed the
jetty and got under the lee of the causeway wall.
That meant of course that one of us would be put
out of action, but unless we tried something of
the kind we should both fail.

I put the thing to him, as we lay among the
scrubby arbutus, and though he clearly did not
like the proposal, since his notion was to man-

handle somebody on Maris's behalf, he was too good a soldier not to see the sense of it. He pointed out various difficulties, and then shook his head like a dog and said that he agreed. For his own sake I forbade any shooting. If he were merely hunted and captured, it was unlikely that any harm would befall him. He could explain that he was one of the survey party who had lost the others, and at the worst he would be shut up temporarily in some barn. He might even find the means to make himself useful later in the day.

So it was settled that I should try to worm my way as near to the jetty as the cover would allow. He was to watch my movements and when he saw my hand raised three times he was to march boldly towards the jetty. I would not be able to see what was happening, so when he was pursued and started up the little valley he was to shout as if in alarm. That would be the signal to me that the sentry had left the jetty and that I might try to cross it.

I started out at once on my first stage. As I have said, the cover was good—boulders overgrown with heath and vines, and patches of arbutus and a very prickly thorn. I tried to behave as if I were on a Scotch hill stalking alone, with deer where the sentries stood. It was not a very difficult passage, for my enemies had no eyes for the ground on my side, their business being to prevent egress from the House. After about half an hour's careful crawling, I found myself within six yards of the jetty looking through the tangle to the rough masonry of it, with a sideway view of the point where it joined the causeway. I could see none of the guards, but I heard distinctly the sound of their speech. I had marked the spot where I now lay before I started, and knew that it was within sight of Janni. So I straightened myself and thrice raised my arms above the scrub.

For a minute or two nothing happened. Janni must have started but had not yet attracted attention. I raised my body as far as I dared, but I could only see the shoreward end of the jetty— neither the jetty itself nor any part of the causeway. I waited for a cry, but there was no sound. Was Janni being suffered to make his way up the little valley unopposed ?

Then suddenly a moving object flashed into my narrow orbit of vision. It must be one of the watchers from the causeway, and he was in a furious hurry—I could hear the scruff of his heel-less boots on the dry stones as he turned a corner. . . . He must be in pursuit of Janni. . . . There would no doubt be others too at the job. Their silence might be a ritual business. *Favete linguis*, perhaps ? If Janni shouted I never heard him.

I resolved to take the chance, and bolted out of cover to the jetty. In two bounds I was beyond it and among the gravel and weed of the farther beach. But in that short progress I saw enough of the landscape to know that I was undiscovered, that there was nobody on the causeway within sight, or at the mouth of the little glen. Janni had certainly been followed, and by this time was no doubt in the hands of the Philistines out of my ken.

I ran close under the lee of the sea-wall, and at first I had a wild hope of getting beyond the causeway into the region of the olive groves before the sentries returned. But some remnant of prudence

made me halt and consider before I attempted the
last open strip of beach.   There I had a view of the
bit of the causeway towards the jetty, and suddenly
figures appeared on it, running figures, like men
returning to duty after a hasty interlude.   If I
had moved another foot I should have been within
view.

There was nothing for it but to wait where I
was.   I crouched in a little nook between a fallen
boulder and the wall, with the weedy rim of the
causeway six feet above me.   Unless a man
stood on the very edge and peered down I was
safe from observation.   But that was the sum of
my blessings.   I heard soft feet above me as the
men returned to their posts, and I dared not move
a yard.   It was now about two in the afternoon ;
I had brought no food with me, though I found a
couple of dusty figs in my pocket ;   the sun
blazed on the white wall and the gravel of the
shore till the place was like a bakehouse ;   I was
hot and thirsty, and I might have been in the
middle of the Sahara for all the chance of a drink.
But the discomfort of my body was trivial compared with the disquiet of my mind.

For I found myself in a perfect fever of vexa-
tion and fear.   The time was slipping past and the
crisis was nigh, and yet, though this was now my
fourth day on the island, I was not an inch farther
forward than the hour I landed.   My worst fears
—nay, what had seemed to me mere crazy imagin-
ings—had been realised.   I was tortured by the
thought of Koré—her innocent audacities, her
great-hearted courage, her loneliness, her wild
graces.   " Beauteous vain endeavour "—that was
the phrase of some poet that haunted me and made

me want to howl like a wolf. I realised now the
meaning of a sacrifice and the horror of it. The
remembrance of the slim victor in the race, beautiful and pitiless, made me half-crazy. Movement
in that place was nearly impossible, but it was
utterly impossible that I should stay still. I
began in short stages to worm my way along the
foot of the wall.

I do not suppose that the heat of that April
afternoon was anything much to complain of, but
my fever of mind must have affected my body,
for I felt that I had never been so scorched and
baked in my life. There was not a scrap of shade,
the rocks almost blistered the hand, the dust got
into my throat and nose and made me furiously
thirsty, and my head ached as if I had a sun-
stroke. . . . The trouble was with the jetty and the
watchers on it, for I was always in view of them.
Had they detected a movement below the wall,
a single glance would have revealed me. So I
had to make my stages very short, and keep a
wary outlook behind. . . . There seemed to be much
astir on the jetty. Not only the guards, but
other figures appeared on it, and I saw that they
were carrying up something from a boat at anchor.
That I think was what saved me. Had the
sentries had nothing to do but to stare about them
I must have been discovered, but the portage
business kept them distracted.

The minutes seemed hours to my distraught
mind, but I did indeed take an inconceivable time
crawling along that grilling beach, with the cool
sea water lapping not a dozen yards off to give
point to my discomfort. When I reached the
place where the causeway ceased, and long ribs

of rock took the place of the boulders of the shore,
I found by my watch that it was nearly six o'clock.
The discovery put quicksilver into my weary
limbs. Looking back I saw that I was out of sight
of the jetty, and that a few yards would put me
out of sight of the causeway. I wriggled into the
cover of a bush of broom, lay on my back for a
minute or two to rest, and then made for the shade
of the oliveyards.

The place was weedy and neglected—I don't
know anything about olive culture, but I could see
that much. There was a wilderness of a white
umbelliferous plant and masses of a thing like a
spineless thistle. I pushed uphill among the trees,
keeping well in the shade, with the west front of
the House glimmering through the upper leaves at
a much higher elevation. Above me I saw a deeper
shadow which I took to be cypresses, and beyond
them I guessed must lie the demesne. I hoped
for a gate, and in any case expected no more than
a hedge and a palisade.

Instead I found a wall. There was a door to be
sure, but it was no use to me, for it was massive
and locked. I might have known that Shelley
Arabin would leave no part of his cursed refuge
unbarricaded. I sat and blinked up at this new
obstacle, and could have cried with exasperation.
It seemed to run direct from the House to the edge
of the cliffs which began about a quarter of a mile
to my right, and was an exact replica of the wall
above the Dancing Floor.

I decided that it was no good trying it at the
House end, for there I should certainly be in view
of some of the guards. The masonry was comparatively new and very solid, and since none of the

olive trees grew within four yards of it, it was impossible to use them as a ladder. Already I felt the approach of night, for the sun was well down in the west and a great tide of sunset was flooding the sky. I do not think I have ever before felt so hopeless or so obstinate. I was determined to pass that wall by its abutment on the cliffs or break my neck in the effort.

My memory of the next hour is not very clear. All I know is that in the failing daylight I came to the cliffs' edge and found an abutment similar to the one at the Dancing Floor. Similar, but not the same. For here some storm had torn the masonry and it seemed to me that it might be passed. The rock fell steep and smooth to the sea, but that part which was the handiwork of man was ragged. I took off my boots and flung them over the wall, by way of a gage of battle, and then I started to make the traverse.

It was a slow and abominable business, but I do not think it would have been very difficult had the light been good, for the stone was hard enough and the cracks were many. But in that dim gloaming with a purple void beneath me, with a heart which would not beat steadily and a head which throbbed with pain, I found it very near the limit of my powers. I had to descend before I could traverse, and the worst part was the ascent on the far side. I knew that, when I at last got a grip of a wind-twisted shrub and tried to draw myself over the brink, it needed every ounce of strength left in me. I managed it and lay gasping beside the roots of a great pine—inside the demesne at last.

When I got my breath I found that I had a view

into the narrow cove where Janni and I had seen the boat. Black George had returned, and returned brazenly, for he was showing a riding light. A lantern swung from the mast, and, more, there was a glow from the cabin skylight. I wondered what was going on in the little craft, and I think the sight gave me a grain of comfort, till I realised that I was hopelessly cut off from Black George. What was the good of a link with the outer world, when unscalable walls and cliffs intervened— when at any moment murder might be the end of everything ?

Murder—that was the word which filled my head as I pushed inland. I had never thought of it in that way, but of course I was out to prevent murder. To prevent it ? More likely to share in it. . . . I had no plan of any kind, only a desire to be with Koré, so that she should not be alone. It was her loneliness that I could not bear. . . . And anyhow I had a pistol and I would not miss the runner. " The priest who slew the slayer and shall himself be slain "—the tag came unbidden to my lips. I think I must have been rather light-headed.

The last fires of the sunset did not penetrate far into the pine wood, the moon had not yet risen, and as I ran I took many tosses, for the place was very dark. There were paths, but I neglected them, making straight for where I believed the House to lie. I was not exact in my course, for I bore too much to the right in the direction of the breach in the wall at the Dancing Floor. Soon I was among shrubberies in which rides had been cut, but there were still many tall trees to make darkness. I thought I saw to the right, beyond where the wall lay, a reddish glow. That would be the torches on the Dancing Floor where the people waited for the epiphany.

Suddenly on my left front a great blaze shot up to heaven. I knew it was the signal that the hour had come. The outbuildings had been fired, and the House would soon be in flames. The blaze wavered and waned, and then waxed to a mighty conflagration as the fire reached something specially inflammable. In a minute that wood was bright as with an obscene daylight. The tree trunks stood out black against a molten gold, which at times crimsoned and purpled in a devilish ecstasy of destruction.

I knew now where the House lay. I clutched my pistol, and ran down a broad path, with a horrid fear that I was too late after all. I ran blindly, and had just time to step aside to let two figures pass.

They were two of the guards—hillmen by their dress—and even in my absorption I wondered what had happened to them. For they were like men demented, with white faces and open mouths. One of them stumbled and fell, and seemed to stay on his knees for a second praying, till his companion lugged him forward. I might have faced them with impunity, for their eyes were sightless. Never have I seen men suffering from an extremer terror.

The road twisted too much for my haste, so I cut across country. The surge and crackle of the flames filled the air, but it seemed as if I heard another sound, the sound of running feet, of bodies, many bodies, brushing through the thicket. I was close on the House now, and close on the road which led to it from the broken wall and the Dancing Floor. As I jumped a patch of scrub and the gloom lightened in the more open avenue, I bumped into another man and saw that it was Maris.

He was waiting, pistol in hand, beside the road, and in a trice had his gun at my head. Then he recognised me and lowered it. His face was as crazy as the hillmen's who had passed me, and he still wore nothing but breeches and a ragged shirt, but his wild eyes seemed to hold also a dancing humour.

" Blessed Jesu ! " he whispered, " you have come in time. The fools are about to receive their Gods. You have your pistol ? But I do not think there will be shooting."

He choked suddenly as if he had been struck dumb, and I too choked. For I looked with him up the avenue towards the burning House.

PART III

THIS part of the story (said Leithen) I can only
give at second-hand. I have pieced it together as
well as I could from what Vernon told me, but on
many matters he was naturally not communicative,
and at these I have had to guess for myself. . . .

Vernon left England the day after the talk with
me which I have already recorded, sending his
boat as deck cargo to Patras, while he followed by
way of Venice. He had a notion that the great
hour which was coming had best be met at sea,
where he would be far from the distractions and
littlenesses of life. He took one man with him
from Wyvenhoe, a lean gipsy lad called Martell,
but the boy fell sick at Corfu and he was obliged
to send him home. In his stead he found an
Epirote with a string of names, who was strongly
recommended to him by one of his colleagues in
the old Ægean Secret Service. From Patras they
made good sailing up the Gulf of Corinth, and,
passing through the Canal, came in the last days
of March to the Piræus. In that place of polyglot
speech, whistling engines and the odour of gas-
works, they delayed only for water and supplies,
and presently had rounded Sunium, and were
beating up the Euripus with the Attic hills rising
sharp and clear in the spring sunlight.

He had no plans. It was a joy to him to be

alone with the racing seas and the dancing winds,
to scud past the little headlands, pink and white
with blossom, or to lie of a night in some hidden
bay beneath the thymy crags. He had discarded
the clothes of civilisation. In a blue jersey and
old corduroy trousers, bareheaded and barefooted, he steered his craft and waited on the passing
of the hours. His mood, he has told me, was one
of complete happiness, unshadowed by nervousness
or doubt. The long preparation was almost at
an end. Like an acolyte before a temple gate, he
believed himself to be on the threshold of a new
life. He had that sense of unseen hands which
comes to all men once or twice in their lives, and
both hope and fear were swallowed up in a calm
expectancy.

Trouble began under the snows of Pelion as they
turned the north end of Euboea. On the morning
of the first Monday in April the light winds died
away, and foul weather came out of the north-
west. By midday it was half a gale, and in those
yeasty shallow seas, with an iron coast to port
and starboard, their position was dangerous. The
nearest harbour was twenty miles distant, and
neither of the crew had ever been there before.
With the evening the gale increased, and it was
decided to get out of that maze of rocky islands
to the safer deeps of the Ægean.

It was a hard night for the two of them, and
there was no chance of sleep. More by luck than
skill they escaped the butt of Skiathos, and the
first light found them far to the south-east among
the long tides of the North Ægean. They ran
close-reefed before the gale, and all morning with
decks awash nosed and plunged in seas which might

have been the wintry Atlantic. It was not till
the afternoon that the gale seemed to blow itself
out and two soaked and chilly mortals could
relax their vigil. Soon bacon was frizzling on
the cuddy-stove, and hot coffee and dry clothes
restored them to moderate comfort.

The sky cleared, and in bright sunlight, with
the dregs of the gale behind him, Vernon steered
for the nearest land, an island of which he did not
trouble to read the name, but which the chart
showed to possess good anchorage. Late in the
evening, when the light was growing dim, they
came into a little bay carved from the side of a
hill. They also came into fog. The wind had
dropped utterly, and the land which they saw
was only an outline in the haze. When they cast
anchor the fog was rolling like a tide over the
sea, and muffling their yards. They spent a busy
hour or two, repairing the damage of the storm,
and then the two of them made such a meal as
befits those who have faced danger together.
Afterwards Vernon, as his custom was, sat alone
in the stern, smoking and thinking his thoughts.
He wrote up his diary with a ship's lantern beside
him, while the mist hung about him low and soft
as an awning.

He had leisure now for the thought which had
all day been at the back of his mind. The night
—the great night—had passed and there had been
no dream. The adventure for which all his life
he had been preparing himself had vanished into
the Ægean tides. The hour when the revelation
should have come had been spent in battling with
the storm, when a man lives in the minute at grips
with too urgent realities.

His first mood was one of dismal relaxedness.
He felt as useless as an unstrung bow. I, the
only man to whom he had ever confided his secret,
had been right, and the long vigil had ended in
fiasco. He tried to tell himself that it was a
relief, that an old folly was over, but he knew
that deep down in his heart there was bitter disappointment. The fates had prepared the stage,
and rung up the curtain and lo ! there was no play.
He had been fooled, and somehow the zest and
savour of life had gone from him. After all,
no man can be strung high and then find his
preparations idle without suffering a cruel recoil.

And then anger came to stiffen him—anger at
himself. What a God-forsaken ass he had been,
frittering away his best years in following a phan-
tom ! . . . In his revulsion he loathed the dream
which he had cherished so long. He began to
explain it away with the common sense which on
my lips he had accounted blasphemy. . . . The
regular seasonal occurrence was his own doing—
he had expected it and it had come—a mere case
of subjective compulsion. . . . The fact that each
year the revelation had moved one room nearer
was also the result of his willing it to be so, for
subconsciously he must have desired to hasten
the consummation. . . . He went through every
detail, obstinately providing some rationalistic
explanation for each. I do not think he can have
satisfied himself, but he was in the mood to de-
face his idols, and one feeling surged above all
others—that he was done with fancies now and
for ever. He has told me that the thing he longed
for chiefly at that moment was to have me beside
him that he might make formal recantation.

By and by he argued himself into some philosophy. He had dallied certain years, but he was still young and the world was before him. He had kept his body and mind in hard training, and that at any rate was not wasted, though the primal purpose had gone. He was a normal man now among normal men, and it was his business to prove himself. He thought in his Calvinistic way that the bogus vision might have been sent to him for a purpose—the thing might be hallucination, but the *askesis* which it had entailed was solid gain. . . . He fetched from his locker the little book in which he had chronicled his inner life, and wrote in it " Finis." Then he locked it and flung the key overboard. The volume would be kept at Severns to remind him of his folly, but it would never be opened by him.

By this time he was his own master again. He would sail for England next morning and get hold of me and make a plan for his life.

He was now conscious for the first time of his strange environment. The boat was in a half-moon of bay in an island of which he had omitted to notice the name but whose latitude and longitude he roughly knew. The night was close around him like a shell, for the fog had grown thicker, though the moon behind it gave it an opaque sheen. It was an odd place in which to be facing a crisis. . . .

His thoughts ran fast ahead to the career which he must shape from the ruins of his dream. He was too late for the Bar. Business might be the best course—he had big interests in the north of England which would secure him a footing, and he believed that he had the kind of mind for

administration. . . . Or politics ? There were
many chances for a young man in the confused
post-bellum world. . . .

He was absorbed in his meditations and did not
hear the sound of oars or the grating of a boat
alongside. Suddenly he found a face looking
at him in the ring of lamplight—an old bearded
face curiously wrinkled. The eyes, which were
shrewd and troubled, scanned him for a second or
two, and then a voice spoke :

" Will the Signor come with me ? " it said in
French.

Vernon, amazed at this apparition which had
come out of the mist, could only stare.

" Will the Signor come with me ? " the voice
spoke again. " We have grievous need of a man."

Vernon unconsciously spoke not in French but
in Greek.

" Who the devil are you, and where do you
come from ? "

" I come from the House. I saw you enter
the bay before the fog fell. Had there been no
fog, they would not have let me come to you."

" Who are ' they ' ? " Vernon asked.

But the old man shook his head. " Come with
me and I will tell you. It is a long story."

" But what do you want me to do ? Confound
it, I'm not going off with a man I never saw before
who can't tell me what he wants."

The old man shrugged his shoulders despairingly.
" I have no words," he said. " But Mademoiselle
Élise is waiting at the jetty. Come to her at any
rate and she will reason with you."

Vernon—as you will admit, if I have made his
character at all clear to you—had no instinct for

melodrama. He had nothing in him of the knight-errant looking for adventure, and this interruption out of the fog and the sea rather bored him than otherwise. But he was too young to be able to refuse such an appeal. He went below and fetched his revolver and an electric torch which he stuffed into a trouser pocket. He cried to the Epirote to expect him when he saw him, for he was going ashore.

" All right," he said. " I'll come and see what the trouble is."

He dropped over the yacht's side into the cockle-shell of a boat, and the old man took up the sculls. The yacht must have anchored nearer land than he had thought, for in five minutes they had touched a shelving rock. Somebody stood there with a lantern which made a dull glow in the fog.

Vernon made out a middle-aged woman with the air and dress of a lady's maid. She held the lantern close to him for a moment, and then turned wearily to the other. " Fool, Mitri ! " she cried. " You have brought a peasant."

" Nay," said the old man, " he is no peasant. He is a Signor, I tell you."

The woman again passed the light of her lantern over Vernon's face and figure. " His dress is a peasant's, but such clothes may be a noble-man's whim. I have heard it of the English."

" I am English," said Vernon in French.

She turned on him with a quick movement of relief.

" You are English . . . and a gentleman ? But I know nothing of you . . . only that you have come out of the sea. Up in the House we women are alone, and my mistress has death to face, or

worse than death. We have no claim on you,
and if you give us your service it means danger—
oh, what danger ! See, the boat is there. You
can return in it and go away, and forget that you
have been near this accursed place. But, O
Monsieur, if you hope for Heaven and have pity on
a defenceless angel, you will not leave us."

Vernon's blood was slow to stir, and, as I have
said, he had no instinct for melodrama. This
gesticulating French maid was like something out
of an indifferent play.

" Who is your mistress ? " he asked. " Did
she send you for me ? "

The woman flung up her hands.

" I will speak the truth. My mistress does not
know you are here. Only Mitri and I saw you.
She will not ask help, for she is foolishly confident.
She is proud and fearless, and will not believe the
evidence of her eyes. She must be saved in spite
of herself. I fear for her and also for myself, for
the whole House is doomed."

" But, Mademoiselle, you cannot expect me to
intrude uninvited on your mistress. What is her
name ? What do you want me to do ? "

She clutched his arm and spoke low and rapidly
in his ear.

" She is the last of her line, you must know—
a girl with a wild estate and a father dead these
many months. She is good and gracious, as I
can bear witness, but she is young and cannot
govern the wolves who are the men of these parts.
They have a long hatred of her house, and now they
have it rumoured that she is a witch who blights
the crops and slays the children. . . . Once, twice,
they have cursed our threshold and made the

blood mark on the door. We are prisoners now, you figure. They name her Basilissa, meaning the Queen of Hell, and there is no babe but will faint with fright if it casts eyes on her, and she as mild and innocent as Mother Mary. . . . The word has gone round to burn the witch out, for the winter has been cruel and they blame their sorrows on her. The hour is near, and unless salvation comes she will go to God in the fire."

There was something in the hoarse excited voice which forbade Vernon to dismiss lightly this extraordinary tale. The woman was patently terrified and sincere. It might be a trap, but he had his pistol, and from an old man and a woman he had nothing to fear. On the other hand there might be some desperate need which he could not disregard. It seemed to him that he was bound to inquire further.

" I am willing to go to your mistress," he said, and the woman, murmuring " God's mercy," led the way up a steep causeway to some rocky steps cut in a tamarisk thicket.

She stopped half-way to whisper an injunction to go quietly. " They cannot see us in this blessed fog," she whispered, " but they may hear us." Then to Vernon : " They watch us like wild beasts, Monsieur ; their sentries do not permit us to leave the House, but this night the kind God has fooled them. But they cannot be far off, and they have quick ears."

The three crept up the rock staircase made slippery by the heavy mist. Presently a great wall of masonry rose above them, and what seemed the aperture of a door. " Once," the woman whispered, " there were three such posterns, but two were walled up by my lady's father—walled up within, with the doors left standing. This our enemies do not know and they watch all three, but this the least, for it looks unused. Behold their work ! "

Vernon saw that tall bundles of brushwood had been laid around the door, and that these had with difficulty been pushed back when it was opened.

" But what . . . ? " he began.

" It means that they would burn us," she hissed. " Now, Monsieur, do you believe my tale, and, believing, does your courage fail you ? "

To Vernon, shy, placid, a devotee of all the conventions, it was beginning to seem a monstrous thing to enter this strange house at the bidding of two servants, primed with a crazy tale, to meet an owner who had given no sign of desiring his presence. A woman, too—apparently a young woman. The thing was hideously embarrassing, the more so as he suddenly realised that he was barefooted, and clad in his old jersey and corduroys. I think he would have drawn back except for the sight of the faggots—that and the woman's challenge to his courage. He had been " dared " like a schoolboy, and after twenty-four hours fighting with storms and the shattering of the purpose of a lifetime he was in that half-truculent, half-reckless mood which is prone to accept a challenge. There was business afoot, it appeared, ugly business.

" Go on. I will see your mistress," he said.

With a key the old man unlocked the door. The lock must have been recently oiled, for it moved easily. The three now climbed a staircase which seemed to follow the wall of a round tower. Presently they came into a stone hall with ancient hangings like the banners in a church. From the open frame of the lantern a second was kindled, and the two lights showed a huge desolate place with crumbling mosaics on the floor and plaster dropping from the walls and cornices. There was no furniture of any kind and the place smelt damp and chilly like a vault.

" These are unused chambers," the woman said, and her voice was no longer hushed but high-pitched with excitement. " We live only on the landward side."

Another heavy door was unlocked, and they entered a corridor where the air blew warmer, and there was a hint of that indescribable scent which comes from human habitation. The woman stopped and consulted in whispers with the old man. Now that she had got Vernon inside, her nervousness seemed to have increased. She turned to him at last :

" I must prepare my mistress. If Monsieur will be so good he will wait here till I fetch him."

She opened a door and almost pushed Vernon within. He found himself in black darkness, while the flicker of the lantern vanished round a bend in the corridor.

FROM his pocket Vernon drew his electric torch
and flashed it round the room in which he found
himself.   It was the extreme opposite of the empty
stone hall, for it was heavily decorated and crowded
with furniture.   Clearly no one had used it lately,
for dust lay on everything and the shutters of the
windows had not been unbarred for months.   It
had the air, indeed, of a lumber-room, into which
furniture had been casually shot.   The pieces were
for the most part fine and costly.   There were
several Spanish cabinets, a wonderful red-lacquer
couch, quantities of Oriental rugs which looked
good, and a litter of Chinese vases and antique
silver lamps.

But it was not the junk which filled it that caught
Vernon's eye.   It was the walls which had been
painted and frescoed in one continuous picture.
At first he thought it was a Procession of the Hours
or the Seasons, but when he brought his torch to
bear on it he saw that it was something very
different.   The background was a mountain glade,
and on the lawns and beside the pools of a stream
figures were engaged in wild dances.   Pan and his
satyrs were there, and a bevy of nymphs, and
strange figures half animal, half human.   The
thing was done with immense skill—the slanted
eyes of the fauns, the leer in a contorted satyr
face, the mingled lust and terror of the nymphs,

the horrid obscenity of the movements. It was a carnival of bestiality that stared from the four walls. The man who conceived it had worshipped darker gods even than Priapus.

There were other things which Vernon noted in the jumble of the room. A head of Aphrodite, for instance—Pandemia, not Urania. A broken statuette of a boy which made him sick. A group of little figures which were a miracle in the imaginative degradation of the human form. Not the worst relics from the lupanars of Pompeii compared with these in sheer subtlety of filth. And all this in a shuttered room stifling with mould and disuse.

There was a door at the farther end which he found unlocked. The room beyond was like a mortuary—the walls painted black and undecorated save for one small picture. There was a crack in the shutters here, and perhaps a broken window, for a breath of the clean sea air met him. There was no furniture except an oblong piece of yellow marble which seemed from the rams' heads and cornucopias to be an old altar. He turned his torch on the solitary picture. It represented the stock scene of Salome with the head of John the Baptist, a subject which bad artists have made play with for the last five hundred years. But this was none of the customary daubs, but the work of a master—a perverted, perhaps a crazy, genius. The woman's gloating face, the passion of the hands caressing the pale flesh, the stare of the dead eyes, were wonderful and awful. If the first room had been the shrine of inhuman lust, this had been the chapel of inhuman cruelty.

He opened another door and found himself in a

little closet, lined to the ceiling with books. He
knew what he would find on the shelves. The
volumes were finely bound, chiefly in vellum, and
among them were a certain number of reputable
classics. But most belonged to the backstairs
of literature—the obscenities of Greek and of
silver Latin, the diseased sidewalks of the Middle
Ages, the aberrations of the moderns. It was
not common pornography ; the collection had
been made by someone who was a scholar in
vice.

Vernon went back to the first room, nauseated
and angry. He must get out of this damned
place, which was, or had been, the habitation
of devils. What kind of owner could such a
house possess ? The woman had said that it
was a young girl, as virtuous as the Virgin. But,
great God ! how could virtue dwell in such an
environment ?

He had opened the door to begin his retreat
when a lantern appeared in the corridor. It was
the woman, and with a finger on her lips she
motioned him back into the room.

" My mistress is asleep," she said, " and it
would not be well to wake her. Monsieur will
stay here to-night and speak with her in the morning ? "

" I will do nothing of the kind," said Vernon.
" I am going back to my boat."

The woman caught his involuntary glance at
the wall paintings and clutched his arm. "But
that is not her doing," she cried. " That was
the work of her father, who was beyond belief
wicked. It is his sins that the child is about
to expiate. The people have condemned her,

but you surely would not join in their unjust judgment."

"I tell you I will have nothing to do with the place. Will you kindly show me the way back ? "

Her face hardened. " I cannot. Mitri has the key."

" Well, where the devil is Mitri ? "

" I will not tell . . . O Monsieur, I beseech you, do not forsake us. There has been evil in this House enough to sink it to hell, but my mistress is innocent. I ask only that you speak with her. After that, if you so decide, you can go away."

The woman was plainly honest and in earnest, and Vernon was a just man. He suddenly felt that he was behaving badly. There could be no harm in sleeping a night in the house, and in the morning interviewing its owner. If it was a case of real necessity he could take her and her maid off in his boat. . . . After all there might be serious trouble afoot. The sight of those hideous rooms had given him a sharp realisation of the ugly things in life.

He was taken to a clean, bare little attic at the top of the house which had once no doubt been a servant's quarters. Having been up all the previous night, his head had scarcely touched the rough pillow before he was asleep. He slept for ten hours, till he was awakened by Mitri, who brought him hot water and soap and a venerable razor with which he made some attempt at a toilet. He noticed that the fog was still thick, and from the garret window he looked into an opaque blanket.

He had wakened with a different attitude towards the adventure in which he found himself. The sense of a wasted youth and defrauded hopes had left him ; he felt more tightly strung, more vigorous, younger ; he also felt a certain curiosity about this Greek girl who in an abominable house was defying the lightnings.

Mitri conducted him to the first floor, where he was taken charge of by the Frenchwoman.

" Do not be afraid of her," she whispered. " Deal with her as a man with a woman and make her do your bidding. She is stiff-necked towards me, but she may listen to a young man, especially if he be English."

She ushered Vernon into a room which was very different from the hideous chambers he had explored the night before. It was poorly and sparsely furnished, the chairs were chiefly wicker, the walls had recently been distempered by an amateur hand, the floor was of bare scrubbed boards. But a bright fire burned on the hearth, there was a big bunch of narcissus on a table set for breakfast, and flowering branches had been stuck in the tall vases beside the chimney. Through the open window came a drift of fog which intensified the comfort of the fire.

It was a woman's room, for on a table lay some knitting and a piece of embroidery, and a small ivory housewife's case bearing the initials " K. A." There were one or two books also, and Vernon looked at them curiously. One was a book of poems which had been published in London a month before. This Greek girl must know English ; perhaps she had recently been in England. . . . He took up another volume, and to his amazement it was a reprint of Peter Beckford's *Thoughts on Hunting*. He could not have been more surprised if he had found a copy of the *Eton Chronicle*. What on earth was the mistress of a lonely Ægean island doing with Peter Beckford ?

The fire crackled cheerfully, the raw morning air flowed through the window, and Vernon cast longing eyes on the simple preparations for breakfast. He was ferociously hungry, and he wished he were now in the boat, where the Epirote would be frying bacon. . . .

There was another door besides that by which he had entered, and curiously enough it was in the same position as the door in the room of his dream. He angrily dismissed the memory of that preposterous hallucination, but he kept his eye on the door. By it no doubt the mistress of the house would enter, and he wished she would make haste. He was beginning to be very curious about this girl. . . . Probably she would be indignant and send him about his business, but she could scarcely refuse to give him breakfast first. In any case there was the yacht. . . . There was a mirror above the mantelpiece in which he caught a glimpse of himself. The glimpse was not reassuring. His face was as dark as an Indian's, his hair wanted cutting, and his blue jersey was bleached and discoloured with salt water. He looked like a deck-hand on a cargo boat. But perhaps a girl who read Beckford would not be pedantic about appearances. He put his trust in Peter——

The door had opened. A voice, sharp-pitched and startled, was speaking, and to his surprise it spoke in English.

" Who the devil are you ? " it said.

He saw a slim girl, who stood in the entrance poised like a runner, every line of her figure an expression of amazement. He had seen her before, but his memory was wretched for women's faces. But the odd thing was that, after the first second, there was recognition in her face.

" Colonel Milburne ! " said the voice. " What in the name of goodness are you doing here ? "

She knew him, and he knew her, but where —when—had they met ? He must have stared blankly, for the girl laughed.

" You have forgotten," she said. " But I have seen you out with the Mivern, and we met at luncheon at Wirlesdon in the winter."

He remembered now, and what he remembered chiefly were the last words he had spoken to me on the subject of this girl. The adventure was becoming farcical.

" I beg your pardon," he stammered. " You are Miss Arabin. I didn't know——"

" I am Miss Arabin. But why the honour of an early morning call from Colonel Milburne ? "

" I came here last night in a yacht." Vernon was making a lame business of his explanation, for the startled angry eyes of his hostess scattered his wits. " I anchored below in the fog, and an old man came out in a boat and asked me to come ashore. There was a woman on the beach—your maid—and she implored my help—told a story I didn't quite follow——"

" The fog ! " the girl repeated. " That of course explains why you were allowed to anchor.

In clear weather you would have been driven away."

She spoke in so assured a tone that Vernon was piqued.

" The seas are free," he said. " Who would have interfered with me ? Your servants ? "

She laughed again, mirthlessly. " My people. Not my servants. Continue. You came ashore and listened to Élise's chatter. After that ? "

" She said you were asleep and must not be wakened, but that I should speak to you in the morning. She put me up for the night."

" Where ? " she asked sharply.

" In a little room on the top floor."

" I see. ' Where you sleeps you breakfasts.' Well, we'd better have some food."

She rang a little silver hand-bell, and the maid, who must have been waiting close at hand, appeared with coffee and boiled eggs. She cast an anxious glance at Vernon as if to inquire how he had fared at her mistress's hands.

" Sit down," said the girl when Élise had gone. " I can't give you much to eat, for these days we are on short rations. I'm sorry but there's no sugar. I can recommend the honey. It's the only good thing in Plakos."

" Is this Plakos ? I came here once before— in 1914—in a steam yacht. I suppose I am in the big white house which looks down upon the jetty. I could see nothing last night in the fog. I remember a long causeway and steps cut in the rock. That must have been the road I came."

She nodded. " What kind of sailor are you to be so ignorant of your whereabouts ? Oh,

I see, the storm! What's the size of your boat ? "

When he told her, she exclaimed. " You must have had the devil of a time, for it was a first-class gale. And now on your arrival in port you are plunged into melodrama. You don't look as if you had much taste for melodrama, Colonel Milburne."

" I haven't. But is it really melodrama ? Your maid told me a rather alarming tale."

Her eyes had the hard agate gleam which he remembered from Wirlesdon. Then he had detested her, but now, as he looked at her, he saw that which made him alter his judgment. The small face was very pale, and there were dark lines under the eyes. This girl was undergoing some heavy strain, and her casual manner was in the nature of a shield.

" Is it true ? " he asked.

" So-so. In parts, no doubt. I am having trouble with my tenants, which I am told is a thing that happens even in England. But that is my own concern, and I don't ask for help. After breakfast I would suggest that you go back to your yacht."

" I think you had better come with me. You and your maid. I take it that the old man Mitri can fend for himself."

" How kind of you ! " she cried in a falsetto, mimicking voice. " How extraordinarily kind ! But you see I haven't asked your help, and I don't propose to accept it. . . . You're sure you won't have any more coffee ! I wonder if you could give me a cigarette ? I've been out of them for three days."

She lay back in a wicker chair, rocking herself and lazily blowing smoke clouds. Vernon stood with his back to the fire and filled a pipe.

" I don't see how I can go away," he said, " unless I can convince myself that you're in no danger. You're English, and a woman, and I'm bound to help you whether you want it or not." He spoke with assurance now, perhaps with a certain priggishness. The tone may have offended the girl, for when she spoke it was with a touch of the insolence which he remembered at Wirlesdon.

" I'm curious to know what Élise told you last night."

" Simply that you were imprisoned here by the people of Plakos—that they thought you a witch and might very likely treat you in the savage way that people used to treat witches."

She nodded. " That's about the size of it. But what if I refuse to let anyone interfere in a fight between me and my own people ? Supposing this is something which I must stick out for the sake of my own credit ? What then, Colonel Milburne ? You have been a soldier. You wouldn't advise me to run away."

" That depends," said Vernon. " There are fights where there can be no victory—where the right course is to run away. Your maid told me something else. She said that the evil reputation you had among the peasants was not your own doing—that of course I guessed—but a legacy from your family, who for very good reasons were unpopular. Does that make no difference ? "

" How ? "

" Why, there's surely no obligation in honour

to make yourself a vicarious sacrifice for other people's misdeeds ! "

" I—don't—think I agree. One must pay for one's race as well as for oneself."

" Oh, nonsense ! Not the kind of thing your family seem to have amused themselves with."

" What do you mean ? "

" I was put into a room last night——" Vernon spoke hesitatingly—" and I saw some books and paintings. They were horrible. I understood—well, that the peasants might have a good deal of reason—something to say for themselves, you know. Why should you suffer for that swinishness ? "

The morning sun had broken through the fog and was shining full on the girl's face. She sprang to her feet, and Vernon saw that she had blushed deeply.

" You entered those rooms ! " she cried. " That fool Élise ! I will have her beaten. Oh, I am shamed. . . . Get off with you ! You are only making me wretched. Get off while there's time."

The sight of her crimson face and neck moved Vernon to a deep compassion.

" I refuse to leave without you, Miss Arabin," he said. " I do not know much, but I know enough to see that you are in deadly danger. I can no more leave you here than I could leave a drowning child in the sea. Quick ! Get your maid and pack some things and we'll be gone."

She stood before him, an abashed obstinate child.

" I won't go . . . I hate you. . . . You have seen—oh, leave me, if you have any pity."

" You come with me."

" I won't ! " Her lips were a thin line, and the shut jaws made a square of the resolute little face.

" Then I shall carry you off. I'm very sorry, Miss Arabin, but I'm going to save you in spite of yourself."

Vernon had his hand stretched out to the silver handbell to summon Élise, when he found himself looking at a small pistol. He caught her wrist, expecting it to go off, but nothing happened. It dropped into his hand and he saw that it was unloaded.

He rang the bell.

" All the more reason why you should come with me if you are so badly armed."

The girl stood stiff and silent, her eyes and cheeks burning, as Élise entered.

" Pack for your mistress," he told the maid. " Bring as little baggage as possible, for there isn't much room." The woman hurried off gladly to do his bidding.

" Please don't make a scene," he said. " You will have to come in the end and some day you will forgive me."

" I will not come," she said, " but I will show you something."

Life seemed to have been restored to her tense body, as she hurried him out of the room, along a corridor, and up a flight of stairs to a window which looked seaward.

The last wreath of fog had disappeared, and the half-moon of bay lay blue and sparkling. Down at the jetty were men and boats, but out on the water there was no sign of the anchored yacht.

" What does that mean ? " Vernon cried.

" It means that your boat has gone.   When the air cleared the people saw it, and have driven your man away. . . .   It means that you, like me, are a prisoner ! "

As Vernon looked at the flushed girl, whose voice
as she spoke had at least as much consternation
in it as triumph, he experienced a sudden dis-
location of mind. Something fell from him—
the elderliness, the preoccupation, the stiff dogma
of his recent years. He recaptured the spirit
which had open arms for novelty. He felt an
eagerness to be up and doing—what, he was not
clear—but something difficult and high-handed.
The vanishing of his dream had left the chambers
of his mind swept and garnished, and youth does
not tolerate empty rooms.

Also, though I do not think that he had yet
begun to fall in love with Koré, he understood the
quality of one whom aforetimes he had disliked
both as individual and type. This pale girl,
dressed like a young woman in a Scotch shooting lodge, was facing terror with a stiff lip. There
was nothing raffish or second-rate about her now.
She might make light of her danger in her words,
but her eyes betrayed her.

It was about this danger that he was still un-
decided. You see, he had not, like me, seen the
people of the island, felt the strain of their expectancy, or looked on the secret spaces of the Dancing
Floor. He had come out of the storm to hear a
tale told in the fog and darkness by an excited
woman. That was all—that and the hideous

rooms at which he had had a passing glance. The atmosphere of the place, which I had found so unnerving, had not yet begun to affect him.

" My fellow will come back," he said, after scanning the empty seas. " He has his faults, but he is plucky and faithful."

" You do not understand," the girl said. " He would be one against a thousand. He may be as brave as a lion, but they won't let him anchor, and if they did they would never let you and me join him. I have told you we are prisoners—close prisoners."

" You must tell me a great deal more. You see, you can't refuse my help now, for we are in the same boat. Do you mind if we go back to where we breakfasted, for I left my pipe there."

She turned without a word and led him back to her sitting-room, passing a woe-begone Élise who, with her arms full of clothes, was told that her services were now needless. The windows of the room looked on a garden which had been suffered to run wild but which still showed a wealth of spring blossom. Beyond was a shallow terrace and then the darkness of trees. A man's head seemed to move behind a cypress hedge. The girl nodded towards it. " One of my gaolers," she said.

She stood looking out of the window with her eyes averted from Vernon and seemed to be forcing herself to speak.

" You have guessed right about my family," she said. " And about this house. I am cleaning it slowly—I must do it myself, Élise and I, for I do not want strangers to know. . . . This room was as bad as the other two till I whitewashed the walls. The old furniture I am storing till I have time to destroy it. I think I will burn it, for it has hideous associations for me. I would have had the whole house in order this spring if my foolish people had not lost their heads."

A "tawdry girl," that was how Vernon had spoken of her to me. He withdrew the word now. "Tawdry" was the last adjective he would use about this strange child, fighting alone to get rid of a burden of ancient evil. He had thought her a modish, artificial being, a moth hatched out of the latest freak of fashion. Now she seemed to him a thousand years removed from the feverish world which he had thought her natural setting. Her appeal was her extreme candour and simplicity, her utter, savage, unconsidering courage.

"Let us take the family for granted," Vernon said gently. " I can't expect you to talk about that. I assume that there was that in your predecessor's doings which gave these islanders a legitimate grievance. What I want to know is what they are up to now. Tell me very carefully everything that has happened since you came here a week ago."

She had little to tell him. She had been allowed to enter the House by the ordinary road from the village, and after that the gates had been barred. When she had attempted to go for a walk she had been turned back by men with rifles —she did not tell Vernon how the rifles had been procured. The hillmen had joined with the people of the coast—you could always tell a hillman by his dress—though the two used to be hereditary enemies. That made her angry and also uneasy; so did the curious methodical ways of the siege. They were not attempting to enter the House—she doubted if anyone of them would dare to cross the threshold—they were only there to prevent her leaving it. She herself, not the looting of the House, must be their object. Mitri was permitted to go to the village, but he did not go often, for he came back terrified and could not or would not explain his terrors. No communication had been held with the watchers, and no message had come from them. She had tried repeatedly to find out their intentions, but the sentinels would not speak, and she could make nothing of Mitri. No, she was not allowed into the demesne. There were sentries there right up to the house wall—sentries night and day.

Vernon asked her about supplies. She had brought a store with her which was not yet exhausted, but the people sent up food every morning. Mitri found it laid on the threshold of the main door. Curious food—barley cakes and honey and cheese and eggs and dried figs. She couldn't imagine where they got it from, for the people had been starving in the winter. Milk, too—plenty of milk, which was another unexpected thing.

Water—that was the oddest business of all. The House had a fine well in the stableyard on the east side. This had been sealed up and its use forbidden to Mitri. But morning and night buckets of fresh water were brought to the door —whence, she did not know. " It rather restricts our bathing arrangements," she said.

She told the story lightly, with a ready laugh, as

if she were once more mistress of herself. Mistress of her voice she certainly was, but she could not command her eyes. It was these that counteracted the debonair tones and kept tragedy in the atmosphere.

Vernon, as I have said, had not the reason which I had for feeling the gravity of the business. But he was a scholar, and there were details in Koré's account which startled him.

" Tell me about the food again. Cheese and honey and barley cakes, dried figs and eggs— nothing more ? "

" Nothing more. And not a great deal of that. Not more than enough to feed one person for twenty-four hours. We have to supplement it from the stores we brought."

" I see. . . . It is meant for you personally—not for your household. And the water ? You don't know what spring it comes from ? "

She shook her head. " There are many springs in Plakos. But why does our commissariat interest you ? "

" Because it reminds me of something I have read somewhere. Cheese and honey and barley cakes—that is ritual food. Sacramental, if you like. And the water. Probably brought from some sacred well. I don't much like it. Tell me about the people here, Miss Arabin. Are they very backward and superstitious ? "

" I suppose you might call them that. They are a fine race to look at, and claim to be pure Greek—at least the coast folk. The hillmen are said to be mongrels, but they are handsome mongrels and fought bravely in the war. But I don't know them well, for I left when I was a child, and since my father died I have only seen the people of Kynætho."

"Kynætho?" Vernon cried out sharply, for the word was like a bell to ring up the curtain of memory.

"Yes, Kynætho. That is the village at the gate."

Now he had the clue. Kynætho was the place mentioned in the manuscript fragment which he had translated for me. It was at Kynætho that the strange rite was performed of the Koré and the Kouros. The details were engraven on his memory, for they had profoundly impressed him and he had turned them over repeatedly in his mind. He had thought he had discovered the record of a new ritual form ; rather it appeared that he had stumbled upon the living rite itself.

"I begin—to understand," he said slowly. "I want you to let me speak to Mitri. Alone, if you please. I have done this work before in the war, and I can get more out of that kind of fellow if I am alone with him. Then I shall prospect the land."

He found Mitri in his lair in the ancient kitchen. With the old man there was no trouble, for when he found that his interlocutor spoke Greek fluently he overflowed in confidences.

"They will burn this House," he said finally. "They have piled faggots on the north and east sides where the wind blows. And the time will be Easter eve."

"And your mistress?"

Mitri shrugged his shoulders. "There is no hope for her, I tell you. She had a chance of flight and missed it, though I pled with her. She will burn with the House unless——"

He looked at Vernon timidly, as if he feared to reveal something.

" Unless—— ? " said Vernon.

" There is a rumour in Kynætho of something else. In that accursed village they have preserved tales of the old days, and they say that on the night of Good Friday there will be *panegyria* on the Dancing Floor. There will be a race with torches, and he who wins will be called King. To him it will fall to slay my mistress in order that the Ancient Ones may appear and bless the people."

" I see," said Vernon. " Do you believe in that rubbish ? "

Mitri crossed himself and called the Panagia to witness that he was a Christian and after God and the Saints loved his mistress.

" That is well. I trust you, Mitri ; and I will show you how you can save her. You are allowed to leave the House ? "

" Every second day only. I went yesterday, and cannot go again till to-morrow. I have a daughter married in the village, whom I am permitted to visit."

" Very well. We are still two days from Good Friday. Go down to the village to-morrow and find out all about the plans for Good Friday evening. Lie as much as you like. Say you hate your mistress and will desert her whenever you are bidden. Pretend you're on the other side. Get their confidence. . . . A madness has afflicted this island and you are the only sane Christian left in it. If these ruffians hurt your mistress, the Government—both in Athens and in London— will send soldiers and hang many. After that

there will be no more Kynætho. We have got
to prevent the people making fools of themselves.
Your mistress is English and I am English, and
that is why I stay here. You do exactly as I tell
you and we'll win through."

It was essential to encourage Mitri, for the old
man was patently torn between superstitious
fear and fidelity to Koré, and only a robust scepticism and a lively hope would enable him to
keep his tail up and do his part. Vernon ac-
cordingly protested a confidence which he was
very far from feeling. It was arranged that Mitri
should go to Kynætho next morning after breakfast and spend the day there.

After that, guided by the old man, Vernon
made a circuit of the House. From the top
windows he was able to follow the lie of the land
—the postern gates to the shore, the nest of stables
and outbuildings on the east with access to the
shallow glen running up from the jetty, the main
entrance and the drive from Kynætho, the wooded
demesne ending at the cliffs, and the orchards and
oliveyards between the cliffs and the causeway.
The patrols came right up to the House wall, and
on various sides Vernon had a glimpse of them.
But he failed to get what he specially sought, a
prospect of any part of the adjoining coast-line
beyond the little bay. He believed that his
yacht was somewhere hidden there, out of sight
of the peasants. He was convinced that the
Epirote would obey orders and wait for him, and
would not go one yard farther away than was
strictly necessary. But he was at a loss to know
how to find him, if he were penned up in this
shuttered mausoleum.

He returned to find Koré sewing by the window of the breakfast room. He entered quietly and had a momentary glimpse of her before she was conscious of his presence. She was looking straight before her with vacant eyes, her face in profile against the window, a figure of infinite appeal. Vernon had a moment of acute compunction. What he had once thought and spoken of this poor child seemed to him now to have been senseless brutality. He had called her tawdry and vulgar and shrill, he had thought her the ugly product of the ugly after-the-war world. But there she sat like a muse of meditation, as fine and delicate as a sword-blade. And she had a sword's steel, too, for had she not faced unknown peril for a scruple ?

"What does Mitri say ? " she asked in a voice which had a forced briskness in it.

" I shall know more to-morrow night, but I have learned something. You. are safe for the better part of three days—till some time on Good Friday evening. That is one thing. The other is that your scheme of wearing down the hostility of your people has failed. Your islanders have gone stark mad. The business is far too solemn for me to speak smooth things. They have resurrected an old pagan rite of sacrifice. *Sacrifice*, do, you understand ? This House will be burned, and if they have their will you will die."

" I was beginning to guess as much. I don't want to die, for it means defeat. But I don't think I am afraid to die. You see—life is rather difficult—and not very satisfactory. But tell me more."

Vernon gave her a sketch of the ritual of Kynætho. " It was your mentioning the name that brought it back to me. I have always been interested in Greek religion, and by an amazing chance I came on this only a month or so ago. Leithen—the lawyer—you know him, I think— gave me a bit of mediæval Greek manuscript to translate, and part of it had this rite."

" Leithen," she cried. " Sir Edward ? Then he found it among the papers I lent him. Why didn't he tell me about it ? "

" I can't imagine."

" Perhaps he thought I wouldn't have believed it. I wouldn't a month ago. Perhaps he thought he could prevent me coming here. I think he did his best. I had to go off without saying good-bye to him, and he was my greatest friend."

" He happens to be also my closest friend. If you had known about this—this crazy ritual, would you have come ? "

She smiled. " I don't know. I'm very obstinate, and I can't bear to be bullied. These people are trying to bully me. . . . But of course I didn't know how bad it was. . . . And I didn't know that I was going to land you in this mess. That is what weighs on my mind."

" But you didn't invite me here. You told me to clear out."

" My servants invited you and therefore I am responsible. . . . Oh, Colonel Milburne, you must understand what I feel. I haven't had an easy life, for I seem to have been always fighting, but I didn't mind it as long as it was my own fight. I felt I had to stick it out, for it was the penalty I paid for being an Arabin. But whatever paying was to be done I wanted to do it myself. . . . Otherwise, don't you see, it makes the guilt of my

family so much heavier. . . . And now I have
let you in for it, and that is hell—simply hell ! "

Vernon had suddenly an emotion which he had
never known before—the exhilaration with which
he had for years anticipated the culmination of
his dream, but different in kind, nobler, less self-
regarding. He felt keyed up to any enterprise,
and singularly confident. There was tenderness
in his mood, too, which was a thing he had
rarely felt—tenderness towards this gallant child.

" Listen to me, Miss Arabin. I have two
things to say to you. One is that I glory in being
here. I wouldn't be elsewhere for the world. It
is a delight and a privilege. The other is that
we are going to win out."

" But how ? "

" I don't know yet. We will find a way. I
am as certain of it as that I am standing here.
God doesn't mean a thing like this to be a blind
cul-de-sac."

" You believe in God? I wish I did. I think
I only believe in the Devil."

" Then you believe in God. If evil is a living
thing, good must be living as well—more indeed,
or the world would smash. . . . Look here, we've
two days to put in together. There is nothing
we can do for the present, so we must find some
way to keep our nerves quiet. Let's pretend
we're in an ordinary English country house and
kept indoors by rain."

So the two of them made plans to pass the time,
while the clear spring sunlight outside turned
Vernon's pretence into foolishness. They played
piquet, and sometimes he read to her—chiefly
Peter Beckford. The florid eighteenth-century

prose, the tags of Augustan poetry, the high stilts, the gusto, carried their thoughts to the orderly world of home. I have no wish to speculate about the secrets of a friend, but I fancy that the slow hours spent together brought understanding. Koré must have told him things which she had kept back from me, for the near prospect of death breaks down many barriers. I think, too, that he may have told her the story of his boyish dream —he must have, for it bore directly on the case. With his sense of predestination he would draw from it a special confidence, and she would be made to share it. He had undergone a long preparation for something which had ended in mist, but the preparation might point to success in a great reality. . . .

Late the following afternoon old Mitri returned. Vernon saw him first alone, and got from him the details of the next evening's ceremonial. There was to be a race among the young men on the Dancing Floor as soon as the moon rose, and the victor would be called the King. Some of the news which Mitri had gathered was unexpected, some incomprehensible, but in the main it agreed with his own version. The victor would choose a victim—a male victim, clearly, for the female victim was already chosen. The two would enter the House, and on the next night—the eve of this grim Easter—the sacrifice would be accomplished. Beyond that Mitri could say nothing except that the people looked for a mighty miracle ; but the manuscript had told what the miracle would be.

" Who will be the runners ? " Vernon asked.

" The fleetest among the young men, both of the village and the hills."

It was characteristic of Vernon's fatalism that
he had not troubled to make even the rudiments
of a plan till he had heard Mitri's tidings. Now
the thing began to unfold itself. The next step
at any rate was clearly ordained.

" Will everybody be known to each other ? "
he said.

" Faith, no. Kynætho till now has had few
dealings with the hill folk, and the villages in the
hills are generally at strife with each other. To-
morrow night there will be many strangers, and
no questions will be asked, for all will be allies in
this devilry."

" Do I speak like a Greek ? "

" You speak like a Greek, but like one from
another island."

" And I look like an islander ? "

Mitri grinned. " There are few as well-looking.
But if your face were darkened, you would pass.
There is a place, a little remote place in the hills,
Akte by name, where the folk are said to have
white skins like you, Signor."

" Well, attend, Mitri. I am a man from Akte
who has been at the wars, and has just returned.
That will account for my foreign speech."

" The Signor jests. He has a stout heart that
can jest——"

" I'm not jesting. I'm going to compete in the
race to-morrow night. What is more, I'm going
to win. I've been a bit of a runner in my time,
and I'm in hard training."

A faint spark appeared in the old man's
eye.

" The Signor will no doubt win if he runs. And
if he ever reaches the Dancing Floor he will not

be troubled with questions. But how will he reach the Dancing Floor ? "

" I intend to get out of the House early to-morrow morning. There are several things I want to do before the race. Have you any rags with which I can imitate the dress of a hillman ? "

Mitri considered. Shirt and breeches he had, but no boots. A cap might be improvised, but boots ?

" Remember I have only just returned to Akte, and have brought the fashion of the war with me. So I can make shift with home-made puttees. Anything else ? "

" The men around the House will not let you pass."

" They'll have to. I'm one of themselves, and you've got to coach me in local customs. You have twelve hours before you in which to turn me into a respectable citizen of Akte. If any awkward questions are asked I propose to be truculent. A soldier is going to stand no nonsense from civilians, you know."

Mitri considered again. " It will be best to go by the main road to Kynætho."

" No, I'm going by the causeway. I want to see what lies beyond it to the west."

" The cliffs are there and there is no road."

" I will find one."

Mitri shook his head. He had apparently little belief in the scheme, but an hour later, after Vernon had given Koré a sketch of his intentions, he arrived with an armful of strange garments. Élise at her mistress's request had collected odd-ments of fabrics, and brought part of the contents of the linen-cupboard.

" We are about," Vernon told a mystified Koré, " to prepare for private theatricals. Puttees are my most urgent need, and that thin skirt of yours will be the very thing."

Since Koré still looked puzzled he added : " We're cast for parts in a rather sensational drama. I'm beginning to think that the only way to prevent it being a tragedy is to turn it into a costume-play."

VERY early next morning, before the blue darkness had paled into dawn, Vernon swung his legs
out of an upper window of the House, crawled
along the broad parapet and began to descend by
a waterpipe in an angle between the main building and the eastern wing. This brought him to the
roof of one of the outbuildings, from which it was
possible for an active man to reach the road which
ran upward from the jetty. He had been carefully prepared by Mitri for his part. The loose
white shirt and the short mountain tunic were in
order. Mitri's breeches had proved too scanty,
but Élise had widened them, and the vacant space
about his middle was filled with a dirty red
cummerbund, made of one of Mitri's sashes, in
which were stuck a long knife and his pistol. A
pair of Mitri's home-made shoes of soft untanned
hide were supplemented by home-made puttees.
He had no hat; he had stained his face, hands and
arms beyond their natural brown with juice from
Mitri's store of pickled walnuts, and—under the
critical eye of Koré—had rubbed dirt under his
eyes and into his finger-nails till he looked the image
of a handsome, swaggering, half-washed soldier.
More important, he had been coached by Mitri in
the speech of the hills, the gossip which might have
penetrated to the remote Akte, and the man-
nerisms of the hillmen, which were unpleasingly
familiar to the dwellers by the sea.

All this care would have been useless had Vernon not been in the mood to carry off any enterprise. He felt the reckless audacity of a boy, an exhilaration which was almost intoxication, and the source of which he did not pause to consider. Above all he felt complete confidence. Somehow, somewhere, he would break the malign spell and set Koré beyond the reach of her enemies.

He reached ground fifty yards south of the jetty and turned at once in the direction of the sea. At the beginning of the causeway he met a man.

" Whither away, brother ? " came the question, accompanied by the lift of a rifle.

Vernon gave the hillman's greeting. He loomed up tall and formidable in the half-darkness.

" I go beyond the causeway to the oliveyards," he said carelessly, as if he condescended in answering.

" By whose orders ? "

" We of Akte do not take orders. I go at the request of the Elders."

" You are of Akte ? " said the man curiously. He was very willing to talk, being bored with his long night-watch. " There are none of Akte among us, so far as I have seen. The men of Akte live in the moon, says the proverb. But . . ." this after peering at Vernon's garb—" these clothes were never made in the hills."

" I am new back from the war, and have not seen Akte these three years. But I cannot linger, friend."

" Nay, bide a little. It is not yet day. Let us talk of Akte. My father once went there for cattle. . . . Or let us speak of the war. My uncle

was in the old war and my young nephew was . . .
If you will not bide, give me tobacco."

Vernon gave him a cigarette. " These are what
we smoked in Smyrna," he said. " They are
noble stuff."

Half-way along the causeway a second guard
proved more truculent. He questioned the orders
of the Elders, till Vernon played the man from
Akte and the old soldier, and threatened to fling
him into the sea. The last sentry was fortunately
asleep. Vernon scrambled over the fence of the
oliveyards, and as the sun rose above the horizon
was striding with long steps through the weedy
undergrowth.

His object was not like mine when I travelled
that road, to get inside the demesne ; he wanted
to keep out of it, and to explore the bit of coast
under it, since it seemed from the map to be the
likeliest place to find his boat. The Epirote, he
was convinced, would obey his instructions faith-
fully, and when driven away from his old anchorage would not go a yard more than was necessary.
So, after being stopped as I had been by the wall
which ran to the cliffs, he stuck to the shore. He
picked his way under the skirts of the great headland till the rock sank sheer into deep water.
There was nothing for it now but to swim, so he
made a bundle of his shirt and jacket and bound
them with the cummerbund on his shoulders, took
his pistol in his teeth and slipped into the cold
green sea. Mitri's breeches were a nuisance, but
he was a strong swimmer, and in five minutes was
at the point of the headland.

He found a ledge of rock which enabled him to
pull up his shoulders and reconnoitre the hidden

bay. There to his joy was the yacht, snugly
anchored half-way across. There was no sign of
life on board, for doubtless the Epirote was below
cooking his breakfast. Vernon had no desire to
make himself conspicuous by shouting, for the
demesne and the watchers were too near, so he
dropped back into the water and struck out for
the boat. Ten minutes later he was standing
dripping on the deck, and the Epirote was welcoming him with maledictions on Plakos.

He stripped off his wet clothes, and put on his
old aquascutum till they should be dried. Then
he breakfasted heartily, while Black George gave
an account of his stewardship. When Vernon did
not return he had not concerned himself greatly,
for the affairs of his master were no business of his.
But in the morning, when the fog began to lift,
men had put off from shore in a boat and had
demanded the reason of his presence. The interview had been stormy, for he had declined to
explain, holding that if his master chose to land
secretly by night, and rude fellows appeared with
the daylight, it would be wise to tell the latter
nothing. His interviewers had been more communicative. They had been very excited and had
tried to alarm him with foolish tales of witches.
But it was clear that they had meant mischief,
for all were armed, and when at the point of
several rifle barrels they had ordered him to depart,
it seemed to him the part of a wise man to obey.
He had feigned fear and deep stupidity, and had
upped sail and done their bidding. Then, looking
for a refuge, he had seen the great curtain of cliff
and had found this little bay. Here he hoped he
was secure, for there was no passage along the

shore, and the people of Plakos did not seem during these days to be sailing the seas. He could be observed, of course, from the cliff tops, but these were shrouded in wood and looked unfrequented.

" Did I not well, Signor ? " he asked anxiously.

" You did well. Have you seen no one ? "

" No islander. Last night two men came about midnight. One was a crippled Greek and the other man, I judge, English.

Vernon woke to the liveliest interest, but Black George told a halting tale. " He swam out and wakened me, and at first, fearing trouble, I would have brained him. Since he could not speak my tongue, I rowed ashore with him and saw the Greek. . . . He was an Englishman, beyond doubt, and a Signor, so I gave him food."

" What did he want with you ? "

" Simply that I should stay here. He had a story of some lady to whom the devils of this island meant mischief, and he begged me to wait in case the lady should seek to escape."

No cross-examination of Vernon's could make Black George amplify the tale. He had not understood clearly, he said, for the English Signor could not speak his tongue and the Greek who interpreted was obviously a fool. But he had promised to remain, which was indeed his duty to his master. No. He had spoken no single word of his master. He had not said he was an Englishman. He had said nothing.

Vernon puzzled over the matter but could make nothing of it. He did not credit the story of an Englishman in Plakos who knew of Koré's plight, and came to the conclusion that Black George had misunderstood his visitor's talk. He had the day

before him, and his first act was to row ashore to
the other point of the bay—the place from which
Janni and I had first espied the yacht. There he
sat for a little and smoked, and it was one of his
cigarette ends that I found the same afternoon.
A scramble round the headland showed him the
strip of beach below the Dancing Floor, but it
occurred to him that there was no need to go
pioneering along the coast—that he had a yacht
and could be landed wherever he pleased. So he
returned to Black George, and the two hoisted
sail and made for open sea.

The day was spent running with the light north-
west wind behind them well to the south of
Plakos, and then tacking back till about sunset
they stood off the north-east shore. It was a day
of brilliant sun, tempered by cool airs, with the
hills of the island rising sharp and blue into the
pale spring sky. Vernon found to his delight that
he had no trepidation about the work of the
coming night. He had brought with him the copy
he had made of his translation of Koré's manuscript, and studied it as a man studies a map,
without any sense of its strangeness. The madmen
of Plakos were about to revive an ancient ritual,
where the victor in a race would be entrusted with
certain barbarous duties. He proposed to be the
victor, and so to defeat the folly. The House
would be burnt, and in the confusion he would
escape with Koré to the yacht, and leave the
unhallowed isle for ever. The girl's honoui
would be satisfied, for she would have stuck it out
to the last. Once he had convinced himself that
she would be safe, he let his mind lie fallow. He
dreamed and smoked on the hot deck in the bright

weather, as much at his ease as if the evening were
to bring no more than supper and sleep.

In the early twilight the yacht's dinghy put
him ashore on a lonely bit of coast east of the
village. Black George was ordered to return to
his former anchorage and wait there; if on the
following night he saw a lantern raised three times
on the cliff above, he was to come round to the
oliveyards at the far end of the causeway. At
this stage Vernon's plan was for a simple escape
in the confusion of the fire. He hoped that the
postern gate at the jetty would be practicable;
if not he would find some way of reaching the
oliveyards from the demesne. The whole affair
was viewed by him as a straightforward enterprise—provided he could win the confounded race.

But with his landing on Plakos in the spring
gloaming his mood began to change. I have
failed in my portrayal of Vernon if I have made
you think of him as unimaginative and insensitive.
He had unexpected blind patches in his vision and
odd callosities in his skin, but for all that he was
highly strung and had an immense capacity for
emotion, though he chose mostly to sit on the
safety valve. Above all he was a scholar. All
his life he had been creating imaginative pictures
of things, or living among the creations of other
men. He had not walked a mile in that twilight
till he felt the solemnity of it oppressing his mind.

I think it was chiefly the sight of the multitude
moving towards the Dancing Floor, all silent, so
that the only sound was the tread of feet. He had
been in doubt before as to where exactly the place
was, but the road was blazed for him like the
roads to Epsom on Derby Day. Men, women,

children, babes-in-arms, they were streaming past
the closes at the foot of the glade, past the graveyard, up the aisle of the Dancing Floor. It was his
first sight of it—not as I had seen it solitary under
the moon, but surging with a stream of hushed
humanity. It had another kind of magic, but one
as potent as that which had laid its spell on me.
I had seen the temple in its loneliness, he saw it
thronged with worshippers.

No one greeted him or even noticed him; he
would probably have passed unregarded if he
had been wearing his ordinary clothes. The
heavy preoccupation of the people made them
utterly incurious. He saw men dressed as he was,
and he noted that the multitude moved to left
and right as if by instinct, leaving the central
arena vacant. Dusk had fallen, and on the crown
of the ridge on his right he saw dimly what he
knew to be the trees of the demesne. He saw,
too, that a cluster seemed to be forming at the
lower end of the arena, apart from the others, and
he guessed that these were the competitors in the
race. He made his way towards them, and found
that he had guessed rightly. It was a knot of
young men, who were now stripping their clothes,
till they stood naked except for the sashes twisted
around their middle. Most were barefoot, but one
or two had raw-hide brogues. Vernon followed
their example, till he stood up in his short linen
drawers. He retained Mitri's shoes, for he feared
the flints of the hillside. There were others in
the group, older men whom he took to be the
Elders of whom Mitri had spoken, and there was
one man who seemed to be in special authority
and who wore a loose white cassock.

It was now nearly dark, and suddenly, like the
marks delimiting a course, torches broke into
flame. These points of angry light in the crowded
silence seemed to complete the spell. Vernon's
assurance had fled and left behind it an unwilling
awe and an acute nervousness. All his learning,
all his laborious scholarship quickened from mere
mental furniture into heat and light. His imagination as well as his nerves were on fire. I can only
guess at the thoughts which must have crowded
his mind. He saw the ritual, which so far had
been for him an antiquarian remnant, leap into a
living passion. He saw what he had regarded
coolly as a barbaric survival, a matter for brutish
peasants, become suddenly a vital concern of his
own. Above all, he felt the formidableness of
the peril to Koré. She had dared far more than
she knew, far more than he had guessed ; she was
facing the heavy menace of a thousand ages, the
devils not of a few thousand peasants but of a whole
forgotten world. . . . And in that moment he has
told me that another thing became clear to him—
she had become for him something altogether rare
and precious.

The old man in the white ephod was speaking.
It was a tale which had obviously been told before
to the same audience, for he reminded them of
former instructions. Vernon forced himself to
concentrate on it an attention which was half
paralysed by that mood of novel emotion which
had come upon him. Some of it he failed to grasp,
but the main points were clear—the race twice
round the arena outside the ring of torches, the
duty of the victor to take the last torch and
plunge it in the sacred spring. The man spoke

as if reciting a lesson, and Vernon heard it like a lesson once known and forgotten. Reminiscences of what he had found in classical by-ways hammered on his mind, and with recollection came a greater awe. It was only the thought of Koré that enabled him to keep his wits. Without that, he told me, he would have sunk into the lethargy of the worshippers, obedient, absorbed in expectancy.

Then came the start, and the race which Janni and I watched from our hiding-place in the shadows under the wall. He got off the mark clumsily, and at first his limbs seemed heavy as lead. But the movement revived him and woke his old racing instinct. Though he had not run for years, he was in hard training, and towards the close of the first round his skill had come back to him and he was in the third place, going well within his powers. In the second round he felt that the thing was in his hands. He lay close to the first man, passed him before the final straight, and then forged ahead so that in the last hundred yards he was gaining ground with every stride. He seized the torch at the winning-post and raced to where in the centre of the upper glade a white figure stood alone. With the tossing of the flame into the well he straightened his body and looked round, a man restored to his old vigour and ready for swift action.

His account of the next stage was confused, for his mind was on Koré and he was going through a violent transformation of outlook. The old man was no longer repeating a rehearsed lesson, but speaking violently like one in a moment of crisis. He addressed Vernon as " You of the

hills," and told him that God had placed the fate
of Kynætho in his hands—which God he did not
particularise. But from his excited stammering
something emerged that chilled Vernon's blood. . . .
He was to wait in the House till moonrise of the
next night. The signal was to be the firing of
the place. With the first flames he was to perform
the deed to which he had been called. " Choose
which way you please," said the old man, " provided that they die." Then he would leave the
House by the main door and join the young men
without. " They will be gathered there till they
come who will come." The door would be closed
behind him till it was opened by the fire. . . .
" They who will come are Immortals."

The man's voice was high-pitched with passion,
and his figure, solitary in the bright moonshine
in that ring of silent folk, had something in it of
the awful and the sacramental. But Vernon's
thoughts were not on it, but on the news which
meant the downfall of his plans. His mind worked
now normally and sanely ; he was again a man of
the modern world. The young men—of course
they would be there—the Kouretes to greet the
Kouros. He might have known it, if he had
only thought. But how was Koré to escape from
those frenzied guardians ? He had imagined that
with the fire the vigilance of the watch would be
relaxed and that it would be easy to join Black
George and the boat. But with the fire there was
to be a thronging of the hierophants towards the
House, and what was inside would be kept inside
till the place was a heap of ashes.

The man was speaking again. He had made
some signal, for three figures had approached the

well. " The woman is within," he said, " and
it is for you to choose the man. Your choice is
free among the people of Plakos, but we have one
here, a young man, a Greek, but a stranger. He
would doubtless be acceptable."

The half-clad Maris cut an odd figure as, in the
grip of two stalwart peasants, he was led forward
for inspection. His face was white and set, and
his eyes were furious. " No willing victim this,"
thought Vernon, " but so much the better, for he
and I are in the same boat and I must make him
an ally." From the way he carried himself he
saw that Maris had been drilled, and he considered
that a soldier might be useful. " I choose this
man," he said.

A jar was given him, and he filled it from the
spring and emptied it on Maris's head and shoulders.
His own clothes were also brought, but he contented himself with Mitri's sash, of which he made
a girdle and into which he stuck his own pistol
and Mitri's knife. " I have no need of the rest,"
he said, for he was beginning to enter into the
spirit of the part. Then he knelt while the old
man laid a hand on his head and pronounced
some consecration. " Come," he said to Maris,
and the two moved up the slope of the Dancing
Floor towards the breach in the wall.

He had almost forgotten his anxiety in the
wonder of the scene. He seemed to be set on a
stage in a great golden amphitheatre, and Maris
and the guards who accompanied him were no more
than stage properties. All human life had for
the moment gone, and he was faced with primordial
elements—the scented shell of earth, the immense
arch of the sky and the riding moon, and, as he

climbed the slope, an infinity of shining waters. The magic weighed on him, a new magic, for the ruthlessness of man was submerged in the deeper ruthlessness of nature. . . . And then, as he passed the fringe of the spectators and caught a glimpse of pallid strained faces, he got his bearings again. It was man he had to cope with, crazy, fallible, tormented man. He felt the pity and innocence of it behind the guilt, and in an instant he regained confidence. . . . Maris was stumbling along, walking painfully like one unaccustomed to going on bare feet, casting fierce startled glances about him. As they approached the breach in the wall Vernon managed to whisper to him to cheer up, for no ill would befall him. " I am your friend," he said ; " together we will make an end of this folly," and the man's face lightened.

It was this look on Maris's face which I saw from my hiding-place and which made me forbid Janni's pistol shot.

THE great doors clanged behind them, and Vernon, who had been given the key by the guards, turned it in the lock. In spite of the reassuring word he had spoken to Maris he thought that his companion might attack him, so he steered wide of him and in the inky darkness fell over a basket of logs. The mishap wrung from him a very English expletive. Then he shouted on Mitri to bring a light.

He heard Maris's excited voice. " Who are you ? Who in God's name are you ? Are you English ? "

" Of course I am English. Confound it, I believe I have cracked my shin. Mitri, you idiot, where are you ? "

The old man appeared from a corridor with a lantern shaking in his hand. He had no words, but stared at the two as if he were looking on men risen from the dead.

" Where's your mistress ? In her sitting-room ? For God's sake, get me some clothes—my old ones, and bring something for this gentleman to put on. Any old thing will do. Get us some food, too, for we're starving. Quick, man. Leave the lantern here."

By the slender light, set on a table in the great stone hall, the two men regarded each other.

" You want to know who I am," said Vernon. " I'm an Englishman who came here three nights ago in a yacht. I happened to have met Miss Arabin before. I found out what the people of Plakos were up to, and it seemed to, me that the best thing I could do was to win the race to-night. I needn't tell you about that, for you saw it. . . . Now for yourself. I gather that you also are unpopular in this island ? "

Maris gave a short sketch of his career, and Vernon convinced himself by a few questions that he spoke the truth, for the Greek had served alongside the British at Salonika.

" I came here to protect the lady," Maris concluded.

" Who sent you ? "

" Mr Ertzberger. I had a companion, an English colonel who is also in your Parliament, and a great milord. Leithen is his name."

" God bless my soul ! Leithen ! Oh, impossible ! Quick ! Tell me more. Where is he now ? "

" That I do not know. Yesterday evening we separated, each seeking to find some way of entering this House. I blundered badly, and was taken by the guards on the seaward front. My friend must also have failed, or he would be here, but I do not think he has been taken."

The knowledge that I was somewhere in the island gave Vernon, as he told me, a sudden acute sense of comfort. I must have been the visitor to the yacht. He cross-examined Maris, who knew nothing of the boat's existence, and Maris agreed that the stranger who had gone aboard must have been myself. " The Greek who was with him," he said, " was doubtless my corporal,

Janni, the one man in my batch of fools who kept his head."

Mitri returned with Vernon's clothes, and an ancient dressing-gown for Maris. He also brought a bowl of milk and some cakes and cheese. Questions trembled on his lips, but Vernon waved him off. " Go and tell your mistress that we will come to her in a quarter of an hour. And have a bed made ready for this gentleman."

As Vernon dressed he had a look at his companion, now grotesquely robed in a gown too large for him, and dirty and scratched from his adventures. It was the mercy of Providence that had given him such a colleague, for he liked the man's bold hard-bitten face and honest eyes. Here was a practical fellow, and he wanted something exceedingly prosaic and practical to counteract the awe which still hovered about his mind. He fought to keep at a distance the memory of the silence and the torches and the shining spaces of the Dancing Floor. This man did not look susceptible.

" I need not tell you that we are in the devil of a tight place, Captain Maris. Do you realise precisely the meaning of the performance we have just witnessed ? "

Maris nodded. " Since yesterday. It has been most pointedly explained to me. I am one victim for the sacrifice, and the lady of this house is the other, and you are the priest."

" We have the better part of twenty-four hours' grace. After that ? "

" After that this House will be burned. You may go forth, if you have the nerve to play the part. The lady and I—no. We are supposed

19

to die when the fire begins, but if we do not die by your hand we will die in the flames."

" There is no way of escape ? "

" None," said Maris cheerfully. " But with your help I think we will do some mischief first. God's curse on the swine ! "

" And the lady ? "

Maris shrugged his shoulders.

" Till this evening," said Vernon, " I thought I had a plan. I was pretty certain I could win the race, and I proposed to reason with the male victim who came back with me, or club him on the head. I thought that when the fire began there would be confusion and that the people would keep outside the wall. My boat is lying below the cliffs and I hoped to carry the lady there. But now I know that that is impossible. There will be a concourse of the young men outside the door at the moment of the burning, and the House will be watched more closely than ever. Do you know what the people expect ? "

Maris spat contemptuously. " I heard some talk of the coming of Gods. The devil take all priests and their lying tales."

" They await the coming of Gods. You are not a classical scholar, Captain Maris, so you cannot realise, perhaps, just what that means. We are dealing with stark madness. These peasants are keyed up to a tremendous expectation. A belief has come to life, a belief far older than Christianity. They expect salvation from the coming of two Gods, a youth and a maiden. If their hope is disappointed, they will be worse madmen than before. To-morrow night nothing will go out from this place, unless it be Gods."

" That is true. The lady and I will without doubt die at the threshold, and you also, my friend. What arms have we ? "

" I have this revolver with six cartridges. The lady has a toy pistol, but, I think, no ammunition. The men without are armed with rifles."

" Ugly odds. It is infamous that honest folk and soldiers should perish at the hands of the half-witted."

" What about Leithen ? He is outside and has come here expressly to save the lady."

Maris shook his head. " He can do nothing. They have set up a cordon, a barrage, which he cannot penetrate. There is no hope in the island, for every man and woman is under the Devil's spell. Also the telegraph has been cut these three days."

" Do you see any chance ? "

Maris cogitated. " We have twenty-four hours. Some way of escape might be found by an active man at the risk of a bullet or two. We might reach your boat."

" But the lady ? "

" Why, no. Things look dark for the poor lady. We came here to protect her, and it seems as if we can do no more than die with her. . . . I would like to speak with that old man about clothes. A soldier does not feel at his bravest when he is barefoot and unclad save for pants and a ragged shirt. I refuse to go to Paradise in this dressing-gown."

Maris's cheerful fortitude was balm to Vernon's mind, for it seemed to strip the aura of mystery from the situation, and leave it a straight gamble of life and death. If Koré was to be saved it must be through Maris, for he himself was cast for another part.

" Come and let me present you to the lady," he said. " We must have some plan to sleep on."

Koré was in her sitting-room, and as she rose to meet them he saw that her face was very white.

" I heard nothing," she said hoarsely, " though Mitri says that there are thousands in the glade beyond the wall. But I saw a red glow from the upper windows."

" That was the torches which lined the stadium. I have been running a race, Miss Arabin, and have been lucky enough to win. Therefore we have still twenty-four hours of peace. May I present Captain Maris of the Greek Army ? He asks me to apologise for his clothes."

The Greek bowed gallantly and kissed her hand.

" Captain Maris came here to protect you. He came with a friend of ours, Sir Edward Leithen."

" Sir Edward Leithen ? " the girl cried. " He is here ? "

" He is in the island, but he is unable to join us in the House. Captain Maris tried, and was unfortunately captured. He was handed over to me as the victor of the race, and that is why he is here. But Sir Edward must be still scouting around the outposts, and it is pretty certain that he won't find a way in. I'm afraid we must leave him out of account. . . . Now I want you to listen to me very carefully, for I've a good deal to say to you. I'm going to be perfectly candid, for you're brave enough to hear the worst."

Vernon constructed three cigarettes out of his pipe tobacco and tissue paper from the illustrations in Peter Beckford. Koré did not light hers, but sat waiting with her hands on her knees.

" They think you a witch, because of the habits of your family. That you have long known. In the past they have burned witches in these islands, and Plakos remembers it. But it remembers another thing—the ancient ritual I told you of, and that memory which has been sleeping for centuries has come to violent life. Perhaps it would not have mastered them if the mind of the people had not been full of witch-burning. That, you see, gave them one victim already chosen, and in Captain Maris, who is of their own race and also a stranger, they have found the other."

" I see all that," the girl said slowly. " Of course I did not know when I left London—I couldn't have guessed—I thought it was a simple business which only needed a bold front, and I was too vain to take advice. . . . Oh, forgive me. My vanity has brought two innocent people into my miserable troubles. . . ."

" I told you yesterday that we were going to win. You must trust me, Miss Arabin. And, for Heaven's sake, don't imagine that I blame you. I think you are the bravest thing God ever made. I wouldn't be elsewhere for worlds."

Her eyes searched his face closely, and then turned to Maris, who instantly adopted an air of bold insouciance.

" You are good men. . . . But what can you do ? They will watch us like rats till the fire begins, and then—if we are not dead—they will kill us. . . . They will let no one go from this House—except their Gods."

These were the very words Vernon had used to

Maris, and since they so wholly expressed his own belief, he had to repudiate them with a vehement confidence.

" No," he said, " you forget that there are two things on our side. One is that, as the winner of the race, I am one of the people of Plakos. I can safely go out at the last moment and join their young men. I speak their tongue and I understand this ritual better than they do themselves. Surely I can find some way of driving them farther from the House so that in the confusion Maris can get you and your maid off unobserved. Mitri, too——"

" Mitri," she broke in, " has permission from our enemies to go when he pleases. But he refuses to leave us."

" Well, Mitri also. The second thing is that I have found my boat and got in touch with my man. He is lying in the bay below the cliffs, and I have arranged that on a certain signal he will meet you under the oliveyards. There is a gate in the wall there of which Mitri no doubt has the key. Once aboard, you are as safe as in London."

" And you ? "

" Oh, I will take my chance. I am a hillman from Akte and can keep up the part till I find some way of getting off."

" Impossible ! " she cried. " When they find that their Gods have failed them they will certainly kill you. Perhaps it is because I was born here, but though I have only heard of this ritual from you, I feel somehow as if I had always known it. And I know that if the one sacrifice fails, there will be another."

She rang the little silver bell for Mitri. " Show this gentleman his room," she looked towards Maris. " You have already had food ? Good night, Captain Maris. You must have had a wearing day, and I order you to bed."

When they were alone she turned to Vernon. " Your plan will not work. I can make a picture of what will happen to-morrow night—I seem to see every detail clear, as if I had been through it all before—and your plan is hopeless. You cannot draw them away from the House. They will be watching like demented wolves. . . . And if you did and we escaped, what on earth would become of you ? "

" I should be one of them—a sharer in their disappointment—probably forgotten."

" Not you. You are their high-priest, and an angry people always turns on their priest."

" There might be a bit of a row, but I dare say I could hold my own."

" Against thousands—mad thousands ? You would be torn in pieces even though they still believed you were a hillman from Akte."

" I'll take the risk. It is no good making difficulties, Miss Arabin. I admit that the case is pretty desperate, but my plan has at any rate a chance."

" The case is utterly desperate, and that is why your plan is no good. Desperate cases need more desperate remedies."

" Well, what do you suggest ? "

She smiled. " You are very tired and so am I. We have a day and a night left us and we can talk in the morning. . . . I told you when you first came here that I refused to run away. Well, I—don't—think—I have changed my mind. . . ."

.   .   .   .   .

The difficulty of telling this part of the story (said Leithen) is that it must be largely guess-work. The main facts I know, but the affair had become so strange and intimate that neither Koré nor Vernon would speak of it, while Maris was only vaguely aware of what was happening. It must have been some time on the Friday morning that the two met again. I can picture Vernon racking his brains to supplement his fragile plan, turning sleeplessly in his bed, hunting out Maris in the early morn to go wearily over the slender chances. Koré, I imagine, slept dreamlessly. She had reached her decision, and to her strong and simple soul to be resolved was to be at peace. Vernon was a fine fellow—I have known few finer—but there were lumpish elements in him, while the girl was all pure spirit.

But I can reconstruct the meeting of the two in the bare little sitting-room—without Maris—for that much Vernon has told me. I can see Vernon's anxious face, and the girl's eyes bright with that innocent arrogance which once in my haste I had thought ill-breeding.

" I am not going to run away from my people," she said. " I am going to meet them."

Vernon asked her meaning and she replied :

" I said yesterday that no one would be permitted to leave the House, unless in the eyes of the watchers they were Gods. Well, the Gods will not fail them. . . . Listen to me. I have tried to purify this place, but there can be only one purification and that is by fire. It had to come, and

it seems to me right that it should come from the
hands of those who have suffered. After that I
go out as a free woman—and to a free woman
nothing is impossible."

I think that for a little he may not have understood her. His mind, you see, had been busy
among small particulars, and the simplicity of her
plan would not at once be comprehended. Then
there came for him that moment of liberation,
when the world clarifies and what have been
barrier mountains become only details in a wide
prospect. The extreme of boldness is seen to be
the true discretion, and with that mood comes a
sharp uplift of spirit.

"You are right," he cried. "We will give
them their Gods."

"Gods?" She stopped him. "But I must go
alone. You have no part in this trial. But if
I win all this household will be safe. Most of
these people have never seen me, and Kynætho
knows me only as a girl in old country clothes
from whom they kept their eyes averted. I
can dress for a different part, and they will
see someone who will be as new to them as if
the Panagia had come down from Heaven. But
you——"

"They will not be content with one divinity,"
he broke in. "They await a double epiphany,
remember—the Koré and the Kouros. That is
the point of the occasion. We must be faithful
to the letter of the rite. After all they know less
of me than of you. They saw me win a race, a
figure very much like the others in the moonlight. . . . To those who may recognise me I am an
unknown hillman of Akte. Why should not the

Kouros have revealed himself the day before, and be also the Basileus ? "

She looked at him curiously as if seeing him for the first time as a bodily presence. I can fancy that for the first time she may have recognised his beauty and strength.

" But you are not like me," she urged. " You have not an old burden to get rid of. I am shaking off the incubus of my youth, and going free, like the Gods. What you call the epiphany is not only for Plakos but for myself, and nothing matters, not even death. I can play the part, but can you ? To me it is going to be the beginning of life, but to you it can only be an adventure. Chivalry is not enough."

" To me also it is the beginning of life," he answered. Then he returned to the tale of his boyhood's dream. " When it vanished in the storm a few nights ago I hated it, for I felt that it had stolen years from my life. But now I know that nothing is wasted. The door of the last of the dream-rooms has opened and you have come in. And we are going to begin life—together."

A strange pair of lovers, between whom no word of love had yet been spoken ! By very different roads both had reached a complete assurance, and with it came exhilaration and ease of mind. Maris during the long spring day might roam about restlessly, and Mitri and Élise fall to their several prayers, but Vernon and Koré had no doubts. While I, outside the wall, was at the mercy of old magics, a mere piece of driftwood tossed upon undreamed-of tides, the two in the House had almost forgotten Plakos. It had become to them no more than a background for their own

overmastering private concerns. The only problem was for their own hearts ; for Koré to shake
off for good the burden of her past and vindicate
her fiery purity, that virginity of the spirit which
could not be smirched by man or matter ; for
Vernon to open the door at which he had waited
all his life and redeem the long preparation of his
youth. They had followed each their own paths
of destiny, and now these paths had met and must
run together. That was the kind of thing that
could not be questioned, could not even be thought
about ; it had to be accepted, like the rising sun.
I do not think that they appreciated their danger,
as I did, for they had not been, like me, down in
the shadows. They were happy in their half-
knowledge, and in that blessed preoccupation
which casts out fear.

But some time in the afternoon he drew for the
girl a picture of the ancient rite, and he must
have been inspired, for, as she once recounted it
to me, he seems to have made his book learning
like the tale of an eye-witness.

" Why do you tell me this ? " she asked.

" Because if we are to play our part we must
understand that there is beauty as well as terror
in this worship."

" You speak as if you were a believer."

He laughed. " There is truth in every religion
that the heart of man ever conceived. It is because of that that we shall win."

But I think his confidence was less complete
than hers. I judge from what Maris told me that,
though Vernon was what the Scotch call " fey "
during those last hours, he retained something of
his old careful prevision. As the twilight fell he

took Maris aside and gave him his pistol. " Mitri has orders as soon as he gets out of the House to take a lantern to the cliffs and make the signal for my boat. He has a key and will open the door in the oliveyard wall. Miss Arabin and I are staking everything on a mighty gamble. If it succeeds, I think that the people will be in a stupor and we shall have an opportunity to join you. But if it fails—well, they will tear us to pieces. You must be close to us and await events. If the worst happens, one of these bullets is for the lady. Swear to me on your honour as a soldier."

I TAKE up the tale now (said Leithen) at the point where I fell in with Maris in the avenue which led to the gap in the wall. As I have told you, I had stumbled through the undergrowth with the blazing House making the place an inferno of blood-red aisles and purple thickets. Above the roar of the flames I heard the noise of panic-driven feet, of men plunging in haste—two indeed I had met, who seemed to be in the extremity of fear. For myself I was pretty nearly at the end of my tether. I was doddering with fatigue, and desperate with anxiety, and the only notion in my head was to use the dregs of my strength to do something violent. I was utterly in the dark, too. I did not know but that Koré might be already beyond my help, for that crimson grove seemed to reek of death.

And then I blundered into Maris, saw something in his face which gave me a surge of hope, and with his hand on my arm turned my eyes up the avenue.

The back part of the House and the outbuildings were by this time one roaring gust of flame, but the front was still untouched, and the fan of fire behind it gave it the concave darkness of a shell—a purple dark which might at any moment burst into light. The glow beyond the façade was reflected farther down the avenue, which was as bright as

day, but the House end was shadowed, and the two
figures which I saw seemed to be emerging from a
belt of blackness between two zones of raw gold.
I therefore saw them first as two dim white forms,
which, as they moved, caught tints of flame. . . .

Put it down to fatigue, if you like, or to natural
stupidity, but I did not recognise them. Besides,
you see, I knew nothing of Vernon's presence
there. My breath stopped and I felt my heart
leap to my throat. What I saw seemed not of the
earth—immortals, whether from Heaven or Hell,
coming out of the shadows and the fire in white
garments, beings that no elements could destroy.
In that moment the most panicky of the guards
now fleeing from the demesne was no more abject
believer than I.

And then another fugitive barged into me, and
Maris caught him by the arm and cuffed his ears.
I saw that it was Janni, but the sight meant
nothing to me. The corporal seemed to be whim-
pering with terror, and Maris talked fiercely to
him, but I did not listen. He quieted him, and
then he took us both by an arm and hurried us
with him towards the gap. It was what I wanted
to do. I dared not look again on that burning
pageant.

The next I knew I was beyond the wall on the
edge of the Dancing Floor. I do not know how I
got there, for my legs seemed to have no power
in them, and I fancy that Maris dragged us both.
The scared guards must have preceded us, for
behind was emptiness, save for the presences in the
avenue. The thick trees partly blanketed the fire,
but the light from the burning roof fell beyond
them and lit up redly the scarp on which we stood.

A rival light, too, was coming into being. The rising moon had already flooded the far hills, and its calm radiance was sweeping over the hollow packed with the waiting multitude.

At first I saw only the near fringes of the people —upturned faces in the uncanny light of the fire. But as I looked, the unfeatured darkness beyond changed also into faces—faces spectral in the soft moonshine. I seemed to be standing between two worlds, one crimson with terror and the other golden with a stranger spell, but both far removed from the kindly works of men.

Maris had pulled us aside out of the line of the breach in the wall, where the avenue made a path for the glow of the fire. We were in full view of the people, but they had no eyes for us, for their gaze was concentrated on the breach. The fugitive guards had by this time been absorbed, and their panic had not communicated itself to the great multitude. For a second I forgot my own fears in the amazing sight before me. . . . The crowded Dancing Floor was silent ; in face of that deep stillness the crackle and roar of the fire seemed no more than the beating of waves on a far-away coast. Though the moon made the hills yellow as corn, it left the upturned faces pale. I was looking down on a sea of white faces —featureless to me, masks of strained expectation. I felt the influence from them beat upon me like a wind. The fierce concentration of mingled hope and fear—wild hope, wilder fear—surged up to me, and clutched at my nerves and fired my brain. For a second I was as exalted as the craziest of them. Fragments of the dithyramb which Vernon had translated came unbidden to my

lips—" Io, Kouros most great. . . . Come, O come,
and bring with thee—holy hours of thy most holy
Spring."

The spell of the waiting people made me turn,
as they had turned, to the gap in the wall. Through
it, to the point where the glow of the conflagration
mingled with the yellow moonlight, came the two
figures.

I think I would have dropped on my knees,
but that Maris fetched me a clout on the back,
and his exultant voice cried in my ear. " Bravo,"
he cried. " By the Mother of God, they win !
That is a great little lady ! "

There was something in the familiarity, the
friendly roughness of the voice which broke the
spell. I suddenly looked with seeing eyes, and I
saw Koré.

She was dressed in white, the very gown which
had roused Vernon's ire at my cousin's dance the
summer before. A preposterous garment I had
thought it, the vagary of an indecent fashion.
But now—ah now ! It seemed the fitting robe
for youth and innocence—divine youth, heavenly
innocence—clothing but scarcely veiling the young
Grace who walked like Persephone among the
spring meadows. *Vera incessu patuit Dea.* It
was not Koré I was looking at, but *the* Koré, the
immortal maiden, who brings to the earth its
annual redemption.

I was a sane man once more, and filled with
another kind of exaltation. I have never felt so
sharp a sense of joy. God had not failed us. I
knew that Koré was now not only safe but tri-
umphant.

And then I recognised Vernon.

I did not trouble to think by what mad chance he had come there. It seemed wholly right that he should be there. He was dressed like the runner of the day before, but at the moment I did not connect the two. What I was looking at was an incarnation of something that mankind has always worshipped—youth rejoicing to run its race, that youth which is the security of this world's continuance and the earnest of Paradise.

I recognised my friends and yet I did not recognise them, for they were transfigured. In a flash of insight I understood that it was not the Koré and the Vernon that I had known, but new creations. They were not acting a part, but living it. They, too, were believers; they had found their own epiphany, for they had found themselves and each other. Each other! How I knew it I do not know, but I realised that it was two lovers that stood on the brink of the Dancing Floor. And I felt a great glow of peace and happiness.

With that I could face the multitude once more. And then I saw the supreme miracle.

People talk about the psychology of a crowd, how it is different in kind from the moods of the men who compose it. I dare say that is true, but if you have each individual strained to the extreme of tension with a single hope, the mood of the whole is the same as that of the parts, only multiplied a thousandfold. And if the nerve of a crowd goes there is a vast cracking, just as the rending of a tree-trunk is greater than the breaking of a twig.

For a second—not more—the two figures stood on the edge of the Dancing Floor in the sight of the upturned eyes. I do not think that Koré and Vernon saw anything—they had their own inward vision. I do not know what the people saw in the presences that moved out of the darkness above them.

But this I saw. Over the multitude passed a tremor like a wind in a field of wheat. Instead of a shout of triumph there was a low murmur as of a thousand sighs. And then there came a surge, men and women stumbling in terror. First the fringes opened and thinned, and in another second, as it seemed to me, the whole mass was in precipitate movement. And then it became panic —naked veritable panic. The silence was broken by hoarse cries of fear. I saw men running like hares on the slopes of the Dancing Floor. I saw women dragging their children as if fleeing from a pestilence. . . . In a twinkling I was looking down on an empty glade with the Spring of the White Cypress black and solitary in the moonlight.

I did not doubt what had happened. The people of Plakos had gone after strange gods, but it was only for a short season that they could shake themselves free from the bonds of a creed which they had held for a thousand years. The resurgence of ancient faiths had obsessed but had not destroyed the religion into which they had been born. Their spells had been too successful. They had raised the Devil and now fled from him in the blindest terror. They had sought the outlands, had felt their biting winds, had had a glimpse of their awful denizens, and they longed with the passion of children for their old homely shelters. The priest of Kynætho would presently have his fill of stricken penitents.

Maris was laughing. I dare say it was only a relief from nervous strain, but it seemed to me an impiety. I turned on him angrily. " There's a boat somewhere. See that everybody is aboard —the whole household. And bring it round to the harbour where we first landed."

" Not to the oliveyards ? " he asked.

" No, you fool. To the harbour. Plakos is now as safe for us as the streets of Athens."

Koré and Vernon stood hand in hand like people in a dream. I think they were already dimly aware of what had happened, and were slowly coming back to the ordinary world. The virtue was going out of them, and with the ebbing of their exaltation came an immense fatigue. I never saw human faces so pale.

Vernon was the first to recover. He put his arm round Koré's waist, for without it she would have fallen, but he himself was none too steady on his feet. He recognised me.

" Ned," he said, in a stammering voice, like a sleep-walker's. " I heard you were here. It was good of you, old man. . . . What do you think . . . now . . . the boat . . ."

" Come along," I cried, and I took an arm of each. " The sooner you are on board the better. You want to sleep for a week." I started them off along the edge of the Dancing Floor.

" Not that way," he gasped. " Too risky . . ."

" There is no danger anywhere in this blessed island. Come along. You want food and clothes. It's getting on for midnight and you're both only half-dressed."

They were like two children pulled out of bed and too drowsy to walk, and I had my work cut

out getting them along the ridge. The Dancing
Floor was empty, and when we entered the road
which led from Kynætho to the main gate of the
House there was also solitude. Indeed, we had
to pass through a segment of the village itself,
and the place was silent as the grave. I knew
where the people were—in and around the church,
grovelling in the dust for their sins.

Our going was so slow that by the time we
looked down on the harbour the boat was already
there. I stopped for a moment and glanced back,
for far behind me I heard voices. There was a
glow as from torches to the south where the
church stood, and a murmur which presently
swelled into an excited clamour. Suddenly a
bell began to ring, and it seemed as if the noise
became antiphonal, voices speaking and others
replying. At that distance I could make out
nothing, but I knew what the voices said. It
was " Christ is risen—He is risen indeed."

The moon had set before we put to sea. My
last recollection of Plakos is looking back and
seeing the House flaming like a pharos on its
headland. Then, as we beat outward with the
wind, the fire became a mere point of brightness
seen at a great distance in the vault of night.

I had no wish or power to sleep. Koré and
Vernon, wrapped each in a heap of cloaks, lay in
the bows. It was the quietest place, but there
was no need of precautions, for they slept like
the drugged. Élise, whose nerves had broken
down, was in Vernon's berth, Black George had
the helm, and old Mitri and Janni snored beside
him.

I sat amidships and smoked. When the moon went down a host of stars came out, pale and very remote as they always seem in a spring sky. The wind was light and the water slid smoothly past ; I knew roughly our bearings, but I had a sense of being in another world and on seas never before sailed by man. The last week had been for me a time of acute anxiety and violent bodily exertion, but a sponge seemed to have passed over the memory of it. Something altogether different filled my mind. I had with my own eyes seen Fate take a hand in the game and move the pieces on the board. The two sleepers in the bows had trusted their destiny and had not been betrayed.

I thought with contrition of my cynicism about Vernon's dream. No doubt it had been a will-o'-the-wisp, but it had been true in purpose, for it had made him wait, alert and aware, on something which had been prepared for him, and if that something was far different from his forecast the long expectation had made him ready to seize it. How otherwise could he, with his decorous ancestry and his prudent soul, have become an adventurer ? . . . And Koré ? She had stood grimly to the duty which she conceived Fate to have laid upon her, and Fate, after piling the odds against her, had relented. Perhaps that is the meaning of courage. It wrestles with circumstance, like Jacob with the angel, till it compels its antagonist to bless it.

I remembered a phrase which Vernon had once used about " the mailed virgin." It fitted this girl, and I began to realise the meaning of virginity. True purity, I thought, whether in woman or man, was something far more than the narrow sex thing which was the common notion of it. It meant keeping oneself, as the Bible says, altogether unspotted from the world, free from all tyranny and stain, whether of flesh or spirit, defying the universe to touch even the outworks of the sanctuary which is one's soul. It must be defiant, not the inert fragile crystal, but the supple shining sword. Virginity meant nothing unless it was mailed, and I wondered whether we were not coming to a better understanding of it. The modern girl, with all her harshness, had the gallantry of a free woman. She was a crude Artemis, but her feet were on the hills. Was the blushing sheltered maid of our grandmother's day no more than an untempted Aphrodite ?

These were queer reflections, I know, for a man like me, but they gave me contentment, as if I had somehow made my peace with life. For a long time I listened to the ripple of the water and watched the sky lighten to dim grey and the east flush with sunrise. It had become very cold and I was getting sleepy, so I hunted about for a mattress to make myself a bed. But a thought made me pause. How would these two, who had come together out of the night, shake down on the conventional roads of marriage ? To the end of time the desire of a woman should be to her husband. Would Koré's eyes, accustomed to look so masterfully at life, ever turn to Vernon in the surrender of wifely affection ? As I looked at the two in the bows I wondered.

Then something happened which reassured me. The girl stirred uneasily as if in a bad dream, turned to where Vernon lay, and flung out her hand. Both were sound asleep, but in some secret way the impulse must have been communicated to Vernon, for he moved on his side, and brought an arm, which had been lying loosely on the rug which covered him, athwart Koré's in a gesture of protection.

After that both seemed to be at peace, while the yawl ran towards the mainland hills, now green as a fern in the spring dawn.